Cells boiled, flesh burned, organs burst. Muscles melted away and reappeared, only to melt anew. His phenomenal metabolism sped up to compensate for the magnitude of the physical damage.

Finally, some unknown tipping point was reached; the regenerative process hit critical mass. Logan's flesh vanished, only to reappear, phoenixlike, a microsecond later.

Flesh disintegrated and reformed again and again. Through it all, the only constant was the pain—an anguish so intense it seemed impossible for Logan to bear.

Logan opened his mouth, but his tongue burned away before he could shout. The raging trauma turned every microsecond into an aeon of torment. His jaws stretched wide, his mouth gaping, the sound that emerged seemed to spring from the primal core of Logan's being.

Soon, his screams filled the blasted clearing. His tortured howls echoed across the mountainside and drifted down, into the valley and the settlement far below.

Read these other exciting Marvel novels from Pocket Books!

WOLVERINE®

VIOLENT TENDENCIES

a novel by
Marc Cerasini

based on the
Marvel Comic Book

POCKET **STAR** BOOKS

NEW YORK   LONDON   TORONTO   SYDNEY

Pocket Star Books
A Division of Simon & Schuster, Inc.
1230 Avenue of the Americas
New York, NY 10020

This book is a work of fiction. Names, characters, places, and incidents either are products of the author's imagination or are used fictitiously. Any resemblance to actual events or locales or persons, living or dead, is entirely coincidental.

First Pocket Star Books paperback edition November 2007

POCKET STAR BOOKS and colophon are registered trademarks of Simon & Schuster, Inc.

For information about special discounts for bulk purchases, please contact Simon & Schuster Special Sales at 1-800-456-6798 or business@simonandschuster.com.

Cover design by John Vairo Jr.; art by Bill Sienkiewicz

Manufactured in the United States of America

10 9 8 7 6 5 4 3 2 1

ISBN-13: 978-1-4165-1074-1
ISBN-10:   1-4165-1074-5

I'd like to thank my wife, Alice Alfonsi,
for pretty much everything.

Ay me! What perils do environ
That man that meddles with cold iron!

—Samuel Butler, *Hudibras,* 1663

EYES WIDE, NOSTRILS FLARING, THE RUST-BROWN stag scrambled along the edge of the granite cliff. The red deer was an "imperial," its fourteen-point antlers spreading like the branches of an ancient oak. Wispy vapor rose from its panting mouth as it vaulted to the summit of a low hill, then paused in the frozen air to survey the snow-draped mountains.

The animal remained still under the slate winter sky, until the whistling winds shifted, and the stag caught scent of the beast that stalked it. Chin tucked, the deer bounded over a tangle of branches and charged into a shallow valley of twisted, wind-blasted trees.

A moment later, a grizzled timber wolf crested the hill. Larger by half than other members of its pack, the alpha male's body was etched with scars from a hundred battles for food, for territory, for a mate. The wolf sniffed out the deer's trail, its snout leaving wet prints on the frost-covered rock.

The breeze shifted again, and the wolf became aware of another predator on the hunt.

Wary now, the wolf paced back and forth. then crouched on its haunches and issued a frustrated whimper. Head low, the predator sniffed the ground once more. Its cold eyes scanned the surroundings; one ear, half torn in some long-forgotten fight, twitched apprehensively.

Finally, the aggression that had driven this male to push forward after his pack had broken off overrode any fear of threat. Lifting its blocky muzzle, the wolf chuffed once and loped into the valley in pursuit of the deer's trail.

The stag was moving quickly now, running full out along a narrow ravine until it crashed into the branches of a fallen tree. Like clutching claws, the brittle wood snared the animal's antlers. The stag bucked wildly but only became more entangled.

Hearing the commotion, the wolf slunk into the canyon, crouching low, its white underbelly brushing the barren ground. Sensing the predator's approach, the deer kicked frantically, its head wrenching back in a futile effort to break loose.

The wolf padded closer. Its slavering lips curled back into a toothy snarl. Then it leaped—and fell. A howl ended in a wet gurgle as the animal was struck in midair by a hurtling ball of diamond-sharp blades and tight, raging muscle.

An explosion of black blood and hot entrails spilled onto the cold rocks. With only a few stubborn bits of cartilage, bone, and skin keeping the half-sundered body together, the wolf was dead before it struck the earth.

The hunter loomed over the twitching carcass, waiting for the gutted predator to do battle. But the wolf failed to rise. Frustrated by the beast's inactivity, the hunter lashed out with a heavily muscled arm. For a moment, the fading sunlight glinted off curved metal tapered to a point. The arm descended in a slashing cut, then another. A flurry of ripping blows followed, each accompanied by a savage grunt of animal satisfaction. Blood splattered the walls of the crevasse, and great gouts of flesh dangled from the clutching branches.

The red deer smelled the wolf's hot blood and kicked wildly, its broken hooves gouging the earth, its eyes black pools of horror. The helpless deer's explosive panic somehow shook the killer from his murderous trance. Beneath dirt and blood and unkempt hair, stony eyes glanced up from the carnage. With a grunt, the naked wild man rose to his full height and shook gore from his blood-soaked claws. Then one more slash—

Wood splintered, and a severed antler tumbled to

the ground. Freed at last from the ensnarling branches, the imperial stag bounded along the ravine until it was no longer visible.

The hunter watched the deer's flight, his claws retracting with a dull hiss. As the sun began to set behind the mountains, the man squatted on his haunches and noisily began to feed.

Logan thrashed and cried out.

Another nightmare.

He opened his eyes, expecting chemical vats, intravenous tubes, piercing needles. But the sterile lab was gone. No green lab smocks. No bland faces. Instead, a full moon glared in the purple night.

Logan moaned and covered his eyes. The moon was a burning sun, the starlight lasers piercing his retinas. He closed his eyes, but it didn't help. Lancing agony was already slicing his brain. The throbbing expanded until Logan thought his head would explode.

Groaning, he rolled onto his side and realized he was lying at the bottom of a frigid ravine—somewhere in the Canadian Rockies, by the look of the terrain. He heard the wind's howl, felt its biting sting, a pleasure compared with the intense spasms inside his skull.

Finally, Logan's headache receded, but he lay still, fearing one movement would bring back the torment.

How long was I blacked out this time? Hours? Days? Weeks?

When the bloodlust came, it overwhelmed him.

More than some momentary wave, it flooded his entire being. Like a tsunami, the need drowned everything human within him, pushing it into a dark place, until the blood storm passed and the violence receded.

When did it happen?

Logan searched his memory, trying to remember his last sane, human moment.

Well, sane, anyway, he amended. *I haven't felt human in a while.*

Thinking caused the pain in his head to return, so Logan gave up. He knew from experience that the memories would come . . . or not. In the end, it didn't matter. So he focused on his physical condition and let the rest slide.

Licking his lips, he tasted metal, his mouth encrusted with bits of raw flesh and coppery blood. Blindly, he tried to wipe away the gore, but his fingers wouldn't obey the commands from his brain.

Once again, he opened his eyes. The light from the moon and stars no longer felt like nails hammering into his eyes, and Logan counted that as a plus. But as soon as he moved, his whole body began to shiver. His hands were black, the flesh puffy from frostbite, and he felt a dull, throbbing ache in every joint and muscle.

Finally, the reasoning part of his brain took hold, told him what had happened. As he'd lain naked and senseless on the frozen ground for who the hell knew how long, the relentless arctic cold had seeped into his body. Because of his phenomenal metabolism, he usually didn't require heat to survive—not even in the subzero temperatures here in the mountains. His hypermetabolism always battled the temperature . . . but the shiny steel skeleton encased inside his flesh couldn't compensate this time. Logan's bones were now chilled to a temperature that approximated the refrigerated metal slab at the morgue.

Exhaling hard, Logan rejected the pain and sat up. Still woozy, he discovered a coating of sticky blood had soaked into the thick layer of filth that clung to his body. The blood was fresh, and Logan could smell the acrid stink of death even before he saw the shattered bones, the ripped cartilage, and the gnawed flesh scattered around the ravine.

Still shivering, Logan spied the bloody carcass and crawled on all fours to reach it. With hands stiff as frozen claws, he wrapped the wolf's ragged pelt around his broad shoulders, clothing himself in the spoils of his hunt. The wolf's wedge-shaped head dangled from Logan's bull neck like a grim talisman, its jaws slack, its tongue lolling.

Logan stumbled to his feet and promptly heaved up the contents of his stomach. The retching continued for many minutes, but he felt better after the purge.

Throat parched, he sniffed the air. Then he moved toward the valley below, where the smell of water was strong.

His shivering quickly abated. Now that he was

awake and moving, Logan's extraordinary metabolism restored his internal body temperature. His fingers, which had been withered by frostbite, were warm and supple again. But his brain still felt as if it were battering itself against the walls of his skull.

If only I could stop these freakin' headaches, too.

Logan belched, tasted wolf's blood and, beneath it all, a medicinal tang, the taint of the lab that had tortured him. After all these months, unholy drugs still coursed through his veins, defying even the workings of his fierce metabolism.

Logan continued to negotiate the craggy trail, and soon his nausea and headache vanished. By the time he climbed down from the mountain, the last vestiges of cold had been dispelled from his adamantium bones.

At last, Logan reached an icy creek at the base of the hill. Under the crust, the water flowed freely. He shattered the ice with callused feet, jumped into knee-deep water, crouched low. The current washed away some of the filth that coated him. He guzzled for long minutes. The water tasted sweet and fresh; it cleansed his palate.

Minutes later, Logan climbed out of the creek on the opposite shore. He took a deep breath, tensing at the faintest scent of wood smoke. Either he'd ranged unusually far during his last bloodlust blackout—far enough to reach the raw edges of civilization—or some stupid Boy Scout had picked a bad place to go camping.

Logan followed the trail left by the wispy vapors. After paralleling the creek for more than a kilometer, he spied a rude log cabin perched on a low rise. Smoke drifted from its stone chimney, and a flickering lantern glowed on the other side of a frosted window. Beyond the cabin, Logan saw more crude structures, perhaps a dozen. They were nestled in a shallow valley, clustered around a stone well in the middle of a snow-packed clearing.

Since he'd fled that abattoir of a laboratory all those months ago, where a pack of depraved scientists had poured molten adamantium into his skeleton and scrambled the neurons in his brain, Logan hadn't encountered a single human being. Now he'd accidentally stumbled upon an entire village.

Lucky for them, everyone was asleep. Logan could slip away before anyone knew he was there, before he could do any damage.

Turning to leave, he was startled by a sound both familiar and unsettling—a human voice crying out in the night. The shouted curse was followed by a crash and the tinkle of breaking glass. The acrid stink of alcohol entered Logan's hypersensitive nostrils.

Someone in this no-horse hick town was awake, drunk, and royally pissed off.

Common sense told Logan to run away. But curiosity, and maybe a sliver of loneliness, won out. Despite the danger, Logan cautiously moved toward the rough-hewn cabin.

2

THOMAS SWIMMING HORSE WANTED TO SMASH THE book against the cabin wall.

He *wanted* to, but he knew if he did, the Librarian would cut him off—maybe permanently this time. So he threw the mason jar he clutched in his other hand instead.

Waste of good moonshine, not to mention the jar.

Thomas lurched to his feet. Powerfully built under his tattered wool sweater and patched denims, he was tall enough that the knot of his ebony ponytail brushed the smoke-stained rafters. The Native American's muddy brown, slightly slanted eyes bespoke his heritage. Now, however, they were glassy and unfocused.

Still gripping the heavy book, Thomas glanced at the title—*The Decline of the West,* by Oswald Spengler. The urge to tear it up returned with a vengeance. Before he did something he would regret later, Thomas tossed the volume on top of the stack he would return to the Librarian in the morning. Though he would gain a small measure of gratification from pulverizing the book, there was no point in making the old man angry. Thomas was already on thin ice after tossing *The Collected Works of Jean-Paul Sartre* into the fireplace.

Thomas had nothing against books. Far from it. He wanted to learn as much as he could about a world he found baffling and infinitely frustrating. But as far as he was concerned, Spengler's cynical blathering was another dead end.

He'd read hundreds of books in the five years since he left the U.S. Army, became a drifter, and eventually settled in this hermit camp—a town called Second Chance by the collection of misfits and misanthropes who set up residency there. Most of the books he'd read were great works of Eastern and Western philosophy, or so the Librarian claimed. The philosophies varied from the nihilistically cynical to the wildly optimistic, but none of them jibed with reality as Thomas saw it.

That disconnection was the reason he'd left the reservation in the first place. The rituals and traditions of his tribe had been drummed into his head from birth, but they'd failed to inspire him.

Thomas was the grandson of a chief, in line to take over a leadership position in his tribe, yet he felt no affinity for his culture or his people. So when he came of age, Thomas left the small world of his tribe to seek a place in the wider one.

For a while, Thomas was simply directionless. He lived on the road, then on the beach in Southern California, then in a commune in the Northwest. Finally, he joined the military. He was a fine soldier and eagerly volunteered for combat duty—more for the adrenaline rush than from any sense of patriotism.

He wasn't at all patriotic. If he got drunk enough, Thomas would admit that he found modern America to be as baffling and meaningless as his own culture.

But the problem wasn't the culture's. After all he'd seen and been through, he knew his lack of belief was his own problem.

He'd spent years humping the sand with an assault rifle in his hand and all kinds of American boys at his side: corn-fed Kansas farm sons, Bronx-raised Puerto Ricans, homeboys from Detroit. Those guys could *fight,* and they were willing to die—for their country, for their fellow soldier, for *him,* if he asked them to. They believed in something bigger than themselves.

If you listened to the yacking class on television or read their ad-packed newspapers, it was easy to conclude people were no damn good and the world was going to hell in a handcart. Intellectuals like Spengler felt the need to gas on about the loss of values in our modern world. But virtue really was alive and well. It just existed in places the cerebral class feared to tread.

Thomas belched a foul taste left by the moonshine. Suddenly, the low ceiling and rough wood-beam walls made him feel claustrophobic. He gasped and the pervasive odor of burnt wood and badly distilled alcohol sent a wave of nausea through him. Thomas stumbled through the unbarred door and into the frozen night.

But when he crossed the threshold, Thomas heard the crackle of frozen branches, spied movement in the shadows. He figured he'd startled some creature lurking in the brush—a bear, wolf, raccoon, maybe even a wolverine.

Just in case, he reached behind him for the rifle he kept inside the door. Raising the cold weapon, Thomas peered into the darkness. Then something ran across the clearing—on two legs. Thomas got a good look at the mysterious intruder and stumbled back a step.

Either Thomas was drunker than he thought, or a naked, hairy creature that walked very much like a man was dashing through the center of town and up the path toward the mountain. Before he could register many details, the thing vanished. But not completely. Thomas could still hear the stranger, crashing through the forest. He could still see snow falling from disturbed trees. He'd spooked something—the proof was there. So he knew he hadn't imagined the whole thing.

"Hey!" he shouted into the night. But there was no answer, just a return to stillness.

Thomas continued to scan the dark forest beyond the town. After several minutes, the cold settled into his lungs and crept through the soles of his boots.

He coughed and began to shiver. With a grunt of frustrated bafflement, he went back inside.

Only this time, he barred the heavy door after he closed it.

3

THE DIRECTOR OF DEPARTMENT K WAS SEATED IN an Italian leather chair behind a massive desk beautifully fashioned from polished oak. A fire roared inside a carved stone fireplace, bathing the vaulted ceiling in a golden glow. A massive standing globe with bronzed fixtures rested in the corner, and full-sized portraits of the great men of science—Johannes Kepler, Isaac Newton, Copernicus, Albert Einstein, Wernher von Braun—adorned the wood-paneled walls

His spacious office in Administrative Headquarters was silent, save for the crackling of the fire and the methodical ticking of an antique grandfather clock. Then the soft robotic Voice broke the stillness.

"Satellite KS-2 is almost on station, Director," the Voice announced, interrupting the stream of mathematical formulas coursing through the room's sole occupant. "Twenty seconds and counting."

The man behind the desk blinked once. His concentration broken, the Director consciously shut down the mathematical part of his magnificently trained mind. He sighed and shifted in his chair, then ran long fingers through a wild shock of snow-white hair.

"Put it on screen, please."

"At once, Director."

A hatch opened in the gilded ceiling. A high-definition monitor slid out of a hidden compartment and clicked into place directly in front of the Director. The screen immediately sprang to life, displaying a long stream of numbers, symbols, and letters.

More easily deciphered was a countdown box in the upper-left-hand corner of the display, where scarlet numbers ticked down the seconds as the orbital satellite moved into position. At zero, the data scroll vanished, and the screen was filled with the green-tinted, night-vision image of rugged hills, deep, tree-lined valleys, and a winding, half-frozen creek.

"Magnify fifty times. Place the target center screen," ordered the Director.

The digital image froze, then pixilated. A reformed image showed the half-naked figure of a man climbing a steep, icy path up the side of a mountain.

The Director watched the screen for a moment, elbows on his desk, hands steepled, the tips of his spidery fingers brushing his clean-shaven chin.

"Spectrometer," he commanded.

The image shifted again. Now the figure seemed to

be bathed in X-ray, its skeleton glowing a fluorescent blue against the dark green background.

"It's him . . . I mean, *it,*" the Director said, correcting himself.

"Yes, Director. The evidence is indisputable," the disembodied Voice replied. "You are watching real-time images of Weapon X in the Canadian wilderness, photographed by orbital surveillance satellite."

Eyes unblinking, the Director licked thin lips as he stared at the screen. The urge to possess what he was witnessing burned in his chest like a physical hunger.

"Where is its precise location?" the Director asked.

"Forty-nine miles from the laboratory where it was forged. If Weapon X climbed the highest peak, it could see the dam and the hydroelectric plant that once powered Professor Thorton's facility with the naked eye."

The Director accepted the information with a curt nod. "So many questions," he muttered.

"Pardon, sir?"

"Never mind. I want you to activate the crisis center," the Director commanded. "Then notify the staff that all current operations at Department K will cease, effective immediately."

"But why, sir?"

"Until further notice, all resources are to be diverted to monitor, record, and analyze the movements and activities of Weapon X."

The Voice registered surprise. "Monitor? Not *capture*?"

The Director waved the question aside. "How effective are our real-time surveillance capabilities?"

"Even if we use all six surveillance satellites allocated to Department K's Intelligence Center—"

"We will be dedicating *all* of our resources to this project," interrupted the Director.

"It will still be impossible to monitor Weapon X for more than seventy percent of the time," the Voice continued.

The Director swept a lock of wispy white hair from his high-domed brow. "That should be sufficient. Just so long as we don't lose track of him."

"*It*, sir."

The Director blinked. "What?"

"Weapon X is properly referred to as *it*."

"Yes."

"Will we capture it?"

"Eventually," said the Director. "But there are some things I need to learn first."

The display box appeared on the screen again, glowing numbers counting down from ten. When zero appeared, the digital image broke up, and the screen faded to static.

"Weapon X is out of range of our satellite, sir. We've lost contact," the Voice explained. "We should locate it again in approximately forty-six minutes—just as soon as KS-5 is repositioned over the Rocky Mountains. Meanwhile, I'll calculate the trajectory of Weapon X based on its current movements."

The Director was silent for a long time; respectfully, the Voice did not intrude on his thoughts. After many minutes, the man finally spoke.

"Despite all the resources the Department lavished on Professor Thorton's experiment, in the end, the Weapon X Program was an unmitigated disaster."

The Voice immediately protested. "But, sir, surely it was not a total waste. The strides in the biological sciences alone are—"

"Are impressive, it's true," the Director interrupted. "The Professor's goals were murky and his methods unconventional, but no one could deny the man's genius."

"Don't dismiss the contribution made by others," the Voice insisted. "Dr. Zander Rice and Sarah Kinney contributed their own research; and the late Dr. Abraham Cornelius. It was his nanotechnology, along with Dr. Hendry's pioneering surgical techniques, that made the fusion of living bone and adamantium steel feasible."

"Brilliant achievements," the Director said. "And if Weapon X hadn't annihilated those esteemed scientists and destroyed the lab, and if by some miracle the Department were to locate another subject with the same peculiar mutant abilities possessed by this man Logan, then someday we *might* be able to create another Weapon X."

The Director placed the palms of his hands on the desk. "But I have my doubts. At a cost of ninety billion U.S. dollars per single unit, Weapon X is far more expensive than a stealth bomber—"

"But infinitely more useful, sir," the Voice argued.

"You are not incorrect," conceded the Director. "But beyond the considerable expense, there is still a flaw in the creation process. A *fatal* flaw . . ."

"You're referring to control," said the quiet, robotic Voice. "Mind control."

The Director pounded his desk. "Precisely! Without control, Weapon X is less than useless. It's a danger to itself and others."

"Weapon X was certainly a danger to those men and women who created it," the Voice observed.

Though devoid of irony, the comment elicited a grunt of dismay from the Director. "That aspect of the program was always . . . dicey," he confessed. "Weapon X was a man once, and tinkering with the human mind is always fraught with peril."

"What happened, if I may ask?"

The Director frowned. "Weapon X . . . resisted reprogramming. Though it appeared he'd been . . . subdued, some aspect of the man's core personality survived the brain wipe. I blame the woman."

"You are referring to Carol Hines? The technician the Professor recruited from NASA?"

"I knew her father well," the Director said with a nod. "Dr. Benton Hines was a great scientist. Sterling reputation. A giant in his field. I always thought there was something wrong with the daughter, though.

Takes after her mother, perhaps. Mrs. Hines was a bit of a . . . hysteric."

"So you believe the process went awry during the personality-elimination phase?"

"I'm certain of it," the Director said. "Machines, you see, are easily controlled, even the most powerful and intelligent ones. Computers are designed with defaults and built-in inhibitors. The creator has absolute control over his creation from the moment of inception. Artificial intelligence is incapable of disobedience or betrayal, by *design*. Humans are not so blessed."

The Voice remained silent, processing the Director's words.

"It's so perplexing," the man said after a long pause. "I can build a doomsday machine with steel and copper, plastic and silicon. My device would be indestructible and infallible and so durable it would outlive the civilization it was designed to protect. I could begin construction tomorrow. And with the technicians and funds I have on hand, I could guarantee the program's ultimate success."

The Director paused, closed his eyes, and stroked his high forehead with the tips of his fingers. "Unfortunately, turning something as contrary and complex as a human being into a near-invincible weapon is a wee bit trickier. But despite the warning signs, Professor Thorton tried anyway—and we both know how *that* went, don't we?"

"And yet Department K flourishes," the Voice replied. "The money flows. The quest for the perfect biotechnological warrior proceeds at an accelerated pace."

"Thanks to the military, my friend. It's not the scientists but the generals who drive this Department. Right now, those generals are breathing down our necks, and *that* is a problem."

"But since the early days, when Department K was funded by DARPA, the military has always been involved regarding our programs."

The Director nodded. "The military has its uses. They fund our research without fully understanding it, and they forgive us our occasional mistakes. Best of all, they have very deep pockets. But as long as I am in charge, the generals will be kept at arm's length. That's where Professor Thorton and I parted company. The Professor embraced the military's values, and look what happened to him."

"A tragedy, surely," said the Voice. "But is it fair to blame the military for Thorton's mistakes?"

"The military demanded progress. Professor Thorton's frenzied quest for results led to the mistake that is Weapon X."

"Then perhaps the military should step in and take control of the situation," the Voice suggested.

"No. Never," the Director declared. "As messy as things have become since the Professor's demise, the situation would be infinitely worse if the military assumed control. Funds would be reallocated. Pure research would be sacrificed on the altar of expediency. And in a mad dash to achieve results, more mistakes would be made—the kind of mistakes that led to the massacre of the Professor and his staff."

"That puts you in a unique position, Director."

"What are you getting at?"

"You are the only thing that stands between order and chaos."

For the first time in the conversation, the corners of the Director's razor-thin lips curled into something resembling a smile. "Very perceptive of you, my friend," he said. "I never looked at the situation in quite that way before."

"Have you considered your next move, Director?"

"The military must be presented with a prize. Once they are busy playing with their new toy, they will leave us alone to pursue our own agenda."

"That 'toy' being Weapon X? Again, sir, I am not following your logic. The Weapon X Program was the most expensive project ever undertaken by Department K—"

"And more resources will be required to evaluate the capabilities of Weapon X and then *recapture* it," the Director declared. "What is your point?"

"Why give it up?" the Voice asked.

"Because . . . by the time we turn Weapon X over to the generals, we'll know everything we need to know about its function, its capabilities, its advantages, and its shortcomings. We will prod it, probe it, take it apart, and put it back together again. By the time we're done, Weapon X will be of no more use to science than a disease-ridden laboratory rat. But the military will see things differently. To them, the prototype will be invaluable. So we will demand a massive increase in our budget, and the generals will give it to us—in exchange for Weapon X."

"Now I understand. Brilliant plan, sir, but I do foresee one problem."

The Director frowned. "Go on."

"Until we turn over Weapon X, our resources will be strained to the limit."

"So we must tighten our belt." The Director stroked his chin. "What is the largest drain on Department K's current fiscal budget?"

"Well, Director. Project Ubermensch is three hundred percent over budget. Professor Philip and Doctor Wylie are convinced they can replicate the original Super-Soldier serum based on notes left by—"

"I'm not concerned with ongoing *research*," the Director said impatiently. "I'm referring to operational expenses."

"In that case, Department K's largest financial drain is the CCRC unit at Shroud Lake, Ontario," the Voice replied, "formerly known as the Weapon Null Program."

"As I suspected," the Director said with a nod. "So I'm reactivating Weapon Null, effective immediately.

You will notify the Matron personally, while I coordinate logistics with the Canadian Air Force."

"But, sir—"

"Enough. Dispatch Dr. Vigil to act as liaison. The Matron can be . . . most difficult. However, the doctor's unique handicap should elicit a measure of sympathy from the woman. I hear the Matron is . . . *enamored* by freaks."

"I shall notify Dr. Vigil at once," said the Voice.

"I want Weapon Null on site and within striking distance of Weapon X within twenty-four hours," the Director ordered.

"I shall carry out your command, sir. But I cannot see the purpose of this hasty and expensive deployment."

"It's really quite simple, my friend," the Director replied. "The Matron's collection of misbegotten misfits will face off against Weapon X, one at a time, as per my rules of engagement. They will test the weapon's capabilities, while we monitor those confrontations via satellite, recording and evaluating the data."

"But, Director, surely you are aware that Weapon Null is a product of outmoded research and antiquated technology. The members of that unit stand no chance against a creation as advanced as Weapon X."

"Indeed. I predict Weapon X will annihilate those earlier test subjects with ease, effectively ending the Weapon Null Program. You see, my friend, I've now reduced Department K's operating expenses by half."

"But, sir . . . with all due respect . . . wouldn't your plan be tantamount to . . . murder?"

The Director raised an eyebrow as he glanced out the dark, rain-spattered window. "I prefer to call it an efficient use of available resources."

4

NEAR THE ROCK-STREWN SUMMIT OF A RUGGED mountain, Logan spied the entrance to a cave. He'd almost missed the opening in the darkness. It was small, nestled between two massive boulders.

Logan calculated that he was less than three kilometers from the settlement he'd stumbled upon—too close for comfort to other human beings—but the blood storm had drained him of energy, so he decided to hole up for the night.

Once he angled his broad shoulders through the narrow gap between the rocks, Logan found himself in a chamber roughly the size of an average boxcar. He'd ridden the rails decades before, when he was a drifter and, sometimes, a fugitive. That chunk of memory came back to him as the others did, in hazy pieces. Sometimes he remembered places, sometimes people, sometimes just emotional impressions.

Often, there was sudden awareness. He would know a thing but not why he knew it or when and how he'd learned it.

The cave's ceiling was high enough for him to stand up to his full height, the dirt floor smooth, dry, and only slightly uneven.

Logan sniffed the dusty air and immediately detected the lingering stench of big cat. Even his keen eyes had difficulty seeing in the nearly absolute darkness of the cave, but he managed to discern animal bones heaped in the corner, probably from some long-ago feast. The animal smell was faint, the traces old. The cave had long been abandoned. It was a good enough place to rest until Logan had the strength to move on.

There was enough kindling around to start a fire, and the wind whistling through the cave provided natural ventilation, so he took a few minutes to gather up wood and create a pile.

The sharp sting from the release of his adamantium claws elicited a grunt of pain. Logan ignored the discomfort and scraped the blades along the rock wall, producing a shower of sparks. A few more minutes of huffing and puffing, and he soon had a roaring fire. He found a measure of peace watching the flickering light, and as the sun rose outside, the warmth of the crackling flames lulled him to sleep.

● ● ●

Combat Casualty Rehabilitation Center
Shroud Lake, Ontario

Stacked heels clicking on the windswept tarmac, Dr. Megan Vigil sidestepped another automated power carrier—the third vehicle to roll by since she'd exited the belly of the C-130 transport. From behind the oversized sunglasses perched on her pale, heart-shaped face, the young woman observed more carriers lined up on the edge of the airstrip.

That's a lot of equipment for such a small unit. Now I understand why the Director dispatched a Hercules. A smaller aircraft couldn't accomplish the mission.

A sudden blast roared off Shroud Lake, ripping the hat off her head and sending it down the runway. Freed from confinement, her long hair fluttered like a scarlet flag. Dammit, though, she loved that hat. Dr. Vigil shivered and pulled her collar tight around her slim neck. She picked up the pace as she headed for an assembly of boxy, windowless concrete structures at the edge of the single runway.

Megan searched for something that resembled a security checkpoint, a reception area, or even a front door. But the buildings were nondescript, just gray, featureless walls. Finally, she spied movement in a distant section of the compund, vehicles clustered around a loading dock.

Megan was told that the CCRC was a top-secret facility, so she found it strange that she had not been challenged by sentries—an unacceptable lapse of security protocol, in her judgment. When she finally reached the loading dock minutes later, Megan made an eerie discovery. There were no humans present, only more machines.

She stepped around a flatbed carrying a large metal cylinder and noticed an active biomedical monitor had been connected to the coffin-shaped container. Though she was not a physician, Megan recognized the device because she'd been hooked up to one herself not long ago.

Shivering from the cold—or was it from the unwanted memory?—Megan entered the building. Inside the cavernous interior of the loading dock, she finally spied something made of flesh and blood. In the center of the massive space, surrounded by five more of the hermetically sealed metal cylinders, a frowning middle-aged woman in a spotless white laboratory smock watched Megan approach, arms folded in front of her.

"Excuse me," Megan called. "I'm looking for the operating director of this facility—"

"You found me, Dr. Vigil. I'm glad you've arrived with my cargo plane. My team has been expecting you."

"Ah, yes," Megan said, flustered. "Then you must be—"

"The Matron."

"A pleasure to meet you." Megan offered the woman her hand. The Matron's grip was firm.

"You'll see that the Director's instructions have been carried out to the letter." The Matron's tone was coolly professional but not unfriendly. "Once the C-130 is loaded and refueled, the unit can depart. Things will be delayed somewhat, because we'll have to switch to helicopters for the final leg of the journey. Our destination is not equipped to handle large aircraft, you see."

"You have the situation in hand," Megan observed.

"We're well ahead of schedule, Doctor," the Matron said with a hint of pride.

The Matron was a striking woman, though she took little care to accentuate her attractiveness. She wore no makeup, and her gray-streaked hair was pulled back into a tight bun. But her cheekbones were high, her eyes large and blue, her lips full. It was obvious that this woman had been a great beauty in her younger days.

"Where is your unit?" Megan asked. "I'd like to meet them, if possible."

"It's not possible. Not at the moment. But they are here, right in front of you," the woman replied. "Sealed inside these cryostasis chambers."

Behind her dark glasses, Megan blinked in surprise. "All of them?"

The Matron shook her head. "Not all of them. Lieutenant Benteen is the CCRC's head of operations and security. Though he's also a member of my unit, the lieutenant will not be deployed on this mission.

He has other duties, specific to this facility. It was Benteen who notified me of your arrival."

"But I saw no one," Megan replied. "In fact, I found base security to be quite lax."

An electronic crackle echoed inside the giant space, followed by the hollow, tinny sound of a mechanical voice. "I beg to differ, Dr. Vigil. I have been observing your movements since you exited the Hercules aircraft and crossed the tarmac."

Megan heard the quiet rumble of metal wheels, then a hiss that resembled the hydraulic brakes on a bus. She glanced up, and her mouth opened in surprise.

A steel and glass box the size of an elevator car rolled along a monorail system high above the loading area. Through the glass, Megan saw a human brain drifting in a bubbling pink liquid. The long nerve cluster that had once been housed inside a spinal column was still linked to the twin lobes. Smaller nerves flowed outward from the spinal cluster like branches on a tree, each connected to an electronic circuit. More circuits penetrated various sections of the gray brain matter, and two thick bundles of digital feeder cable were wired to the optic nerves. The container rumbled to a halt above the two women.

"Amazing," Megan gasped.

A speaker crackled, and the electronic voice spoke again. "Lieutenant Frank Benteen at your service, Doctor. I knew you were coming because it was I who guided the aircraft in during the approach—"

"Along with air traffic control duties, the lieutenant is also operating the mechanical loaders and the automated refueling system that is replenishing your aircraft," the Matron explained.

"There are no more . . . humans here?" Megan asked.

"I have a dozen technicians on duty full-time. They are monitoring the physical condition of the Weapon Null team members currently in stasis—"

The robotic voice interrupted the Matron, speaking in a hollow monotone that Megan found disturbing.

"By the way, Dr. Vigil, I have located your hat—the one you lost crossing the runway. I've dispatched a loader to retrieve it."

"Thank you." Megan replied.

"Please excuse me," the brain box said after a pause. "There is an oxygen leak in cylinder five, and I must correct the problem."

With another hiss, the brakes released. The container rolled along the track until it passed through a door near the ceiling.

"The elevated monorail system gives Lieutenant Benteen access to the entire facility," the Matron explained. "He will remain behind to safeguard headquarters in our absence."

Megan couldn't shake the image of the living brain encased in a box. "How . . . how did he get that way?" she asked.

The Matron frowned. "War, Doctor. Benteen and

his men blundered into an enemy ambush during the Battle of Ia Drang."

"Vietnam? But I thought Canada remained neutral during that war," Megan replied.

"Twelve thousand Canadian citizens joined the United States military and served in Vietnam. There are seventy-eight Canadians listed on the Vietnam War Memorial in Washington, D.C."

"But where is his body?"

The Matron lifted her chin. "A human being is more than a body, Dr. Vigil. There is also memory, intellect, and perhaps even a soul."

Megan shook her head. "But how can he live like that?"

"When the medics found him in the jungle, Lieutenant Benteen was close to death," the Matron explained. "He'd lost both arms, both legs. His eyes were burned away, his jaw and eardrums shattered. Though he was alive, the lieutenant was locked in a prison of his mind, with no way to communicate with his fellow human beings."

The Matron paused. "Thanks to funding by the U.S. Defense Advance Research Project and the brilliant researchers here at the CCRC, Lieutenant Benteen is now free from his prison and has become a useful and productive member of society."

"I . . . see."

The Matron lifted her chin. "That's what we do here at the CCRC, Dr. Vigil. We take the shattered human debris of war, and, through technology, we give them new potential, new skills, new *lives*."

"But what they did to Lieutenant Benteen . . ." Megan whispered. "It's obscene. Grotesque."

The Matron stepped forward, stared Megan in the face. "Given similar circumstances, what life would you choose?"

Megan frowned but did not reply.

"Dr. Vigil, surely you're not prejudiced against someone because of their physical appearance?" the Matron challenged. "I would expect someone with her own handicap to possess a little empathy."

Inwardly, Megan cringed. But her face remained impassive.

"May I see the prosthetic, Doctor?" asked the Matron.

Without waiting for permission, she slipped the glasses off Megan Vigil's face. The doctor blinked against the glare. The fluorescent lights on the loading dock felt as if they were burning a hole into her skull. But soon the advanced ocular sensors implanted in her brain detected the neural overstimulation, and filters kicked in to compensate. The pain subsided, and Megan's vision cleared.

The Matron leaned forward to examine the blank red lenses. Megan permitted the intrusion for a moment. Finally, she snatched the glasses from the older woman's hand and put them on again.

"A digital optical system with interfacing electronics at the level of the retina, optic nerve, thalamus, and cortex. An astounding achievement, Dr. Vigil. Do they mimic the functionality of real eyes, or are there limitations?"

"In most ways, they are much better than my original eyes. But they are not perfect," Megan replied. The Matron waited to hear more. Megan paused, stubbornly refusing to elaborate further.

"Do you find the devices uncomfortable? Or perhaps even painful?" the Matron asked.

But Megan's patience with the woman was at an end. "I'm not here to talk about my condition, Matron."

"I'm sorry to pry, Doctor. My interest in your bionic modifications is professional, not personal."

"Nevertheless, my assignment is to observe the deployment and evaluate the operational effectiveness of the Weapon Null unit," Megan said through tight lips.

The Matron nodded. "I see. Well, then. By all means, you must begin at once. . . ."

5

THOMAS SWIMMING HORSE BALANCED A STACK OF books on his left arm and pushed through the rickety wooden door with his right. Immediately, the smell of dusk, mildew, wood smoke, and old paper assaulted his nostrils. He sneezed once, and the books tumbled to the crude wooden floor.

"Pretty nice outside," Thomas observed while he scooped them up. "Above zero, and the wind has died down. You might consider airing this place out."

In the center of the book-lined cabin, a bearded old man closed volume five of Gibbon's *The Decline and Fall of the Roman Empire* and rose to greet his visitor.

"Might do that, if I thought it was worth the effort. But I probably won't, 'cause I think it's a waste of time," the Librarian replied.

Thomas set the books down on an art deco counter salvaged from some long-demolished roadside eatery. Then he shrugged off the hunting rifle that was strapped to his left shoulder and leaned it against the counter. The old man limped to Thomas's side.

"Going hunting?" the Librarian asked.

Thomas shrugged.

"Want some coffee before you go, Chief?"

Thomas nodded. "So long as you don't call me Chief."

"Your wish is my command, Kimosabe."

The old man grabbed a stained rag and used it to grip the red-hot handle of the metal coffeepot, snatching it from the smoking hearth. He filled two dented metal mugs and handed one to Thomas.

"So, what did you think of Oswald Spengler?" the Librarian asked.

Thomas blew across the surface of the hot black liquid, then took a cautious sip.

"If I wanted to fill my head with crap, I could listen to Marvin the Silicon Valley Zen Naturalist," he replied. "Failing that, I could give Ben and Jerry a piece of my time. Those whacko survivalists have been waiting for the end of the world since *Newsweek* predicted a new ice age back in the 1970s."

The Librarian stroked his long beard. "I take it you weren't impressed. Well, I got some *Reader's Digest* Condensed Books. Maybe an abridged Danielle Steel potboiler is more your speed."

"Maybe," Thomas replied, refusing to rise to the bait.

The door opened again. A man in a bright yellow

parka entered, huffing against the cold. The newcomer had wide shoulders and short legs but compensated for his diminutive stature with a stride like an aggressive rooster's. Forty-something, he had eyes that flashed nervously under curly black hair. He stopped in his tracks, wide mouth curling into a sneer when he noticed the rifle at Thomas's arm.

"Going on patrol, Soldier Boy?" he asked, his tone snide.

Thomas ignored the jibe, took another gulp of steaming brew, but the Librarian shook his finger at the newcomer. "What's the matter, Marvin? Get up on the wrong side of the futon?"

"No," Marvin replied, his gaze still on Thomas's rifle. "I just don't like living around killers, soldiers, or cops. That's why I came here. That's why we all came here, isn't it? To find a place away from nihilists, destroyers, *pigs*."

"He's going hunting, that's all. If you don't like it, don't eat the meat," the Librarian replied.

"I *won't*, and I *don't*," the other man replied. "And I also don't like this guy shooting up the forest and gunning down the local wildlife, either. I've said again and again, that—"

"I spotted an intruder last night," Thomas said, slapping the cup down on the counter with a loud thunk, hot coffee threatening to slosh over onto the counter. Both men stopped bickering to stare at him.

"Where?" Marvin asked, eyes bulging.

"Outside my cabin. Past midnight. A stranger, and not friendly. As soon as he saw me, he took off up the mountain."

"He? You're sure it was a man?" Marvin asked. "What was he wearing?"

Thomas shrugged. "He was real hairy, or he was wearing animal skins. Either way, the guy was nearly naked."

The Librarian blinked. "Naked? That's crazy. It was fifteen below last night."

Marvin burst out laughing. "You had me fooled for a minute, Chief."

Thomas's dark eyes flashed. "I'm not making this up."

Marvin pulled off his parka, hung it on a set of antlers mounted on the wall. "Either you saw Sasquatch, or you were drinking firewater. Try meditation instead of booze. You people never could handle alcohol."

Thomas grinned, exposing sharp teeth. "We're damn good at scalping, though. Want a demonstration?"

The Librarian placed his lanky body between them. "Okay, boys, enough jawboning."

Thomas rose and moved to the door. "Thanks for the coffee."

The Librarian frowned. "You want to take home some more books, Tommy?"

"Later," Thomas called over his shoulder as he went through the door.

6

A few years ago

"SEPARATIST BOMB INJURES GRADUATE STUDENT."
That's what the headline claimed. Or so Megan Vigil
imagined. In truth, she never saw the newspapers or
the television reports. She never saw them because
she was lying in a hospital, blind and barely clinging
to life.

Her job had been to create virtual-reality models
for use in military training simulators. In exchange
for her work, the Canadian Defense Ministry paid
Megan's graduate-school tuition and offered her a
small stipend.

Megan had never been political. That kind of stuff
bored her. All she cared about was the virtual world.
She loved computers, and at twenty, her only goal in
life was to get a degree and design computer games.

She'd never even heard of the radical group called Anarchistes pour l'Indépendance du Québec. But in the end, that didn't matter. The group decided Megan's tenuous connection to the "oppressive government" made her fair game.

The bomb was planted on her office door over the weekend. Megan sprang the trap on a sunny Monday morning, 9:11 A.M.

When she awoke from her coma weeks later, she begged the doctors to remove her bandages so she could see. They told her the bandages were gone and that she would never see again.

Learning there was no hope of recovery, she fell into a deep depression. Then one night—or it could have been day—Megan gathered enough courage to slit her wrists. Unfortunately, she lacked the skill to do the job properly, and a quick-thinking nurse saved her life.

When Megan woke up again, she was in a different hospital. It was there that a stranger came along.

He revealed to Megan that he was the director of a top-secret military program called Department K. Through the use of advanced bionic devices, he and his surgeons would try to restore her sight—if she volunteered to be their guinea pig. The Director was honest, warning her that the procedures would be extensive and painful and that there was no guarantee the experimental prosthetics would work.

Megan agreed to the procedure. She decided she

was willing to suffer any agony, pay any price, if there was even a slight chance to restore her normal vision.

She paid. Dearly. The suffering continued for endless weeks. Finally, after thousands of procedures and a half-dozen major surgeries, the day came.

"I'm about to activate the bionics, Director," a technician said, his tone hushed.

"Dim the lights, nurse," the Director commanded. "No. Not enough. Even dimmer than that."

"But, Director, surely *we* need to see—"

"I realize it will be difficult for us, but Ms. Vigil's optical sensors need time to adjust, her sensitive nerves time to grow accustomed to the stimulation. Once the prosthetics are activated, there will be no turning back."

"The brain scan is normal, Director," another voice said. "We're ready."

"Feed power to the bionics, on my count. Three. Two. One—"

"Power on."

Megan heard a sound in the darkness. But she felt nothing. *Saw* nothing.

"Director! The neurons are active and flowing from the prosthetic eyes to her brain."

Still she felt nothing. Megan licked her lips nervously. Then she felt hands touching the cumbersome optical blinders strapped to her bald, scarred head.

"Are you ready, Ms. Vigil?" the Director whispered.

She nodded.

"Keep your eyes closed, my dear."

Megan nodded again. Her head was jostled, and Megan heard a faint click. Then, for the first time in weeks, the optical blinders were removed. The weight she had carried for so long suddenly gone, Megan felt light-headed.

"You may open your eyes now, Ms. Vigil," the Director said softly. "Don't be afraid."

Trembling, Megan did as the man asked. Slowly, tentatively, she lifted her eyelids—and the light stabbed her brain like a million diamond-hard, razor-sharp nails. Within seconds, the torment intensified, and so did her screams.

Megan's howls of agony continued, filling the room and echoing through the antiseptic corridors until someone finally jabbed a needle into her arm, and her world mercifully faded to black again.

Somewhere over British Columbia
Today

Megan awoke, startled and disoriented. Soon she regained her senses, realizing that the rumble of the C-130's massive engines had lulled her into sleep. She sat up, catching the files in her lap before they spilled onto the deck. Megan straightened her coat and adjusted the dark glasses on her face. Then she looked up and discovered that the Matron had been watching her all along.

"Yes?" Megan said sharply.

"I was wondering if you were finished reviewing the personnel files, Doctor?"

"Almost," Megan replied.

Uninvited, the Matron sat down next to her on the canvas seat, a notebook computer on her lap. Megan shifted uncomfortably and glanced away.

Within a few feet of them, lined up along either side of the cargo aircraft's Spartan interior, the members of the Weapon Null unit were imprisoned inside metal cylinders, locked in a dreamless cryosleep.

"Is it necessary to transport your unit like this?" Megan asked. "Couldn't this time be used better? Perhaps to interact with them? Conduct mission briefings, engage in strategic planning?"

"They need no briefing or planning, Doctor. When the time comes, my team will know what to do."

Then the Matron smiled.

"In fact, I'm delighted to have the opportunity to demonstrate the usefulness of my unit. In the past, the potential of the Weapon Null Program has been grievously overlooked."

"If you care so much about your unit, why keep them penned up? Why can't they move freely?"

The Matron sighed. "You must think of them as high-precision instruments, Doctor. Advanced tools of war such as fighter jets, nuclear submarines, and attack helicopters require many man-hours of maintenance time for every hour of combat operations. The same is true of my unit."

"But—"

"You have no idea what it takes to maintain my people, Dr. Vigil. The drugs alone cost millions of dollars. Deactivation during downtime cuts costs considerably. The members of my unit understand the necessity of these measures. And I'm sure the Director appreciates our frugality."

Megan glanced at the files in her lap. From the notes she'd read, she imagined the appearance of the Weapon Null unit to resemble the ghastly figures in a Hieronymus Bosch painting—a twisted collection of biomechanical human grotesqueries, their flesh fused with weaponry, brains linked to computers, human matter twisted and reengineered by scientists bent on destruction without any consideration of the consequences.

"I . . . I understand your point," Megan said. "Some of these . . . modifications—they seem extreme. The aesthetic impact alone—"

"You're saying they're ugly—"

"I'm not commenting on their physical appearance, Matron. There are no images in these files beyond photographs taken during the induction process."

The Matron opened the laptop. "I'm not hiding anything, Doctor. There are thousands of images of my team stored here. You're welcome to—"

Megan waved the device aside. "I'm sorry, Matron. My prosthetic eyes don't function quite like the real thing. There are subtle differences—a hypersensitivity to light, for instance, and a few blind spots when dealing with electronic devices."

"Please elaborate, Doctor."

Megan sighed. "To be frank, computer screens, televisions, any kind of monitor . . . all I see when I look at them are flashes of light and rippling waves of color. A blur, basically."

"Oh. Oh, well." The Matron closed the computer and set it aside. "We all lived perfectly contented lives before computers and television were invented. In truth, your limitation . . . it's a small thing, really."

"Yes," Megan replied. "A small thing."

"In any case, you'll meet my team soon enough. Then you can see for yourself."

The Matron rose, then turned to face her.

"Don't judge my people too harshly, Dr. Vigil. Military hardware is not designed for beauty or grace, only effectiveness. Theirs is a fearful symmetry. But if you look closely enough, under the grotesque technology, the chaotic redesign of their bodies . . . you might recognize their splendor, too. "

7

THOMAS SWIMMING HORSE TURNED HIS BACK TO the blasting wind and looked upward to the steep trail that ran along the side of the mountain. A quick scan of the path, and his sharp eyes spied a slight depression in the crusty snow—another footprint left by the stranger he'd been pursuing all afternoon.

Breathing hard, Thomas climbed to the top of a jutting rock. He sank down, letting his booted feet dangle over the cliff's edge. Glancing at the sun, he estimated the time. He'd have to start back soon or risk getting stuck in the mountains overnight. He was far enough away from home that if a sudden winter storm were to blow in, he'd be finished. Up here, he doubted even his mountain warfare training could save him.

Thomas coughed and wiped his nose, wondered about the man he was pursuing. He had no doubt he was hunting a human being. And whoever this SOB was, he was wise to the ways of a tracker. Thomas knew that because of the spoor he'd been following.

At first, he'd easily detected the stranger's footprints. But as Thomas continued to climb, weather became a factor. Whipping winds obliterated snow tracks, and the packed ice barely registered the stranger's passing.

Thomas soon realized that his quarry was deliberately masking his trail. The stranger left the path, to move across rocks that left no footprints. He doubled back on his own tracks, left false trails, and even crossed a dangerous stretch of bare cliff to avoid leaving his path in the snow. Thomas had to backtrack a half-dozen times, which was endlessly frustrating.

This guy was good. But Thomas was a trained tracker, too, and a Cherokee of the Wind Clan to boot. There was no way this brave was going to lose the trail if he didn't want to—despite the fact that his quarry consistently took the most difficult road available in an effort to shake off any pursuit.

Now, who does that remind me of? Thomas mused, recalling the words of his grandfather, now dead and buried.

A sly horse runs, and a smiling fish swims, Thomas, the old man used to say. *So our grandmothers named us the Swimming Horse people, because we always choose the most difficult path through life.*

Thomas debated whether to continue the chase or

head back to Second Chance, where a warm fire and a can of pork and beans was waiting for him. Finally, he rose, intent on heading home. But his sudden movement startled a fawn that had been lurking unseen among the rocks. The young deer bolted, scrambling up the path toward higher ground.

It's fate. The deer's going in the same direction as the man.

Thomas dragged the rifle from his shoulder, loaded it, and continued up the trail.

He climbed for another hour, while the sun moved across the sky and his shadow grew longer. Three times, Thomas almost turned back. But always the fawn reappeared—too far away for a clear shot but always within sight.

Against his better judgment, Thomas pushed on, the thought of fresh meat too tempting. Fortunately, the steep trail ran along the bottom of a deep crevasse etched into the side of the mountain. The deer was forced to remain on the path, and it had nowhere to go but up.

Thomas knew from a previous climb that the ravine dead-ended. He also recalled that there was a cave nestled among the rocks and that the last time he'd hiked through this area, a cougar had taken up residence there.

The big cat might still be around, so he should have proceeded with caution. Instead, Thomas decided to speed up, determined to bag the deer before the cougar snatched it out from under his nose.

Winded, Thomas reached a blind corner in the trail a few minutes later. From the other side of the bend, he heard the soft pounding of hooves on hard frozen ground. The deer had shifted direction and was coming toward him. Thomas raised his rifle and just touched the cold metal trigger with his index finger.

Before he expected it, the deer rounded the corner. Fawn and man both stopped dead in their tracks.

The deer's nostrils flared, its white-tipped tail flickering back and forth. Thomas could see the animal was spooked—so spooked it raced into the arms of its hunter.

Must have gotten a whiff of the big cat's scent and took off frantically, in a blind run, Thomas figured. In any case, the animal was so close he couldn't possibly miss. Thomas aimed and squeezed the trigger.

The shot took the deer between the eyes. The impact knocked the creature backward. It tumbled end over end before landing on its side. Its legs kicked once, then stilled.

Concerned about the possibility of a big cat lurking around, Thomas kept his rifle ready as he warily approached the carcass.

But as careful as he was, nothing could prepare him for the nightmare that lurched around the bend as Thomas crouched to check his kill.

He saw the shadow first. Misshapen, with thick-muscled, apelike arms. Thomas looked up—and stared a demon in the face.

It was a man, or looked like one, short and powerfully built, with broad shoulders covered in black, wiry hair. He was filthy, a ragged wolf pelt encrusted with dried blood wrapped around his waist. Strangest of all, the hair on the man's head peaked into two points, just above the ears, like a devil's horns.

Thomas yelped in surprise, stumbled backward, and slipped on the ice. His legs flew out from under him, and down he went. With a loud grunt, he landed on his tailbone, the rifle still pointed at the stranger. The impact jarred his trigger finger, and the weapon discharged.

The rifle blast echoed off the mountains, shattering the stillness. He saw the stranger's head jerk backward in a shower of blood. Hot liquid splashed across Thomas's face. The wild man dropped to one knee.

The recoil tore the rifle out of Thomas's grip. As he fumbled to catch it, the weapon bounced off the ice-slick rocks and slid down the hill.

On the ground, unarmed and helpless, Thomas could only watch as the stranger clutched his ruined head with large, beefy hands.

Thomas waited for the stranger to topple dead to the ground—surely, the wound was fatal? Instead, the creature squared his shoulders, lowered his arms, and stared straight ahead. Under a Niagara of gushing blood, Thomas saw the grisly wound on the man's scalp, spied a glimmer of metallic silver where white bone and gray brain tissue should have been. He watched, incredulous, as the fountain of gore slowed, then ceased. Finally, the gash began to close before his eyes.

The stranger's eyes seemed to refocus, and he saw Thomas on the ground. With a roar, the man threw his arms wide.

A hiss, and six long, curled metal blades slid out of hidden sheaths in the man's wrists.

"Sonofa—" Thomas croaked. Eyes locked on the monster, he scrambled backward, crab-walking over the deer carcass. Snarling, the creature took a step forward.

Thomas threw up his hands in surrender. "You win! I'm unarmed," he cried. The creature took another step toward him.

Desperate, Thomas kicked the dead fawn toward the thing.

"Here!" he yelled, his back against the wall of the ravine. "You want the meat? Take it. It's yours."

He curled himself into a ball and waited for the end. But for some reason, his attacker paused and stared at him for a moment. Then the claws slowly retracted, until they disappeared beneath the flesh on the man's wrists. Thomas wanted to breath a sigh of relief, but he didn't trust the creature.

"I won't hurt you," Thomas whispered, hoping the thing understood him. "Just take the deer and go, okay?"

The man's hand reached out and closed on the

deer's hind legs. Then the stranger planted a dirty, callused foot on the dead animal's abdomen. With a quick jerk, the wild man yanked the rear leg out of its socket. Another twist, and the tendons snapped. Grunting, the creature draped the deer haunch over his shoulder like a baseball bat, leaving the rest of the meat for Thomas.

Then the wild man turned, raced along the ravine, and vanished around the bend. Trembling, Thomas scrambled to his feet and found his rifle, the barrel plugged with snow. He almost cast the useless weapon aside, then hung it over his shoulder. Heart pumping, knees weak, Thomas hefted the carcass the wild man had left for him and draped it over his shoulders, too.

Without looking backward, Thomas made a hasty retreat.

8

LOGAN TOSSED THE DRIPPING SHANK INTO THE CAVE and squeezed through the narrow entrance. In the gloom, the ashes from last night's fire still glowed, and he stoked the smoldering coals into a healthy blaze.

He extended his claws, wincing as cold steel punched through the skin on his arm. There was not much blood, and the wound immediately closed around the adamantium steel blades. The pain, and the healing, occurred each time he extended those blades.

You'd think I'd get used to it, but it always hurts.

Using the blades, he stripped the hide off the deer leg, then retracted his claws and dangled the meat over the fire. Soon the juices began to flow, and the venison sizzled and popped. Logan's belly rumbled as the smell of scorched flesh filled the cave.

While he waited to enjoy his first cooked meal in

many weeks, Logan gazed into the flickering flame, recalling his confrontation with the hunter. Life to him
was neither sacred nor special, but Logan never liked
to kill anyone who didn't deserve it. That had almost
happened today.

It was a close call, he mused. *I almost gutted that rube
like a pig, and all the guy was doing was hunting for a little
meat, maybe to feed his family.*

Logan turned the deer shank and added wood to
the fire.

He'd had target fixation. That much he knew. He'd
been so intent on chasing supper that he hadn't even
noticed the other guy was there.

Until he shot me, and I almost lost it—

Logan blinked . . . then the corners of his lips curled
into a smile. Yeah, he'd almost lost it. But he hadn't.
He'd fought the urge to lash out. He'd kept his head.
Even after he was shot, he didn't tear the guy apart,
which he remembered doing in the past, and for a lot
less reason than a gunshot wound to the skull.

An unfamiliar noise interrupted his thoughts. It
took a moment for Logan to realize it was the sound of
his own laughter.

Despite all the things they did to me, and all the things they
tried *to do, those lab-coat bastards failed.*

He was still here. He was still human.

*Maybe I'm living like a wild beast, but I'm not some beast
that kills on command. I'm a man, not an animal.*

Smiling under the filth, Logan flicked his wrist.

With a *snikt,* a single steel claw dropped out of its sheath. Logan used it to skewer a piece of sizzling venison. Saliva flowing, he brought the cooked meat to his mouth and began to feast.

It was well past sunset when Thomas came off the mountain. He had to move cautiously for the last half mile, since a curtain of almost total darkness descended over the forest. The deer carcass weighed heavily on his aching shoulders; the coppery scent of fresh-spilled blood attracted hungry wolves.

Thomas redoubled his pace when he heard their echoing howls. By the time he reached his log cabin, the predators were practically nipping at his heels. Stomping his boots to shake off the snow, Thomas slipped the carcass into the rafters above his porch, where the animals couldn't reach it. He knew he should dress the carcass before it froze solid, but he was too rattled for that.

Thomas stumbled through his front door, stoked the coals in the hearth, and tossed on more logs. Finally, he tore the near-frozen, sweat-stained clothing off his back and tossed it into the corner.

While the fire roared, Thomas unscrewed a mason jar and took a deep swig of home-brewed whiskey. The liquid burned his throat, and he shivered, but soon the alcohol and the blazing hearth worked their magic.

Still trembling from cold and shock, he opened a

tin of pork and beans with a survival knife and heated the meager meal right in the can. After he spooned the beans down his throat—and drank a lot more whiskey—Thomas began to feel human again.

At least my hands stopped shaking. . . .

Thomas used to laugh at the stories of spirits and gods told by his grandfather, but his brush with the stranger on the mountain almost made a believer out of him.

What the hell did I see? A demon? A Sasquatch? he asked himself, groping for an answer that made some kind of reasonable sense.

With a blanket over his shoulders, Thomas dismantled his weapon, relieved to discover there was no permanent damage to the hunting rifle. That was fortunate, because he owned only one other weapon, a remnant of his days as a U.S. Ranger. The Colt Commando assault rifle and hundreds of rounds of ammunition were hidden in a waterproof plastic container under the floorboards of his cabin.

Thomas kept the automatic weapon out of sight because it wasn't appropriate for hunting, and the citizens of Second Chance weren't your average gun-collecting mountaineers. The offbeat village wouldn't approve of a military-style weapon in their midst. Even so, Thomas considered digging out that Colt. Just as quickly, he rejected the idea.

I shot him in the head, and the wound was healing inside of a minute. What good would the Colt do against something like that? And anyway, if he'd wanted to kill me, he would have, with those weird knives that popped out of his wrists. . . .

It was long past midnight when Thomas reassembled the rifle and put away his cleaning kit. He doused his face with water warmed on the hearth, then prepared for bed.

But a few minutes after Thomas stretched out on his bunk, he was shaken from a fitful sleep by the beating thunder of helicopter engines—lots of them. They roared high overhead, so many that their noise shook dust loose from the rafters.

Thomas threw the covers aside and leaped out of bed. Half-naked, he burst through the front door and peered into the cloudless sky. He strained to see the aircraft, but with hills and tall trees surrounding the settlement, much of the sky was obscured, and all Thomas saw was a mantle of stars.

Soon the noise faded, and the night was still again.

Shivering, Thomas listened intently for the sound of other aircraft, but all he heard was the wind whistling through the valley and the baying of a ravenous wolf.

9

THE BOEING CH-47 CHINOOK BANKED SHARPLY,
the abrupt shift in gravity causing Megan Vigil to slide
across the seat. Her body came to rest against the hull,
her face pressed against the window.

Megan turned her head to peer through the cold
glass. She could discern mountains in the distance, the
stars reflected off the smooth surface of a lake or river
far below.

She stole a glance at the Matron, who occupied a
seat on the other side of the dark, shadowy cargo bay.
The woman was asleep, curled inside an olive drab
wool blanket, her thick arm thrown across her face.

Megan faced the window again and now saw only
a black void.

Because their mission was clandestine, the helicopters flew "dark"—no running lights, cabins illuminated by red emergency lighting. Megan slipped the

dark glasses off her face and folded them in her lap.

Closing her eyes, Megan used tiny muscles under her eyelids to manipulate the controls of her bionic optical system. When she opened them again, her "eyes" operated through a separate circuit implanted in her brain—a passive, self-contained image-intensifier device that amplified existing ambient light. In layman's terms, Megan was operating in night-vision mode, magnifying the available light to illuminate her surroundings.

Suddenly, the mountains around her and the valleys below were fully revealed in an eerie green glow. She watched as forests rolled by under the chopper's belly, and for a moment, Megan thought she saw a small settlement nestled in a valley next to a winding creek.

But the twin-rotor Chinook was traveling at better than a hundred and fifty miles an hour, too fast for her to make out many details before the scenery changed.

The helicopter banked again, and Megan craned her neck until she could see the other five aircraft following closely behind, in a precise V formation. Then the aircraft leveled off to fly over a deep valley between two mountain ranges, and she saw a partially frozen river snaking its way along the bottom of the canyon.

Megan knew their destination, of course, but she wondered where they were, exactly, in the Canadian Rockies.

Everyone in Department K was familiar with the Weapon X Program. They knew about the Hive and about the tragedy that occurred there months ago. The information was "eyes only," of course, but even within top-secret organizations, people tended to talk. The story was too astonishing—and too horrific—to remain hidden for long.

But despite all the rumors and speculation, one thing was certain. No one knew the exact location of the hidden biomedical facility except the Director himself.

Still peering through the window, Megan activated the telescopic system in her right eye. Like powerful binoculars, this device magnified more than fifty times the images being transmitted to her optic nerves. With it, she examined the terrain in far more detail.

In the green glow of ambient light, Megan saw the river below widen to become an artificial lake. Then she saw the dam and the small hydroelectric plant at its base—the facility that once powered the Professor's laboratory complex.

Minutes later, as they flew directly over the dam, the engine pitch altered, and Megan felt the helicopter slow. Battling unpredictable winds that buffeted the helicopter, the Chinook approached a mountain peak high above the dam. Only when they were close to the ground did Megan see the runway, partially obscured beneath an inch of windswept snow.

The tarmac was cracked and pitted from neglect, the small hangar half-collapsed. On the opposite side of the runway, on top of a steep rise and surrounded by pine trees, Megan spied a line of gray concrete buildings, their roofs and entrances covered with drifting snow.

As the helicopter circled for a landing, Megan saw a kennel or zoo, deserted now but with cages and bars still intact. One outbuilding, crowned by a two-hundred-foot chimney, was scorched by fire. She saw many abandoned vehicles scattered about, all of them frozen in place.

The entire compound was circled by chain-link fencing, much of it blown down by winter winds and collapsed by drifting snow. Security checkpoints stood at each entrance, but they were as deserted as the rest of the complex.

It was once the most advanced biomedical research facility in the world. Now it was nothing but a ghost town. Megan found it hard to believe it had been depopulated by a single entity, the thing called Weapon X.

Death weighed heavily on the place, and Megan decided she'd seen enough. Using the muscles in her eye sockets, she toggled her bionic implants to restore "normal" vision. Then she slipped the dark glasses over her eyes—just in time. Cabin lights sprang to life, filling the cargo hold with brilliant light.

The Matron stirred, blinking against the unexpected glare. The woman sat upright, yawned, and stretched. Then they both felt a jolt and heard a dull thump as the helicopter's wheels touched the frozen tarmac. Outside the window, powdery snow billowed in sparkling clouds as the other helicopters touched down inside the landing zone.

The Matron rose and faced Megan. "We're here at last," she declared, her voice laced with excitement.

Megan nodded but did not reply.

The Matron peered through her window and frowned. "After all the amazing things that have been accomplished here, it's sad to see this compound in such disrepair." Her expression then brightened. "However, for the duration of our mission, we will deploy from here. Our occupation should bring a little bit of life to this tragic place."

With the grinding of gears and the whine of an electric motor, the helicopter's rear ramp descended. The warm cabin filled with a frigid blast of arctic air. The Matron faced the onslaught unruffled, hands on hips.

"To see this place functional again . . . it's like a dream come true," she declared.

Megan shivered against the heavy shroud of cold that descended on her.

Not a dream, Matron. More like a nightmare.

"Director?"

The tone was gentle, soothing. The Director opened his eyes and blinked in surprise. Then he straightened in his chair and ran his left hand through his unruly hair.

"I . . . I must have dozed off," he said.

"You're tired, Director," the robotic Voice replied. "You haven't left this office in two days, and you've barely slept four hours since the operation began."

The Director frowned. "Too many details. Too much to do."

"You need to delegate some of your responsibilities."

"I do far too much of that already. A man should mind his own business, not let others do it for him."

"Speaking of delegates, Dr. Vigil has made her first report."

The Director pushed aside the file he'd been reading. "Good news, I trust."

"I'm pleased to report that the Matron is on-site. Royal Air Force technicians, along with Dr. Vigil, are working to power up a small portion of the facility. Weapon Null's base of operations should be running in two or three hours."

The Director chuckled and slapped the desk. "The Royal Air Force squawked when I commandeered their entire Chinook fleet, but it was worth it. We're well ahead of schedule."

"What next, Director?"

"As soon as the base is fully operational, release all the Chinooks. Allow the aircraft and crew to return to their home base—"

"But, sir! That will leave the Matron and her team isolated."

"As they should be," the Director replied. "No one

from the Royal Air Force should be present when the Matron activates her unit."

"But the Matron will require helicopters for tactical duties, insertions and extractions, resupply—"

"I've already dispatched Major Sallow and his special forces squads, along with three Blackhawk helicopters. His men should arrive at the facility within the hour."

"Very good, sir."

The Director shifted in his chair. "You have something more to say?" he asked.

"Unfortunately, Dr. Vigil has experienced a curious reaction to her surroundings. She is uncomfortable inside the ruins of the Professor's lab. She won't be happy to learn she's trapped there—"

"Unfortunate, but we can't risk word about the existence of Weapon Null leaking to the world," the Director insisted. "You can imagine the result if one of those air force men ended up spilling his guts to the media. I'm afraid the average person will not understand our motives for creating such . . . things." He sighed. "Sometimes it's hard not to feel persecuted, my friend. Our goals are noble, but I'm afraid the public would focus on the grotesquerie itself. And their reaction would be outrage, not understanding."

10

OVERHEAD, THE FULL MOON GLEAMED BEHIND A thin veil of clouds. Far below, a bonfire roared at the mouth of a dry creek bed. Whipped by the desert wind, the blaze illuminated the parched valley in a flickering, red-orange glow.

The creek bed, carved into the earth by ancient waters, was a sacred place to the Wind Clan. Living on the shore of a lake or a river was a Cherokee tradition. But in the Arizona desert, waterways were rare, so Thomas's people made do with what they had.

Thomas watched while the males of the tribe gathered around the fire to dance and chant the sacred words. Strangely, he heard no sounds. Not the crackling fire. Not the frenzied chanting. Not the howling wind or even the hiss of shifting sands that sang him to sleep as a child.

But even without ears, Thomas recognized the

celebration. It was the Festival of the New October Moon—Nuwtiegwa—a sacred time marked by all Cherokee nations, East and West. To the Wind people, this was the most holy festival of them all, celebrated with mysterious rituals that were unique to the clan.

On this special night, the young men displayed Mohawks fashioned from the soft belly fir of porcupines. Their faces were stained with streaks of vermilion paint concocted from bright red mercuric sulfide. Red was an important color, according to Cherokee tradition, signifying triumph in battle and success in life.

Ironic, Thomas believed, because the reservation's soil was red, too—a dusty, blood-hued sand that sustained little life beyond fleas, scorpions, mice, coyotes, and cacti.

Thomas pulled his eyes away from the silent revelers to scan the hills that ringed the valley. Somewhere up there, above the smoke and fire, the women congregated. They celebrated the coming of the new moon, too, but in their own way.

Each gender had its own traditions, and those legacies were not shared. The Divide was one way the Wind Clan maintained harmony, balance—and that balance, between the physical and spiritual worlds, was what his people treasured above all things. So the women listened from the hills while the men in the valley beat drums, rattled gourds filled with stones, stomped the ground with their bare feet.

Still, despite all the frenetic activity he saw, Thomas heard nothing but an oppressive, maddening silence.

He scanned the faces in the crowd and spied many familiar faces. He greeted each man, calling out his name. But everyone he spoke to acted as deaf as he.

In desperation, Thomas jumped up and down and waved his hands in front of their faces. But no one noticed.

Close to the silent fire, he spied his grandfather. The old man wore the ceremonial garb of the tribal medicine man, his shoulder-length gray hair rippling like a faded banner. The man's eyes were closed, and his lips moved as he muttered the sacred words.

Frantic now, Thomas stood in front of the old man, shouted until his throat hurt. He beat his own ears with his fists to show his grandfather that he could not hear. But even when the old man's milky gray eyes opened wide, he stared right through Thomas as if his grandson were not there.

Thomas was like the ghost of a murdered man, doomed to walk the earth forever but no more substantial than a wisp of fog.

Thomas wept. It was unmanly, but he could not control his overwrought emotions. He raged to the heavens and then prayed to the Apportioner, begging the Creator Spirit to let him hear again, live again.

And then the stillness was shattered. A bolt of lightning shot out of the night sky and struck the ground at Thomas's feet. The blast stunned him, and Thomas reeled.

When the smoke cleared, the revelers were gone. The bonfire still blazed, wood popped, the wind whistled. Then Thomas heard his grandfather's gravelly voice.

The old man stood with his back to the fire. His hands were raised to ward off evil spirits. Eyes on the ground, he danced back and forth, chanting the same phrase over and over.

"Wi-na-go, Wi-na-go, Wi-na-go . . ."

His grandfather seemed afraid, and that frightened Thomas, too. He reached for the old man, but before they touched, Thomas was knocked off his feet by a blood-soaked vision that rushed between them, carried on a shrieking gust of wind.

Thomas recognized the wolf pelt, the filth, the dripping steel claws, and the stench of spilled blood. It was the wild man from the mountain.

The chanting became louder, until it echoed off the dry hills and boomed throughout the parched valley.

"Wi-na-go, Wi-na-go, Wi-na-go . . ."

The words were spoken loudly enough for Thomas finally to comprehend them. His grandfather was calling down curses on the Winago—the Cherokee personification of spiritual evil, the origin of all human disease and suffering.

"Wi-na-go, Wi-na-go, Wi-na-go!" the old man cried, dancing and waving his arms to repel the beast.

According to the old ways, wrongful killing—violence done for profit or pleasure—caused an imbalance in the universe. Each violent act caused a new disease to enter the physical world from the spiritual realm, forever to plague mankind.

"Wi-na-go, Wi-na-go, Wi-na-go!"

The words hammered against Thomas's eardrums like gunshots. He clutched his ears to shut out the sound, but the words still penetrated his brain.

"Wi-na-go, Wi-na-go, Wi-na-go!" his grandfather cried.

Then, as suddenly as he appeared, the wild man was gone—banished by the old man's prayers. Trembling, Thomas sank to his knees, awed by the old man's powerful medicine.

To his surprise, the chanting continued. His grandfather danced to magical dances and waved his arms to ward off evil.

"Wi-na-go, Wi-na-go, Wi-na-go . . ."

But this time, his words and gestures were directed at Thomas.

Thomas opened his eyes, shocked back to consciousness by the strange dream.

He lay trembling on the sweat-soaked bunk, stared at the smoke-stained rafters for a long time, until the final traces of the nightmare faded like a poisonous fog. Finally, Thomas sat up and rubbed his eyes.

Still agitated by his dream, Thomas rose and filled the coffeepot with the water he'd drawn from the well yesterday morning. Then he prodded the fire and put on his morning mud.

He'd just had time to splash the final dregs of cold water on his face when someone knocked on his door.

11

The Hive

MEGAN VIGIL EMERGED FROM A NARROW CONDUIT
in the ceiling, startling a young airman. He stared,
openmouthed, at Megan. The airman had been running power cables from this subbasement, up to a satellite communications console in the main laboratory.
That's where the Matron established her command
center, among the ruins of the Professor's grim instru-
mentality.

"Sorry, airman. I was just finishing up a job."

"My fault, ma'am," the man replied with a dis-
tinct French-Canadian accent. "This joint, it has me
spooked, that's all."

Megan smiled. "This place has us all spooked."

The airman smiled gamely. "We'll have the lights

on pretty soon, though. That should brighten things up considerably."

"Are the Matron's people helping out?" Megan asked.

The man snorted. "A worthless bunch of orange-suited geeks, if you'll pardon my bluntness. They haven't left the lab. Been hovering over those cylinders like bees around a hive."

Behind her dark glasses, Megan scanned the area. "Is your boss around?"

"Corporal MacKenzie? I'll buzz him."

Using the radio on his vest, the airman summoned his commanding officer. The man arrived mere moments later and greeted Megan by touching his cap.

"I've restarted the emergency generator," Megan told him. She noticed he was older, around forty with gray threading through his light brown hair. He was tall and lanky, had a kind face, no wedding ring. "The system is powered by a Stark Industries Fusion Twelve battery, so we should have enough juice to operate for several weeks before we'll need replenishment."

"I hope we're out of here long before that," the corporal replied. He gave her a little smile.

"Is there anything else I can do?" she asked.

"Well, there's a broken power coupler between Level A and B," MacKenzie said. "The access tunnel around the break is pretty tight, but you're small enough to fit inside if you're not claustrophobic."

"Not at all."

"Then perhaps you'll give it a try."

"Lead on," Megan replied.

They descended a narrow stairwell, lit by red emergency lighting. At the base of the stairs, Megan saw the unbolted panel, the narrow tunnel behind the wall.

"You'll need a flashlight from here," MacKenzie warned. "It's pretty dark through there."

Megan smiled. "I think I'll manage."

Fifteen minutes later, she located the problem and began to replace a tangle of half-melted wiring with brand-new cable.

The Weapon X facility had been a shambles when they arrived. Emergency lighting that was supposed to be functional was not, and systems they believed they could turn on were fried and needed replacing.

Megan welcomed the work and had thrown herself into it. She enjoyed utilizing her second education in cyberengineering, but she also used the task as an escape—a way to push away thoughts of her grim and oppressive surroundings.

Ironically, the work exposed Megan to the true horror of the facility, for she constantly stumbled upon the grisly evidence of the violence and death that these walls witnessed.

The shocks began three hours before, when an airman opened a maintenance hatch and a human head rolled out, wispy hairs still stuck to the withered scalp. The ghastly relic rolled across the floor in front of an entire air crew.

Corporal MacKenzie took charge of the remains, vowing to take them back to their Royal Air Force base in Halifax for identification and "a proper burial."

Later, while stringing cable through a long ventilation shaft, Megan discovered brown splashes of dried blood and deep tears in the metal walls. She examined the cuts and deduced they'd been made by three-pronged blades of incredible tensile strength. She followed the trail of encrusted blood to another maintenance hatch. She didn't open it.

Bullet holes riddled the walls of another corridor she trekked through, its floor stained with blood from one end to the other. Megan trod lightly and tried not to think about how many deaths it took to spill so much.

Now, inside the tight tunnel, Megan pushed aside those thoughts and concentrated on her task. Ten minutes later, she finished up.

"Okay, Corporal," she said into the radio. "Give it a try."

Megan heard an electronic hum, smelled ozone. Then her radio crackled.

"Good job, lass," MacKenzie said. "Come out now. The Matron is here to see you."

Megan climbed out of the tube, and an airman sealed the hatch behind her. She climbed three flights of concrete stairs to the wrecked laboratory. The Matron waited for her beside the corporal, a thick file in her hand.

"A young airman was kind enough to get one of the printers here up and running," the Matron said. "Here are hard copies of my files. I urge you to examine the top file first. I've already begun the activation process on that particular agent. He will be the first to face Weapon X."

Megan was covered with grease and soot. "I'll clean up and get right on these files," she replied.

"Excellent. Airman Hawkes will show you to your quarters."

"Come along, Doctor," Hawkes said, grinning. "We've got the water heaters working. You've earned a hot shower."

The water was hot, if a bit rusty. Airman Hawkes told Megan it was drawn from the reservoir, down behind the dam. Fortunately, the pumps were in good working order, unlike most of the other machines in the facility.

She showered in near darkness, using only the night-light. The optic nerves behind the bionics throbbed with each beat of her heart, and Megan found the darkness soothing. She'd missed her last several doses of painkillers—on purpose. The daily regimen of opiates had begun to erode her hearing. The Director was already making plans to implant a bionic audio device, complete with various "enhancements," of course.

Megan was determined to avoid the procedure as long as possible.

When the grime was finally washed away, she cut off the spray and stepped out of the shower. The towel smelled musty, so she tossed it into the bin, deciding her assigned quarters were warm enough to drip dry. Still naked, she left the bathroom and stepped in front of a full-length mirror mounted on the door of her sparsely furnished bedroom.

Megan was alarmingly thin, with long, skinny legs, and her head seemed too large for her frail body. Streaks of red hair clung to her slim neck and shoulders like dripping blood. Her complexion was pale and sickly from lack of sunlight. In the muted light, her bionic optical system glowed red, like the eyes of a demonic cat.

Once upon a time, Megan was fit and tanned. But a dozen major surgical procedures in three years and dozens of daily doses of highly toxic antirejection drugs had taken their grim toll on her health. She was scrawny and weak, her body wasted. Megan turned her back on the mirror, found her dark glasses, and slipped them over her eyes. Then she stretched out on the bunk.

The files the Matron had given her were on the night table. Megan snatched the thickest folder off the top of the stack. Inside, she found a file titled "Project Slammer." In the soft glow of the night-light, Megan began to read.

The Librarian sat on a creaky chair, rubbing his chin while he regarded Thomas.

"When the gun went off, you're sure you hit it?"

"*Him,*" Thomas insisted. "It was a man. A man wearing a wolf pelt. Yeah, I hit him, right in the forehead. I felt a hot spray of blood hit my face. I saw the wound, and I saw it healing in a matter of seconds."

Thomas poured the Librarian more coffee. The older man held the tin cup with both hands. "Anything else you recall? Apart from the metal claws he was wearing on his wrists, I mean."

"I'm not sure he was wearing them," Thomas replied.

"Huh?"

"When his scalp was open, I swear I saw metal—"

"Metal?" the other man said. "Like he had a steel plate in his head, you mean?"

Thomas shrugged. "Something like that."

"Are you sure it wasn't a helmet?"

Thomas jumped up, spilling some of the hot coffee on his wrist. "No, hell no," he cried, shaking his scalded hand. "He had hair on his head. A beard and sideburns, too. And his hair came up in points on either side of his head."

The Librarian raised his hands. "Relax, Tommy boy. I believe you. Just don't go telling Marvin. He'll think you're crazier than he thinks you are already. And don't say nothin' to Ben or Jerry, either. They'll figure you saw a Sasquatch, and then they'll be wanting to form a posse to hunt it down."

Thomas doused his hand in a bucket of cold water,

then topped off his cup with the last of the pot. They were quiet for a few minutes, the only sounds the whistling of the wind and the crackling of the fire.

"I wonder if that thing is somehow connected to those helicopters that flew over last night," the Librarian said.

Thomas nodded. "Now that you mention it, I wonder, too. I haven't heard that many birds overhead since I settled here."

The Librarian drained his cup. "Used to be a lot of choppers buzzing around these parts a few years ago. Marvin said they were using some base near the dam."

Thomas blinked. "There's a dam around here?"

"Southeast, maybe forty miles," the Librarian replied. "That base must have closed, though. Haven't heard much air traffic lately—except for last night, that is."

Thomas frowned. "I hope it's not an omen of things to come."

Suddenly, the Librarian slapped his knee. "I almost forgot why I knocked on your door, Tommy boy," he cried. "The trail's fairly clear, so I'm driving the snowcat to Chichak to pick up supplies. I'll be gone all day, which means you'll have to give Rachel her schooling."

Thomas moaned. "Man, not me—"

"It's you or Marvin," the Librarian replied. "And you know the kind of crap he'll fill her head with. Or

I can send her around to the bikers down the creek a ways. Of course, their language might not be suitable for a twelve-year-old girl, but—"

"Why can't she just stay home for the day?" Thomas asked.

"Because Ellie is feeling poorly. At her age, she really should see a doctor. But she's afraid they'll put her in a hospital in Edmonton, and she'll never see Rachel again."

The Librarian set his empty cup down and stood. "Since Rachel's mother died, Ellie's done what she could, but the woman's weakening. Frankly, I think she's dying. In any case, Mr. Carlyle is going to make sure Ellie rests today, and I want them both left alone. Big Rita will be babysitting Rachel—"

"Then why doesn't Big Rita give the girl her lessons?" Thomas demanded.

The Librarian shook his head. "Big Rita isn't up to the task."

"Why not? She speaks three languages: Inuit, English, and some French."

"Sure, she can *speak* three languages," the Librarian replied. "But Rita can't read in *any* language."

Thomas absorbed the news. "Fine, I'll do the schooling," he said. "I just hope I know the lesson. Sometimes I think that kid is a whole lot smarter than me."

"I set everything out on the table in the library. A little history, a little civics, and light reading. I won't trouble you to teach math; you can't do it, anyway."

The Librarian shuffled to the door. "Come by around noon, and she'll be waiting for you. And you're right. Rachel *is* a whole lot smarter than you, Tommy boy, so don't try to match wits with her."

Megan went through every word of the file twice, not quite comprehending what she read. Of course, she understood the basics about the science involved. She could also see why someone with Project Slammer's unique talents would be useful in infantry combat. But there was one piece of information Megan couldn't quite get her mind around: the fact that Herbert "Hank" Gosling had volunteered to become what the Weapon Null Program turned him into.

The code name "Slammer" was apt, if unimaginative.

Gosling was born into a working class family in Quincy, Massachusetts. The older he got, the more trouble he got himself into. After several juvenile arrests and convictions, a judge made Herbert an offer: join the navy, or go to prison for three years. Defiant to the end, Gosling enlisted in the marine corps instead.

He breezed through basic, then specialized in heavy-weapons training. In time, he became very proficient in the use of the SAW, or Squad Automatic Weapon.

Megan found the summary of Gosling's service record unremarkable, until she read about his deployment to Africa during a United Nations peacekeeping mission. After a firefight in the jungle, in which six men from his platoon were killed, along with sixteen rebels and a dozen innocent civilians, Gosling was brought up on charges. Though the records of the subsequent court-martial were sealed, the result was a dishonorable discharge.

This ended his military career, but Gosling immediately found security work with a Canadian firm contracted by the UN to rebuild that same rebellion-torn African nation. It was his work with the Canadian defense contractor that brought Hank Gosling to the attention of the Director's predecessor, the man who created the Weapon Null Program.

After suffering crippling wounds in Africa, Gosling was brought to the Weapon Null facility, and the reconstruction work began. According to his files, Hank Gosling's wounds were not that severe, and he'd only lost part of his right hand. But instead of simple reconstructive bionic repair, Gosling opted to become the living weapon he was now.

Along with the file, the Matron provided photographs. In appearance, Slammer was pretty much as Megan imagined him. She didn't linger on the images. She knew that she would see Slammer in the flesh soon enough.

Megan's communicator buzzed, startling her. She snatched it off the night table. "Hello . . ."

"Dr. Vigil?" The Matron.

"Yes?"

"An insertion team has arrived with three military helicopters. Through the use of orbital surveillance satellites, we've located Weapon X on a mountainside about fifty kilometers from here." The woman paused. "I trust you've read the file."

"Word for word," Megan replied. "I found the information about Slammer . . . astonishing."

"Excellent. Come up to the lab. We're prepping him for the assault right now."

Megan rolled out of bed. "I'll be there in five minutes."

12

The Laboratory

CLAD IN BLACK OVERALLS, HAIR STILL DAMP FROM her shower, Megan left her tiny quarters behind and hurried to the stairwell. Most of the elevators didn't work, and probably never would, but MacKenzie's corps of engineers had strung lights through every hallway, corridor, and stairwell the Matron and her team were likely to use.

Megan thought the light did little to dispel the gloomy, charnel-house atmosphere of this grim and haunted place.

Eyes half-closed behind dark glasses to ward off the harsh glare from the naked lightbulbs, Megan climbed the metal staircase. She was at the top of the first flight of stairs when a deafening cacophony rocked the entire facility, a throbbing sound so powerful the metal floor seemed to quiver under her boots.

When she exited the stairwell, a harsh mechanical whine battered Megan's ears. The noise issued from the medical lab, which more resembled her father's long bankrupt tool-and-die factory in Hamilton, Ontario, than any medical facility Megan had ever seen.

Megan paused at the door of the medical lab, the vibrations rattling her chest and partially disrupting the digital data fed from her prosthetics to her brain through the optic nerves. She used the tiny muscles at the corners of her eyelids to adjust the controls to compensate for the interference, then entered the medical lab.

The man called Slammer lay facedown on a surgical table in the center of the room. The table itself contained a complete biomonitoring system housed within a steel box reinforced with titanium rods to bear Slammer's impressive weight. From three deep gouges slashed into its metal walls, Megan deduced that this same table once had held Weapon X.

It was the massive, ungainly machine beside the lab table that was the source of the ear-splitting racket. The device was topped by a bin filled with large-caliber ammunition. A metal chute below the bin fed the shells into a loading breach surgically implanted near the base of Slammer's spine. Slammer's heavily muscled left arm was limp at his side, IV tubes pumping drugs directly into his bulging purple veins.

Megan searched for the implement that fired the explosive munitions. She was disappointed to discover that the man's right arm, which had been transformed into a high-velocity Vulcan mini-gun, was currently hidden inside a giant metal tube that resembled an old-style iron lung.

A man in an orange jumpsuit operated the ammunition loader, mechanically thrusting the lethal shells through the slot one at a time. Another man in identical attire fed oil-black hydraulic fluid into the iron lung, through a clear plastic tube that rolled out of a fluid tank embedded in the ceiling.

"Ah, you're here."

The Matron was forced to shout to be heard over the din. She stood on a raised catwalk suspended over the laboratory table. The woman wore a tiny headset, with a black plastic communicator attached to the shoulder of her spotless white lab coat.

Another man in a Day-Glo jumpsuit appeared at Megan's shoulder. "Here you go, ma'am," he shouted.

Megan took the headset he offered and slipped it over her ears. To her surprise, the tiny plugs effectively filtered out ninety-nine percent of the machine-shop roar.

"Can you hear me?" the Matron asked through the headset. Megan nodded. "Come on up and observe the procedure. You can see everything here."

Megan crossed the cluttered lab and climbed the metal stairs to stand beside the Matron. The woman had not lied. From this vantage point, much more was revealed. Megan realized that Slammer was unconscious, an oxygen mask covering his nose and mouth. Only the ammunition chute over the man's lower spine covered his nakedness, while biomonitors kept tabs on the man's vital signs.

She observed cords of oversized muscles rippling along the man's thighs and lower legs. His trunk was also covered with thick slabs of rock-hard muscle. Slammer's unnaturally broad shoulders were partially obscured, however, by the grotesquely large bony hump on the man's back.

The uneven lump resembled a turtle's shell, but upon closer examination, Megan realized there were actual ribs inside the sack, the pink flesh stretched balloonlike between each curved bone.

"Slammer is so named because his right arm has been replaced by an organically fabricated mini-cannon," the Matron explained.

"I felt the phrase 'organically fabricated' was imprecise. But there was no clarification in the report," Megan said. "Frankly, the notion puzzled me."

"It's simple, Dr. Vigil," the Matron explained. "The cannon itself has been fashioned out of the subject's own biological material. This feat was accomplished by manipulating the subject's DNA—"

"An amazing accomplishment," Megan said.

"Near the end of the Weapon Null Program, Professor Thorton's medical staff was able to grow bone matter into practically any shape they desired. Unfortunately, his process is lost to us, but at least we have Slammer."

Megan blinked. "Indeed."

"Once all four skeletal gun barrels were fully formed, they were sheathed with rifled titanium steel to maximize muzzle velocity and stopping power," the Matron continued.

Megan already knew this from reading the man's report, but she let the Matron drone proudly on while she observed the hideous arming procedure up close.

"The Slammer's bioweapon was modeled after the military's four-barrel GAU-13/A Gatling gun. Slammer uses thirty-millimeter shells, too, but they are lightweight and specially designed to explode on impact. More than ten thousand rounds are stored in the organic sac on Slammer's upper spine.

"Methane gas manufactured in his digestive system is used to expel the shells out of the sac, into the organic loading tubes. The bullets then move along the man's arm and are fed into the breech through muscular peristalsis—"

"I read about the process," Megan interrupted. "Sections of his lower colon were removed. That intestinal track now links the sac and the gun on his right arm."

The Matron grinned. "I don't want to bore you with details you've already learned. Perhaps—"

Megan raised a hand to silence the woman. "You are

not boring me in the slightest, Matron. In fact, I value your insights. Please continue your explanation."

The Matron nodded. "Well, there are actually two sections of Slammer's lower colon now grafted along his arm. We found that one tube considerably slowed his rate of fire, so we added a second. This second tube also allows us to vary the ammunition. Slammer carries both incendiary and explosive rounds."

Puzzled, Megan shook her head. "Then the sac on Slammer's spine is divided?"

"Yes, Doctor. One sac is actually twice the size of the other. The larger one contains explosive munitions. The smaller sac carries a limited consignment of incendiary rounds." The Matron paused. "We thought reducing the incendiary rounds was a wise precaution. Our goal is to stop Weapon X, not start a forest fire."

Megan watched as one technician opened the long metal cylinder that covered Slammer's right arm, revealing the biogun, still partially submerged in bubbling hydraulic fluid. The gun's ivory base was formed out of bone, tapering off into four long gun barrels coated with metal. Those barrels revolved around a circular titanium mount.

"Does his . . . prosthetic . . . perform like a real Gatling gun? Is there a motor to spin the barrels, or does Slammer somehow physically mimic that function?"

The Matron frowned at the question. "No motors. No smoke or mirrors, either. The muscles in Slammer's right forearm have been reconfigured to do the work. All of Slammer's muscles have been enhanced through the use of myostatin blockers and selectively administered steroids."

"Aren't steroids dangerous, Matron?"

"But necessary," the older woman replied. "The bone matter is dense, the titanium steel coating weighs hundreds of pounds, and the ammunition alone weighs nearly a ton. But to answer your original question, everything except the actual projectiles has been fashioned through either a medical, surgical, or biological process." The Matron faced Megan. "Forgive me for making the distinction, but you, Dr. Vigil, are bionic. The attachments to your optic nerves and brain, which you call eyes, are really machines. Slammer's biological enhancements only mimic the activities of machines. But they consist of flesh and bone."

Megan lifted her chin. "A subtle distinction."

"But one that is very real," the Matron said. "The ultimate goal of the Weapon Null Program was to create human beings that are also self-contained advanced weapons systems."

"You feel the program succeeded?" Megan asked.

"To varying degrees," the Matron said, looking away.

"But these units are hardly self-contained," Megan countered. "Expensive and complex procedures are required to transport and maintain each member of your team."

"I said that was the *goal* of the Weapon Null Program," the Matron replied. "I did not say those targets were always achieved. Unfortunately, just as real progress was being made, Weapon Null was sidelined to make way for more promising projects. I'm sure that situation will be soon be reversed."

Megan thought she sensed a hint of hubris in the woman's tone. "Why?" she asked.

"It's really quite simple, Dr. Vigil," the woman replied. "Slammer is neither the most formidable nor the most powerful member of our unit. But I believe that he, acting alone, is more than capable of neutralizing Weapon X, or even destroying it, if necessary."

The Matron paused to gaze down at the man on the laboratory table. Megan followed her gaze. Strapped to the metal rack, his right arm outstretched, Slammer looked like a victim of some bizarre technological crucifixion.

"I think this will be a momentous day," the Matron declared. "Slammer will prove the value of our program to the Director, once and for all. And then we will see the program generously refunded, the unit moved to active-duty status."

My God, she's clueless, Megan thought. *About the expendable nature of her unit and the contempt the Director feels toward the entire Weapon Null Program.*

Just then, the ammunition loader was deactivated, the sudden silence as jarring as the incessant noise that had preceded it. The loader rolled backward on massive rubber wheels, the orange-suited technician steering it.

"In a few minutes, we'll revive Slammer, and he will be ready to strike," the Matron purred.

"Then you've established the exact location of Weapon X?" Megan asked.

The Matron nodded, her eyes lingering on Slammer's overmuscled form.

"Department K's surveillance satellites have been monitoring its movements almost constantly, and we've confirmed its whereabouts, Dr. Vigil," the Matron replied. "At this moment, Weapon X is following the shore of a winding creek, approximately forty-seven miles from our current position. He's headed west, toward a foothill on the edge of the Rocky Mountains. Our plan is to move Slammer into striking distance by helicopter."

"How soon?" Megan asked.

"The attack should commence in a little more than an hour."

Braced by an icy-cold bath in the near-frozen creek, a clean and refreshed Logan was ready to ascend the mountain once again. He began hiking the same rocky path he'd climbed the day he discovered the cave he now called home, but this time, he had more than the wolf's pelt on his back. He also carried several hollowed-out wooden stumps filled with hundreds of gallons of fresh, potable water drawn from the creek and sealed with deerskin.

Weary of subsisting on melted snow, Logan had already spent the night using his adamantium claws to cut a deep trench into the stone floor of his cave. The pit was designed to hold the snow and ice melted by the heat from his newly constructed hearth. Unfortunately, not enough liquid dripped down from the cracks to meet his needs, so Logan decided to seed his well with hundreds of gallons of water.

In theory, the ready-made pool would facilitate the melting process, which would refill the pool over time. Then Logan would have more than enough water to drink and wash, without the need for a daily journey to the base of the mountain.

Logan had taken other steps to improve his living conditions, as well. He'd cut and collected enough firewood to last several weeks and stored it beside the stone hearth he'd erected. He'd also built a trap and almost immediately snagged another deer. The doe was not as large as the last one he'd tracked. Then again, Logan wouldn't have to share this carcass with some unnamed hunter, either. Tonight and tomorrow, he'd feast on fresh venison; then he'd smoke the leftover meat in anticipation of leaner times.

The trek back up the mountain took more than an hour. Halfway there, he glanced at the sky, reckoning it was around noon. Though the winter days were short, Logan figured he still had several hours of daylight left and considered going on another hunt, then decided against it.

He would fashion some spears instead. He'd already cut and stripped some fairly straight saplings. All he'd have to do was season the wood over his fire, carve a few stone spearheads, and affix them to the handle tips. The next time he hunted, Logan would not have to get within reach of his prey to take it down.

Proud of his achievements, Logan paused on the craggy hillside. He set his brimming wooden buckets on the ground, rolled back the hide covering one of them, guzzled some of the frigid water, and splashed more on his face. Then he stretched out on the rocks and watched the clouds drifting overhead.

The brief rest gave Logan time to consider his activities over the past few hours. His knowledge of woodcraft had come in handy, yet he had no memory of when or where he'd learned any of it.

He closed his eyes, reached around in his mind.

Flashes of images came to him. He saw himself hunting and tracking on the Canadian frontier. Dates came to him, documents and newspapers from long ago, the nineteenth century.

But how can that be? It would make me well over a hundred.

Logan tried to dismiss this strange burst of memory, but it wasn't the first time such thoughts had invaded his mind. Ever since he'd escaped the lab, he'd been struggling to make sense of faces, places, and events from a past he may or may not have had, a life he may or may not have lived.

Who the hell am I, anyway?

A frustrated rumble sounded in Logan's throat. Rising quickly, he hefted his rough-hewn buckets and quickly finished his hike up the hill. He found the cave undisturbed, the fire still smoldering. Logan manhandled the buckets through the narrow cave mouth and dumped their contents into the stone trench. In the end, the pool was not nearly as filled as he'd expected it to be.

Logan cursed. He tossed the buckets through the cave's mouth, intending to fill them with snow from the mountain peak. But as soon as he crawled through the opening, his keen ears picked up a familiar and disturbing sound.

Helicopter. Big one, too. And the sonofabitch is getting closer. . . .

THOMAS OPENED THE MRE POUCH WITH HIS teeth, poured the contents into the tin cup of boiling water, and stirred. Finally, he added the tiny, rock-hard marshmallows from the cellophane-wrapped U.S. government–issue condiment portion.

"Here you go," he said, setting the cup on the rough-hewn table. "Real, honest-to-God, army hot chocolate."

Rachel pulled her golden blond hair back into a ponytail with both hands, snapped a rubber band around it, and stared at the melting, gooey mess in front of her. Her twelve-year-old face was pensive behind big horn-rimmed glasses. She looked cute and puzzled with her plump cheeks and large, dark eyes, like a baby owl with bright yellow feathers.

"Marvin serves green tea," she said.

"Green tea, horse pee . . . what's the difference? Hot

chocolate's the Inca's delight. Now, drink—slowly! That water was boiling."

"It smells . . . sugary," said Rachel, wrinkling her pug nose.

Across the room, Big Rita made a face. "Sugar's no good," she said.

The middle-aged Inuit woman lived next door to the Librarian. Thomas guessed she weighed about ninety pounds in her sealskin parka, so he couldn't figure out where the "Big" moniker came from.

"What's this, a room full of health nuts?" Thomas faced Rita. "And what do you know about health? Your people eat blubber."

Rita licked her lips and winked. "Blubber's good. You should try it."

"Yeah, like you really eat blubber," Thomas said. "You're dining on venison, canned vegetables, and Spam, just like the rest of us."

Rita returned to her knitting. She was there to baby-sit Rachel, not give the girl her lessons, so when the schooling began, she tuned out. She'd go back to her main job of taking care of Rachel's sick aunt when the Librarian returned later today.

Rachel sniffed the cup, then set it down. "Marvin says sugar is bad for your teeth."

Thomas rolled his eyes. "You can't believe everything he says. Marvin practices yoga."

"So what?"

"So nothing. Did you finish reading that chapter

yet? I'm asking because I finished reading that chapter *and* made you hot chocolate. I know you can read faster than me, so you must be finished by now."

Rachel closed the book. "I heard a helicopter."

"Yeah, I heard it, too. Late last night." Thomas sat down on a rickety chair and propped his booted feet on the table.

"I heard one just now," Rachel replied.

"Me, too," said Rita from her chair.

Thomas frowned. "How come I didn't hear it?"

Rachel giggled. "You were too busy cursing Henry's pot, after you burned yourself."

"Who's Henry?"

"The Librarian," Rachel said. "His real name is Henry."

"Now you know everyone's secret name?"

"Not yours."

Thomas leaned forward and tapped the book. "Tell me you finished reading the assigned chapter. I don't have all day."

"I read it," Rachel said. "Twice."

"So what do you think?"

Rachel scrunched up her face. Thomas was surprised at how much she resembled the pictures of her mother. Thomas had never met the woman. He'd blown into town almost a year after she'd died, but he'd seen her picture on the library's wall. It was a Polaroid, snapped during a summer picnic. Rachel was in it, smiling up at her mother, the rest of the townsfolk gathered around them.

No one knew much about Renee—she never told anyone her last name, just said she'd been a cocktail waitress in Las Vegas who took off one day with her kid to get away from a really bad boyfriend. She'd showed up in Second Chance with her eight-year-old daughter in tow and moved into the abandoned cabin next to the bikers. She kept to herself, helped out when asked, and took charity when offered. Six months later, she was dead from pneumonia, and her daughter, Rachel, was an orphan.

That's when old Ellie Warren stepped in. Rachel had been living with the old woman for so long she'd taken to calling Ellie her aunt.

"I think it's kind of crazy for people in the same country to start shooting at each other," Rachel declared. "It's like you and the bikers starting a war. What's the point? You'll only wreck everybody's nice, peaceful town, and for nothing."

Thomas rubbed his chin. "So what if the bikers were keeping old Leroy hostage, and Lilly next door? And your Aunt Ellie, too? And those bikers bossed folks around, made them cook dinner and clean house without paying them? What about that? Huh?"

"You're making a thinly veiled reference to slavery in the United States," Rachel said. "This isn't the United States. This is Canada."

"Tyranny's like a disease. A cancer. It can break out anywhere," Thomas warned. "Wouldn't it be right to start shooting over something as heinous as slavery? Or how about mass murder? That was popular with the Nazis and the Communists. Should we give them a pass or put up a fight?" Suddenly, Thomas blinked. "Hey! Why use me as an example, anyway?"

Rachel pushed her glasses up. "You and the bikers are the only people I know with guns."

"Not true," Thomas replied. "I'll bet Rita has a rifle—"

Rita looked up from her knitting. "I have a thirty-eight. But I haven't fired it in fourteen years."

"I'll bet Ben and Jerry have guns. And *Henry* has a gun, too."

Rachel shrugged. "Anyway, everybody knows that the Civil War wasn't fought over slavery."

Thomas chuckled. "That would surprise Abe Lincoln."

Rachel lifted her chin and folded her arms. "Marvin told me all wars are fought for money. People who start wars get rich. And the people who fight them get to be famous heroes."

Thomas snorted. "Do I look famous to you?"

"Maybe you're rich," Rachel replied.

"Marvin's rich. Or he was before he became a Zen Naturalist," Thomas said. "Do you think maybe Marvin started a war?"

"Not Marvin. He gave all his money to charity."

Rita snorted.

Thomas nodded. "Maybe. But guess what? He had to *make* that money first."

Behind her thick lenses—courtesy of the free-clinic optometrist in Chichak—Rachel's blue eyes caught his own. "Did you really fight in a war?" she asked.

Thomas shrugged. "Hardly a war. More like a political fiasco, but with guns."

"Did you kill anybody?"

Thomas frowned. "I did a lot of shooting."

Rachel let his evasion pass unchallenged. She lifted the cup and sipped the hot chocolate. "Weren't you scared?"

Thomas laughed. "I'm no hero. Let's leave it at—"

A continuous burst of automatic weapons fire interrupted him.

Thomas was out of his chair and through the door before the final echoes faded somewhere in the mountains. Still in his shirtsleeves, he rushed off the porch and into the hard-packed snow. In the middle of the clearing, he dropped to one knee. He cupped his left hand over his ear and pressed the palm of his right hand flat on the frozen ground.

Military maneuvers?

The ordnance he'd heard definitely sounded like it. He wondered if it had come from that secret base near the dam, the place the Librarian had told him about earlier.

Thomas didn't budge during the silence that followed. Seconds stretched into a minute, then two. Then came another burst of gunfire—shorter than the first but enough. A short second shot also helped Thomas pinpoint the origin of the sound. He looked up and spied a puff of black smoke on the mountainside that confirmed the location.

"What's going on?"

Rachel's voice broke his concentration. She and Big Rita stood at Thomas's side, staring down at him. The girl was wrapped in her oversized coat. She held his own parka in her tiny hands.

Thomas rose. He heard voices and realized half the town had come out of their cabins to investigate the noise. While he donned his coat, Thomas scanned the crowd.

He considered Marvin first. The man stood outside his cabin, still in his robe and pajamas. His eyes were wide and darted about nervously, yet he projected the notion that he was unconcerned about the firefight on the mountain, as if it were something happening on the other side of the world.

Next, Thomas eyed Old Herman. The man was on his front porch, hugging the rail to steady himself, a mason jar of moonshine clutched in his grizzled hand.

Up on the hill, Thomas spied Bill Lyons. The big biker clutched a hunting rifle in his beefy, tattooed fists. Lyons took a step forward, but his wife, Betty—who nursed their newborn at her breast—stopped him with a touch.

Thomas locked eyes with Big Rita. The Inuit woman's face was tense, and she looked at him as if she expected something. Protection, maybe.

"Listen, Rachel. Go with Rita. I want you both to stay with Bill and Mrs. Lyons. I'll bet they'll let you hold their baby, too."

"But I don't want to—"

Thomas dropped to his knee and clutched the girl's shoulders. "This is serious. I want you to do what I tell you for once. When the Librarian comes home, you can stay with him. If I get back to town first, I'll come fetch you both."

"Where are *you* going?"

Thomas jerked his head in the direction of the mountain. "Up there, to find out what all the racket is about."

"Rita can watch me, all by herself. Why do you want us to stay with the bikers?"

"Because, Rachel, they have guns."

14

THE ATTACK BEGAN SOON AFTER LOGAN LEFT HIS cave to investigate the sound of the helicopter.

Wrapped in his wolf pelt, he moved down the steep mountain trail, following the sound of chopper blades. Soon he reached a jutting cliff that offered a view of the valley below and the mountains beyond.

The ledge was located near the spot where he'd encountered the lone hunter the day before. Logan wondered if the man he'd spooked had told the authorities about the encounter. Would they even believe him? If they did, then the presence of a helicopter might spell trouble.

Logan paused on the precipice to listen. He could hear the helicopter, but the engine noise reverberated off the hills, and the echo made it impossible for even his ultrasensitive ears to pinpoint the direction of the sound.

Logan scanned the sky and saw nothing, yet he sensed the aircraft was close.

Suddenly, the ground began to quake under his bare feet.

Partially obscured in a blast of snow, a UH-60 Blackhawk helicopter rose from beneath the jutting cliff until it hovered directly in front of Logan. The noise and the downdraft from the whirling rotors battered him. Snow spun in tiny cyclones, icy powder stinging his exposed flesh.

The aircraft's nose was pointed at him—so close Logan could see the shocked expression on the pilot's face, the copilot turn his head and shout to someone in the troop compartment.

Logan turned his back on the aircraft and ran up the path. A machine gun crackled, but he ignored the shots and the orange tracers that danced along the rocks, the stone splinters and bullet fragments that tore the flesh of his calves. Logan ran in a zigzag pattern until he reached the cover of the tree line.

Meanwhile, the whine of the Blackhawk's turbines intensified. The helicopter roared directly over Logan's head, the downdraft flattening trees and kicking up a miniature blizzard. Through a blizzard of powdery snow, Logan watched the aircraft bank, then slow to a hover over a flat clearing on the north face of the mountain.

Logan grunted when a grotesque and malformed figure appeared in the troop compartment door.

Manlike, with oversized hips and heavily muscled legs as thick as tree stumps, the figure was sheathed in plates of titanium armor linked by a night-black steel battle suit. His shoulders were uneven, the right twice the size of the left. The creature was a hunchback, too. Logan spied a bloated hump that seemed to pulsate on the being's back.

The man's barrel chest was as wide as a barn door and shielded by steel plates. Goggles with telescopic lenses covered the man's eyes—a sophisticated digital targeting system, Logan reckoned—and his bullet-shaped head was wrapped in a titanium steel helmet.

The man's left arm was encased in slabs of beefy muscle, and a grenade launcher had been fitted to the thick wrist. But it was the man's right arm that grabbed Logan's attention. As massively overmuscled as the rest of the man, the arm's natural flesh ended below the elbow. It had been replaced by a multi-barreled Gatling gun encased in a sheath of white bone.

Logan barely had time to register these details before the man's head jerked and he turned his goggled eyes in Logan's direction.

"I'm coming for you, wild man!" the figure roared, his electronically amplified voice deafening.

"Who the hell are you?" Logan muttered, barely above a whisper.

To his surprise, the man answered. "The name's Slammer. But to you, I'm death—"

The Blackhawk dipped slightly, and Slammer jumped clear. He landed out of sight, behind a line of swishing trees. The helicopter banked and roared away, ascending until it was nothing more than a dark speck against the blue-gray sky.

Logan took cover among a copse of ancient pines, hoping to ambush the thing that hunted him. But he never got the chance.

A staccato burst of gunfire rattled the silent forest. Logan cried out, and birds scattered. The tall trees he crouched between exploded in a barrage of pine needles and pinprick splinters. Neatly severed by the hail of bullets, trunks separated in a cacophony of loud snaps. Pine trees tumbled to the powdery snow.

Moving on all fours, Logan scrambled across the rocks and dived into a shallow ravine to avoid being crushed by falling timber. Snow covered him in a blanket of white. Over the crackle and snap of breaking branches, Logan heard a taunting voice.

"Where are you, freak machine? Come on out and fight!"

Shaking off the snow, Logan scurried along the bottom of the shallow depression between the rocks. His naked back was riddled with so many wood splinters that he resembled a porcupine. Kicking up snow, he raced along the bottom of the ditch until he reached a dead end.

Without a pause, Logan burst from cover.

"I see you, wild man!" the voice roared.

Red-orange tracers arched over Logan's head and tore up another section of forest. More trees shattered and fell to earth. Panicked, a hawk screeched and took wing. Slammer spied the movement and fired a single shot. The raptor dissolved in a puff of blood and gray-white feathers.

"You're next, monster. And you won't go as quick as that turkey."

The voice echoed off the mountains until Logan was sick of hearing it.

"Why don't you shut up?" he cried.

But Logan didn't wait for an answer. He kept moving until he reached cover behind a tumble of massive boulders. Cowering there, he stilled his breathing and waited for an opening. Meanwhile the frantic bird calls stilled, and silence returned to the mountainside.

I lost him . . . or else he's playing a sniper's game, angling for a better shot. . . .

Either way, Logan knew he had precious few moments to plan his next move. Suddenly, chaotic flashes of memory exploded in his mind. He saw a surreal image of an aircraft carrier floating among the clouds; cybernetic helmets with head-up displays and optical targeting systems; X-ray scopes, heat and night-vision devices; high-intensity lasers for painting targets; sound sensors. . . .

Sonofabitch! Logan realized. *There's no hiding from him.*

Without a doubt, Logan knew that Slammer had a

whole spectrum of imaging systems inside that tin cap of his.

He can locate me anywhere, behind any kind of cover. Hell, he could have me in his sights right now—

An explosion of gunfire shattered the stillness. Bullets tore through Logan's chest, arms, legs. A Kevlar-jacketed shell pinged off his adamantium spine, ricocheted through his guts, tearing him up inside.

Stunned, Logan slammed face-first into the blood-soaked rocks. Still on his feet, he coughed black bile. With an angry snarl, Logan faced his foe, claws extended.

Slammer stepped out from between two rocks and fired again—a single shot that ripped through Logan's jugular vein. Logan's head jerked back as if it had been hit with a baseball bat. His legs buckled, and he dropped to his knees.

Arms hanging limply at his side, claws scratching the cold rocks, Logan stubbornly refused to fall, despite the waterfall of gore that coursed down his torso and stained the snowy earth.

A shadow loomed over him. A powerful hand gripped his hair, and Logan's head was jerked backward, further injuring the hole in his neck. Choking on his own blood, Logan smelled cordite and scorched flesh when the red-hot steel barrel of Slammer's smoking mini-gun seared his temple.

Then he heard laughter.

• • •

"This is remarkably disappointing."

The Director's office was dim, the windows blocked by a giant high-definition screen. Behind his massive desk, the man tugged the ends of his white hair and fretted aloud.

"It appears Dr. Thorton sold us a bill of goods. Weapon X is less than useless. In fact, it's an utter joke if one of the Matron's junkyard dogs can neutralize it."

"I would not have predicted this outcome," the Voice replied in a dispassionate tone. "Despite its tremendous potential, Weapon X has failed its first real test. It's . . . baffling."

The Director watched Weapon X drop to its knees. "Depressing is what it is."

The Voice did not reply.

"What is the Matron seeing?" the Director asked.

"Exactly what we see," the Voice replied. "The real-time feed from Major Sallow's Blackhawk is being relayed to her operational headquarters as well."

"She must be celebrating, then." The Director scowled. "Her discredited department has dealt the rest of us a humiliating defeat."

"This is a scientific experiment, Director," the Voice chided. "There are no winners or losers. We must not expect or even anticipate a particular outcome. Our job is to record and interpret what we observe."

Glancing at the screen, the Director frowned. "There might not be losers, but there are failures; and what we're seeing now is a debacle in the making. *We* have failed."

"Even failure can yield helpful data," said the Voice. "In science, every mistake leads to more discoveries."

"Conscience," the Director said.

"I think we've already established the fact that Weapon X is sentient," the Voice replied.

"Not conscious," the Director replied. "*Conscience*. As in a personal moral code. Tragically, Weapon X may have learned right from wrong. It is trying to recover its latent humanity. In the process, it has lost much of its fighting edge."

"Most alarming," the Voice observed.

The Director nodded. "A tragedy, really. All those resources squandered, and for what? Weapon X is the antithesis of what Professor Thorton set out to achieve. It's supposed to be a remote-controlled killing machine, not—"

"Director," the Voice interrupted, "please observe the monitor."

15

"THIS PATHETIC, BLEEDING PILE OF GARBAGE IS THE legendary Weapon X? The bane of Department K? The savage beast who murdered Professor Thorton and his entire staff?"

Slammer yanked the smoking gun barrel away from Logan's temple and waved it in the air. He did not shut down his amplifier, however, so the man's taunting words battered Logan's ears and reverberated throughout the surrounding forest.

Logan didn't mind. As long as he could hear the man's voice, he knew he was still alive.

Yeah, that's right, asshole. Keep talking. Just a little longer.

"I hope you're recording this, Major Sallow," Slammer roared, eyes skyward. "I want this moment preserved for posterity. I want everyone in Department K to see me annihilate their so-called perfect weapon."

While Slammer raged on, time was healing Logan's wounds. Within seconds, the bloody holes that had been punched through Logan's chest and arms were closing, shredded muscles regenerating. The flow of blood slowed to a trickle, then halted. Like a rising tide, Logan's ebbing strength returned.

With a loud gasp, Logan sucked in a lung full of cold mountain air, then looked up to stare at his own reflection in the bulging lenses of Slammer's telescopic goggles.

Leaping to his feet, Logan lashed out. He crossed both arms in a vicious slashing motion that cut the air in front of Slammer's face. But air wasn't the only thing slashed. Logan's steel claws fractured Slammer's optical targeting system. The oversized goggles exploded in a shower of glass, silicon, and white-hot sparks.

"Put a cap on it, Four Eyes!" Logan roared. "You're giving me a migraine."

Slammer reared back, wailing and clutching his head. Black smoke poured out from under his helmet. Blindly, the man stumbled away, groping for the emergency helmet release with his left hand.

Logan dropped into a fighting crouch to press the attack. But as he prepared to lunge, Slammer's weapon spit deadly fire. Logan jumped away as bullets chipped the rocks, scattering stone splinters that cut his flesh like arrowheads.

To escape the steady stream of hot lead, Logan

executed a standing back flip that sent him sailing over the boulders. He landed on his feet, then dashed for cover while Slammer struggled to remove his shattered headgear.

Behind him, Logan heard a noisy hiss like a ruptured steam pipe. He glanced over his shoulder and saw Slammer's helmet clatter to the ground.

Unmasked, the man's shaved head was seared and pitted by fire. His nose was flat under scorched eyebrows, and tears continued to cloud Slammer's stinging eyes. Logan spied USB ports embedded in his foe's scalp, where severed wires still smoldered and sparked.

"Sonofab—"

Slammer's curse was cut off by the rippling roar of his organic Gatling gun. The hump on his back quivered with each burst of automatic weapons fire. A pair of yellow-brown, organic tubes that connected the sac to the gun on the man's arm seemed to throb and pulsate with unnatural life.

The careless shots went wild, hammering the mountainside and kicking up great gouts of white snow and brown dirt.

Slammer shook the grenade launcher off his left arm and tossed it over the side of the mountain. He used his forearm to wipe the still-flowing tears away from his soot-stained cheeks. By the time his burning vision cleared, Logan was out of sight.

"You think I need fancy eyes to shoot you? Kill

you?" he bellowed. "You're wrong, pal. All I need is this—"

Slammer shook his weapon arm at the heavens. "*I'm* the gun. Do you hear me? *I'm* the gun, and I'm coming for *you*!"

In a frenzied rage, Slammer ran the length of the ravine, then back again.

Meanwhile, Logan crouched, unseen, on an over-hanging cliff far above his head. He'd used his claws to scale the sheer mountain wall that paralleled the ravine.

Claws retracted, he followed the grenade launcher with hungry eyes as it vanished over the side of the mountain. Taking out Slammer's optical targeting system was a coup, but having that launcher would really even the odds.

Slammer roared and stomped the ground. "Where are you hiding? Come out and fight, Weapon X!"

Even without the amplification system, the man's cries reverberated among the rocks until Logan heard the same refrain echoed over and over.

"Weapon X . . . Weapon X . . . Weapon X . . ."

A growl came from Logan as anger overwhelmed him. *Is that what they call me now? A weapon?*

Logan struggled against the beast within, but the rage swelled until his humanity shrank into a tiny, dim thing. The blood tide tinged his vision, steeled his reason, and transformed him into the very thing the madmen in lab smocks had dreamed of, yearned for, and finally created. With a metallic *snikt,* his claws instinctively deployed.

Weapon X snarled, foam flecking its lips.

Slammer heard the sound and looked up. "There you are, freak!" He fired—a long, continuous burst that mixed explosive shells with incendiary bullets. Burning orange tracers ripped into the rocky cliff. Chunks of rocks and soil blew outward. The bullets chipped away at the ledge until it crumbled under Weapon X's feet.

Instinctively, the creature lashed out, embedding its claws in the sheer mountainside. As the ledge fell away, Weapon X clung to the cliff like a spider on a wall.

Through the hail of debris, a single shot got through. The explosive bullet slammed into Weapon X's left leg, struck the adamantium-encased femur, then detonated. Flesh and muscle disintegrated in a red mist. Only the silver adamantium bones remained.

The stunning impact reverberated throughout Weapon X's skeletal system. Nerves jangled, muscles ripped, joints popped. The creature's brain bounced around inside its skull like a coin in a bottle. Though he was stunned, the claws remained embedded in the rock. Weapon X hung limply from those blades. But then, veins and arteries began to creep around the adamantium leg bones like ivy around a tree.

Below the shattered ledge, the only thing that stood between the avalanche and the bottom of the mountain was Slammer. Eyes wide, he scrambled to find cover that did not exist.

A boulder the size of a pickup truck crashed into Slammer's chest. The air flew out of his lungs, and the ammunition sac on his spine burst, spilling bullets onto the rocks. The first massive stone was followed by a granite waterfall. Like a leaf in a snowy cyclone, Slammer was swept over the side of the mountain.

Alarms jangled throughout the Professor's ruined facility. Emergency teams on the airfield and inside the facility responded instantly.

Outside, Weapon Null's medical retrieval unit hurried across the snow-blasted tarmac. Clad in the ubiquitous orange jumpsuits, the men piled into two idling Blackhawks, equipment in tow. Seconds later, the helicopters lifted and headed for the mountain.

Inside, the laboratory was a hive of frenzied activity.

The mission control team worked to restart Slammer's biomonitoring system. Until the man's diagnostic computers were up and running, they couldn't be sure Slammer was even alive.

Meanwhile, others were breaking emergency medical equipment out of metal storage containers and prepping it for immediate use, while Dr. Vigil quickly strung cables from the main emergency generator to power these added devices.

Plasma was brought in from refrigerated units,

along with glass vials and plastic containers filled with highly advanced, experimental bioregenerative and antirejection formulas, all of them top-secret.

A specially trained medical team put the finishing touches on a makeshift surgery that rose out of the ruins of Professor Thorton's operating theater.

The Matron stood in the center of the chaos, making split-second assessments and issuing commands in a calm and even tone.

"Are those biomonitors functioning yet?" she asked.

"The system is coming online now, Matron," the technician replied, eyes locked on his screen. Activity slowed as everyone waited to hear the results from the remote diagnostics system.

"He's alive," the med tech declared. "Unconscious. He's lost a lot of blood. But Slammer is alive."

The tense mood was dispelled, but the activity intensified.

"Dispatch the medical team, if they haven't taken off already—"

"They're gone, Matron," Corporal MacKenzie reported. "Major Sallow has already pinpointed the location of your man. He's guiding the medical team into the landing zone."

The Matron sighed. "Slammer will soon be here, where we can take care of him . . . so what went wrong?"

"It was a mistake, Matron. That's all," the med tech

argued. "Slammer acted out of anger. Fired prematurely. At least he'll live to fight another day—"

"And he's effectively neutralized Weapon X," the mission specialist declared from his chair at the command station. "With respect, Matron. Look at the satellite surveillance monitor. The mission is over."

But the Matron barely glanced at the screen.

"Weapon X is just hanging there, on the side of the cliff, waiting to be plucked," the man cried.

"And how do you propose we 'pluck' it?" the Matron asked. "It would take a team of mountain specialists to get Weapon X off that cliff. By then, it will be functional again, and there will only be more bloodshed."

She glanced once again at the image on the monitor. Weapon X was little more than a black smudge on the sheer cliff.

The mission specialist stared at the screen. "We have to stop it, Matron. Or capture it. Better still, destroy the menace."

The Matron was silent for a long moment. When she finally spoke, her tone was firm with new resolve.

"Weapon X will be stopped," she declared. "But it will be done *my* way. With *my* team."

16

LOGAN AWOKE TO THE TORMENT OF THE RACK.

He opened his eyes to find his arms stretched to their limit, face pressed flat against cold stone. He was dangling from the face of the mountain, his adamantium claws dug into the cliff like climbing mounts. For the life of him, Logan could not remember how he got there.

He moaned and blinked the sweat from his eyes. Then he looked down. Memories flooded his mind, a confusing jumble of images. One involved Slammer, pacing back and forth in a ravine below, Logan watching him from the ledge above.

That ledge was gone now. So was the ravine, and a good chunk of the hillside, too.

How the hell did that happen?

He groped for more memories, but there was nothing more. It didn't matter, anyway; right now, he had nowhere to go but up.

Logan retracted the claws in his left hand. He caught his breath when part of the mountain wall crumbled as the steel slid out of the rock.

He moved his legs in an attempt to find purchase—and new torment exploded in his brain. Grunting, Logan hugged the cliff, then stole a glance at his shredded leg.

Throbbing blue veins ran along pink-brown muscles, yellow tendons stringing the whole mess together like twine on a broken package. Logan looked away, took a deep, shuddering breath. . . .

It was the injury that saved me. Like a shock treatment.

Logan realized the blood tide had taken over his mind. Then Slammer had blasted away, doing enough damage to knock Logan unconscious, which also knocked the killer beast right out of him—at least for a while.

Logan wasn't overly concerned about his crippling injury. It would heal in time. All he had to do was reach his cave and hole up there. In a day or less, he would recover.

He glanced down and saw the heap of rocks and debris at the base of the mountain. The avalanche had felled trees, collapsed ledges, destroyed trails as it swept down. Despite the wind that whipped his naked flanks and stung his throbbing flesh, Logan laughed.

At least I'm still alive to feel pain. I doubt Slammer was so lucky.

Logan stopped laughing when a familiar sound beat against his ears and rolled off the mountain.

Damn helicopters. They're coming back.

Thomas heard the helicopters, too, and dived under a dipping pine branch blanketed with snow.

From his hiding place, he could see the debris-strewn aftermath of the avalanche. Boulders the size of buses had torn a wound in the side of the mountain. The rocks had smashed down trees and completely obliterated the old, familiar trail.

He muttered a curse. If he wanted to reach the peak now, he'd have to find a new way up. Thomas was checking out the damage when he spied a tiny figure clinging to the side of the mountain. He cursed, wishing he'd grabbed the Librarian's binoculars. From his vantage point, he could make out no details, but he was certain it was that wild man.

Meanwhile, the engine noise increased; a helicopter roared over his position, low enough that its downdraft stirred up a storm of snow. Thomas blinked against the icy pelts and dragged the Colt Commando off his shoulder. He felt better once he had the automatic in his hand.

He recognized the chopper—a UH-60 Blackhawk. He'd ridden them into combat at least a hundred times in the Middle East and in Africa. This aircraft was painted matte black—so dark it seemed to absorb light. Ominously, it was unmarked. Not even serial numbers were visible on its armored hull.

He watched the helicopter slow to a hover, about fifty feet over the debris field. The troop compartment opened, and a man in a black battle suit balanced precariously in the doorway. He gripped something that looked like a flashlight, but Thomas wasn't fooled. The man was marking the area, using a laser to illuminate the landing zone. He was guiding more aircraft and personnel onto the scene.

Thomas knew he should get out in a hurry. But curiosity—and the fate of the wild man clinging to the cliff—kept him rooted to his spot.

Within a minute, a second helicopter arrived, closely followed by a third. The original bird continued to hover in a stationary position, while the newcomers set their wheels down on the relatively level clearing.

The doors opened before the aircraft powered down. Men in Day-Glo orange snowsuits jumped out and climbed onto the debris. They searched the area for several minutes, then concentrated their activity on a pile of rocks and snow that had settled at the base of an uprooted pine tree.

Thomas was surprised that everyone ignored the wild man on the cliff. Then he realized that not everyone was indifferent. Standing beside an idling Blackhawk two armed men watched the climber. One man handed the other binoculars; then a third man joined them.

Thomas lifted his head to get a better look at the figure on the cliff. The wild man was still climbing—without the benefit of ropes or climbing gear, apparently. In a few more minutes, he would reach a ledge, and safety.

A competent sniper could take out the climber with a single shot. And since Thomas was convinced that all the shooting somehow involved the wild man, he wondered why the helicopter crew didn't try for it.

Maybe they also know that guns can't kill the wild man.

Thomas shifted his gaze back to the men on the ground. With a start, he realized one man had focused the binoculars in his direction. That man suddenly cried out and gestured toward Thomas.

Thomas turned around and crawled among the trees, the Colt Commando cradled in his forearms. He kept on crawling until he was sure the trees hid him from view. Then he rose and took off in a run, abandoning the mountain as fast as he could.

Thomas's neck prickled when he heard the sound of rotors. They were coming for him!

He redoubled his pace, moving across icy rocks and avoiding snow patches so that he left no tracks behind for others to follow. When he spied a fallen tree covered by drifts, he plunged into the powdery snow, using his gloved hands to dig out a hollow under the log. He'd barely slipped into the shallow depression when the Blackhawk roared over his head. He covered himself with more snow, waiting for the aircraft to return.

For the next hour, the Blackhawk bracketed the area in an obvious search pattern. They had lost his trail, but they hadn't stopped looking for him yet.

It was only a matter of time, Thomas realized. Either the Blackhawk would run out of fuel, or it would get too dark for the hunt to continue, and Thomas would be home free.

Biting back stabbing jets of agony, Logan continued the torturous climb to the top of the cliff. He was determined to retreat to the safety of his cave before those choppers arrived.

Despite his phenomenal strength and restorative abilities, Logan felt wrecked. His fingernails were ripped and his hands bloody when he pulled himself onto the ledge. He collapsed, sucking in gulps of frigid air while he watched his wounded hands heal.

When his fingers were limber again, Logan sat up. The wolf pelt fell away from his shoulders, shredded in the battle against Slammer. He tore the rest of the rough garment away from his body and tossed it over the side.

He examined his injured leg. Though the muscles and tendons had reformed, the epidermis had not yet regenerated. From his left hip to his toes, it was all exposed muscles, tendons, and veins.

Logan dragged himself erect and tried to put weight

on the limb. His leg hurt like a sonofabitch in heat and then gave out. He fell hard, cursing a blue streak as pain coursed through the entire left side of his body.

Determined to find shelter and sleep in front of his own fire, Logan ignored the pain, stumbled to his feet, and limped slowly toward the cave at the top of the mountain.

17

IT WAS DARK WHEN THOMAS FINALLY REACHED
Second Chance. He was cold and tired, and he hadn't
eaten all day. All he wanted was a warm fire, a can of
beans, maybe some Spam—and a stiff shot of moonshine.

He was stopped on the edge of town, where a hair-
trigger reception committee greeted him.

"Who goes there?" Jerry barked, waving a flashlight
in Thomas's face.

"It's me, dumb ass," Thomas replied, shielding his
eyes. "Where's your better half?"

Ben stepped out from behind Old Herman's shack.
Middle-aged and paunchy, he wore a sealskin coat and
a Russian-style hat. The bald, bearded man was armed
with a bear rifle.

"What are you going to shoot with that thing?"
Thomas asked.

"The Librarian says you ran into a wild man in the hills. A Sasquatch, maybe."

"He's not a wild man, and he ain't a Sasquatch," Thomas said. "He's just some crazy old hermit, or maybe a drifter passing through."

"What was all that shooting about?"

The familiar voice came from Old Herman's porch. Thomas spied Marvin immediately. Though he lurked in the shadows, it was hard to miss his bright yellow J. Crew parka.

"I don't know much more than you," Thomas replied.

The little man came down off the porch, clutching a battery-powered lantern that wasn't turned on.

"What happened up there?" he demanded.

Thomas shrugged. "I arrived too late to find out. I heard the shooting, same as you. Then there was an avalanche. Three helicopters came after that, started searching through the mess. I think maybe they were rescuing someone trapped in the landslide."

"Helicopters? What kind of helicopters?" Ben demanded suspiciously.

"Maybe the Canadian military. Or maybe civilian. I didn't get a good look."

It was a necessary deceit. Thomas figured lying made more sense than mentioning black helicopters to a pair of full-time conspiracy theorists.

Suddenly, Marvin turned his lantern on. Thomas was bathed in white light. He raised his arm, blinking against the glare.

"What's that on your arm?" Marvin cried. "You're packing a machine gun? You brought a machine gun to this place?"

His voice was shrill, his outrage palpable. Ben and Jerry both stepped back, away from Thomas.

"What I'm packing is none of your business," Thomas said evenly. "I have a right to bear arms—"

"This isn't the United States, Soldier Boy," Marvin said. "Machine guns aren't legal for you to carry here in Canada."

"It's not a machine gun," Jerry said weakly. "Technically, he's got an automatic—"

"Either way, it's military stuff. Manufactured by war profiteers to kill other human beings." Marvin whirled and shook his finger in Thomas's face. "Guns like that—and the killers who use them—bring nothing but trouble."

Outwardly calm, Thomas pushed past Marvin and strode across the clearing toward home. Marvin followed him up the path. "You're trouble, Swimming Horse. You and your gun. If a war has broken out around here, it's because of men like you."

Thomas reached his cabin and slammed the door in Marvin's face.

• • •

Seven years ago

"Rise and shine, soldier."

Thomas rolled out of the lumpy bunk. His combat boots clicked on the concrete floor. The handcuffs on his wrists rattled when he tried to scratch the stubble that covered his scalp.

Two deputies entered the cell and stood on either side of him. The older of the two men touched his arm gently. He was a potbellied man with sandy brown hair and a bad comb-over.

"Come on, get your butt up." His tone was reasonable. Thomas did as the man asked.

"Turn around," the younger cop said, shoving him. The deputy's voice was shrill, nervous, but he was trying to hide his apprehension, too. Thomas followed his command. He also decided if there was going to be trouble, this was the one to watch.

"Looks like even a rat-tailed tin soldier like you has friends," the young officer said. "Somebody with a chest full of fruit salad is here to bail you out."

Thomas didn't have many friends, so he was curious to know who had come to post bail for him—although not curious enough to ask. He was led out of the cell, then down a long corridor he didn't recall walking through when he was first brought in. But then, he didn't recall much about his arrest—and he hadn't been walking too well, either.

They passed another row of cells, filled with dirty,

desperate men who had raised a little too much hell over the weekend and ended up in the drunk tank, just like him. There were a few soldiers among this bunch, all of them privates. Thomas outranked the lot of them.

Finally, they came to an iron gate. The younger deputy unlocked the door, using a set of keys on his belt. It swung open, and the man shoved Thomas again.

"Wait a minute." The older deputy turned Thomas around to face him. "Let me get these off before you see your friend," he said as he unlocked the handcuffs.

Thomas rubbed his wrists and nodded silent thanks to the man.

"Now, walk," the younger cop barked, pushing Thomas through the door.

They brought him to a small room with cracked green paint and a chipped, graffiti-scarred wooden bench. Captain Howard was there, in his Sunday dress uniform.

He must've driven here straight from chapel, Thomas realized. For the first time, he felt shame about his arrest.

A sad-eyed man with a turkey neck entered behind Thomas. "I'm the bail bondsman," he said, consulting the arrest report in his hand. "The charges against this man are not too serious. Public intoxication. Property damage. Those college boys who tried to rough him up . . . they refused to press charges."

Thomas looked up. "They refused—"

"Shut up, Sergeant," Captain Howard said. Then he faced the court official. "How much?" he snapped.

"Two thousand dollars," the bondsman replied. "Forfeited if Sergeant Swimming Horse misses his court appearance."

"He won't," the captain said.

Thomas kept his eyes on the floor as the captain scribbled a check and thrust it at the bondsman. The man took the scrap of paper and wrote notes in a file. Then he stuck a piece of paper under Thomas's nose and made him sign it.

"Okay, you're free to go, Sergeant. You will receive a letter by certified mail confirming the court date."

Outside, the sun was shining, the weather warm. Captain Howard walked to his Hummer with sure strides. He was a head taller than Thomas, and his legs were long, so Thomas had to hurry to catch up. The captain didn't speak until they were both seated in the car. Clutching the steering wheel with both hands, the officer focused his gray stare on Thomas.

"What the hell happened, soldier?"

"Three punks in a bar threw insults and made threats. Just 'cause I was having a drink with some girl from the university."

"And their behavior gave you the right to beat the hell out of them?"

"They came at me with pool cues, sir. I was only defending myself."

"You're a trained soldier. You could have extracted yourself and the young lady from that situation without resorting to violence."

Thomas's eyes stared at the floorboard. "I was a little intoxicated, sir."

"Look, Swimming Horse. I put my signature on a recommendation that you be accepted into the army Special Forces, and this is how you thank me?"

"This had nothing to do with you, sir," Thomas replied. "They insulted my uniform, and the army, too. One of them called me a mercenary, a paid butcher. Said I was nothing more than a walking weapon—"

"So you showed him your civilized side?" Captain Howard sighed. "You know that beating the crap out of them only proved their point."

"I guess so."

"I'd *say* so, Sergeant."

"But, Captain, I never saw those guys before, yet they acted like they hated me on sight, just because I wore a uniform, and I don't see—"

"Listen, Sergeant, you need to understand something. There are three kinds of people in this world. The first have no capacity for violence. They're innocents and—generally speaking—unable to protect themselves."

"Like sheep?" Thomas said.

"Yes, that's right, and they make up most of the population. Then there's a smaller group who have a hunger for violence and no love for their fellow man.

Dr. Langer, the base psychologist, would label them aggressive sociopaths. Reverend Price, the division chaplain, would call them evil. Either way, they're the predators."

"Wolves?"

Captain Howard locked eyes with his young sergeant. "Lastly, there are people like you and me. We love and respect our fellow man. We serve our country and protect people from harm. But unlike the rest of the population, we have no fear of violence. In fact, we relish the use of it to beat off the predators."

"So what does that make us? The sheep dogs?"

"Yes. And while the sheep may fear the wolf, they don't entirely trust the dog, either, even if the poor animal gives up its life to save the entire flock. Do you understand me?"

Thomas folded his arms. "You're saying some sheep only see the dog's fangs? Its predator's eyes?"

"When some citizens look at us, all they see are the arms we bear, the violence we employ."

Thomas frowned. "But we use it to protect them."

"Doesn't matter, son. Some will always refuse to make the distinction. If this is the life you want, you need to understand that—and get used to it." Captain Howard glanced at his watch. "And we'd better hit the trail; it's almost time for Sunday dinner."

"Sorry I kept you so long, Captain Bob," Thomas said, unconsciously addressing his commanding officer by his nickname. "You can drop me off at the base."

"I'm going home, Sergeant. Lieutenant Hanley and his wife are coming over for supper. I'd like you to join us."

"But, sir, I don't want to impose—"

"Sergeant, didn't your mama teach you manners?"

Thomas blinked. "Excuse me, sir?"

"You heard me, son. *Manners*. A gentleman never refuses an invitation to a sit-down dinner." The captain smiled. "It's just plain rude."

Less than an hour later, they were pulling up to a small house in suburban Maryland.

"This is my daughter, Abigail," said Mrs. Howard in her Tennessee twang. "Abigail, this is Sergeant Thomas Swimming Horse."

Captain Bob's daughter was nineteen, Thomas guessed, with short blond hair and bright green eyes over full lips and a pert nose. From the moment Thomas stepped into the little house, he couldn't stop looking at her. She was pretty, but that wasn't what drew Thomas's attention. Abigail was intense and alive, and she was smart, too—attending Georgetown University. Thomas knew that because the captain sometimes complained about the tuition bills.

Abigail offered her hand. "Nice to meet you, Sergeant."

"A pleasure, Ms. Howard." Thomas lightly grasped her fingers, holding on a moment longer than appropriate. She laughed awkwardly and pulled away.

She hardly looked at me. Probably figures I'm just another one of her daddy's soldier boys.

They sat down for the Sunday dinner—Captain Bob and his wife, Lieutenant Hanley and his wife, and Abigail. She wore a pink blouse and faded jeans with a tiny patch on the leg, a retro hippie logo that read "Love." She closed her eyes and prayed along with her father when Captain Bob said grace. Thomas knew because he was watching her.

Mrs. Howard served soup. Within a few minutes, the conversation flowed in two directions. Captain Bob and the lieutenant spouted army talk; Mrs. Howard, Myrna Hanley, and Abigail chatted about girl stuff.

Thomas remained quiet. He watched Abigail eat her soup. He watched her twist her hair and laugh at one of Myrna Hanley's jokes. He noticed the tiny freckles on the bridge of her nose, the way she rolled her eyes when she thought something she heard was outrageous.

By the time dessert came around, Thomas had caught her glancing at him twice, though she never said a word and looked away as soon as he noticed her stare.

It was like a game, but Thomas also sensed Abigail was becoming uncomfortable with his attention. It didn't matter, though. Thomas had to watch her.

At the end of the meal, the women got up to help clear the table. When they returned with coffee and cake, the two ladies were laughing about something. Bob and the lieutenant were talking about last week's maneuvers and how they'd waxed the tail of the new hotshot West Pointer from Division.

It was Abigail who served Thomas his coffee, in a delicate china cup and saucer. When he took it, their hands touched. Abigail seemed uncomfortable. But then, unexpectedly, she let her hand linger and met his stare with one of her own.

"Sergeant, I've had the strangest feeling you've been wanting to say something to me."

"I do," Thomas quietly replied.

She smiled. "Well, speak your mind, then."

He did, and everything was different after that.

18

"DIRECTOR, I HAVE AN UPDATE FROM THE MATRON. And Major Sallow has also reported in."

The complex numerical calculations that had been dancing inside his mind in bright flashes of incandescent insight ceased their performance. Smiling, the Director opened his eyes. "Excellent."

"Your mood is jovial," the Voice observed.

"You have no idea. I'm still basking in victory's sublime glow."

"Then Weapon X meets with your approval."

"Meets and excels," the Director said.

"The Matron reports that Slammer's condition has stabilized. He has survived his battle with Weapon X and will fight another day—but not this one."

"Good riddance. Slammer survived by luck, not prowess. He was utterly defeated by Weapon X." The Director sat back in his leather chair. "The exhibition was magnificent. Weapon X combines great strength and cunning with survivability. Not even Dr. Thorton could have envisioned his creation's awesome might."

"Did we really see Weapon X?" the Voice asked. "Or has the human side of the project reemerged, perhaps even reasserted a measure of control?"

The Director rubbed the stubble on his chin. "A valid question, but one that probably won't be answered until we bring Weapon X back into the lab for more extensive and invasive testing."

"On that subject, the Matron advised us that she's pitting another member of her team against Weapon X. The operation will begin sometime after dawn. She wishes to strike at Weapon X before it fully recovers."

"Oh, she's a clever witch."

"The Matron has requested the usual technical support. Control of our satellites, operational command of Sallow, his aircraft and personnel."

The Director waved his hand. "Granted. All granted. Do not trouble me with trivia—not when more important information awaits. You mentioned a report from Major Sallow."

"Yes, Director. There's been a new development. Not a positive one, I'm afraid."

"Continue."

"The major claims that a 'local yokel'—his words—was on the mountain. This lone individual observed Slammer's recovery operation."

"How? It's the wilderness. There are no towns, no civilization for miles."

"Actually, Director, that is not precisely true. Years ago, before construction began on the dam, the power plant, and Professor Thorton's facility, there was a security assessment of the region. A routine procedure, but the intelligence team uncovered potential security risks in the vicinity."

The Director frowned. "Please elaborate."

"Two separate communities were discovered, about a mile apart, and both within a fifty-mile radius of the complex."

"But that's impossible. The facility was supposed to be secret. To keep it that way, the government would have invoked eminent domain. The Department would have bought their land and moved the people out of the area long before construction was complete."

"The settlements were not incorporated, Director," the Voice interrupted. "They have never even been recorded in the Canadian census records. There are no property deeds; no survey of the population exists."

The Director blinked, surprised. "In this day and age? Are they members of some religious cult?"

"Both communities were made up of squatters, many of them living in Canada illegally. One settlement began as a counterculture commune in Northern California. Its members crossed the border and took refuge in the wilderness to flee narcotics manufacturing and distribution charges."

"And the other town?"

"A survivalist cult who fled to the wilderness from Denver, Colorado. They were absolutely convinced the final apocalypse was imminent. That was twenty-two years ago."

"And these communities still exist?"

The wall monitor crackled with static, and a satellite image of a tiny, snow-blanketed hamlet appeared on the screen. The wooden structures were centered around a well, and a creek meandered along one end of town.

"Very picturesque." The Director grunted. "I presume this is one of the settlements."

"Actually, Director, in the period between the construction of Professor Thorton's lab and its destruction years later, the two communities merged. This is the only settlement that currently exists. Satellite surveillance shows forty-seven log cabins and three larger structures." The Voice paused. "Our intelligence indicates there are approximately one hundred individuals occupying the town."

The Director brightened. "Then this presents no problem. It may even provide us with an opportunity."

"I don't follow your reasoning, Director."

"It's simple. This is a hamlet full of squatters. Miscreants and antisocial misfits. They have no electricity or running water. They keep to themselves. They don't have jobs. They don't pay income or property taxes, and they don't have credit cards." The Director rubbed his hands together as if washing them. "In short, they don't exist."

There was a long silence. "How do you propose to deal with these people who don't exist, Director?"

"For the time being, we shall ignore them, unless they get in our way. If any one of them spies on us, or attempts to interfere with our activities, I will be forced to take action. If necessary, the entire town will be neutralized. The Weapon Null team will obliterate all traces of that settlement. Or, if necessary, we shall loose Weapon X upon them." The Director nodded. "Yes. Perhaps Weapon X will do the job. That would be *really* interesting. . . ."

Dr. Megan Vigil returned to her dingy quarters and locked the door behind her. She kicked off her boots, dropped her grease-stained overalls on the floor, and tossed her dark glasses onto the bed.

The bathroom was cold and pitch dark, the water freezing, too. Megan stepped into the shower anyway. She had no choice—like Lady Macbeth, she experienced a compulsive need to wash away the evidence of her crimes. Not a murdered king's blood but oil, carbonized rubber, the stench of ozone and burnt insulation.

They rebuilt him. Right before my eyes . . .

The Matron and her staff had put Slammer back together again—with synthetic flesh, steel-reinforced bones, vile chemicals, and bioenhancement treatments that would probably kill him before he reached thirty.

And I helped.

She turned off the water. Even worse, in a couple of hours, she was going to help them again. Then she was going to watch as they sent out another test subject to be slaughtered.

Megan opened the bathroom door and heard the insistent buzzing of her intercom. Blinking against the glare of the five-volt night-light, she crossed the room and hit the button.

"This is Dr. Vigil."

"I've decided to launch Operation Blowtorch," the Matron said without preamble.

"I see."

"You have the agent's file in your stack. If you have time, read about Blowtorch. If you cannot, I'll brief you during each phase of the operation." The Matron paused. "I'm afraid we'll need to begin in less than three hours. If you want to be present for the entire activation process, then—"

"I require very little sleep," Megan broke in. "I'll meet you in the lab at oh-five-hundred hours."

"Very well."

Megan shut off the intercom and dropped into the bunk. She reached for the files on the nightstand, then brushed the stack onto the floor. She was in no mood to read one of the Matron's reports. Not now.

It wasn't that she was tired. What she'd told the Matron was true; since her operation, Megan required very little sleep—and only when the biocells in her bionic eyes needed to recharge—about two hours out of every thirty.

For Megan, one hundred and twenty minutes of deep, dreamless sleep followed deactivation. When the cells were recharged, through a natural chemical process in her brain, an automatic timer inside her optic center awakened her.

Hardworking. Efficient. Uncomplaining. Great at multitasking—and I can see for miles and miles. I'm the perfect freak.

And that's why Megan didn't want to read another case history. She was starting to identify with these poor, hapless creatures who seemed so powerful at first glance but were really quite fragile, helpless, pathetic. Poking and prodding, wiring and dissecting, the Weapon Null Program made each of its members more than they could be—and somehow less than human.

Megan didn't need to read the file to know that Blowtorch, like Slammer and Lieutenant Benteen back at the CCRC headquarters—and probably every other member of Weapon Null—had made a Faustian bargain. They had traded what little humanity they had left after a tragic circumstance for the dubious powers and abilities they now possessed. Megan knew this with certainty for one reason.

I made the same bargain.

• • •

Logan had chewed so much venison jerky his teeth hurt. He'd consumed an entire smoked deer shank the moment his rumbling stomach woke him. Now the meat was gone, but the gnawing hunger in the pit of his stomach still tormented him.

He belched and stoked the fire until the blaze filled the smoky cave with flickering light. Stretching out his left leg, Logan examined it closely. Even he was amazed when he found no visible signs of injury. None. No scars, no discolored skin. Even the hair had grown back.

It was as if the grievous injury had never occurred. And yet, less than twenty-four hours ago, the flesh had been blown away from that leg—all the skin, the muscles, the arteries and veins, right down to his shiny new adamantium bones. Unbelievably, while Logan slept, his phenomenal regenerative abilities fixed things up as good as new.

Logan stood and tested the limb. He walked, stomped his feet, crouched, and stood on one leg— and felt not even a twinge of discomfort. The pangs in his gut were causing him more distress than his formerly shattered leg.

But he was not entirely restored. Logan felt ravenous, of course, and he also felt a bit sluggish. The terrible nature of the injury and the tremendous resources required to repair the physical damage had obviously taxed his system to the limit.

Logan glanced at his reflection in his hand-built water trough and saw his own ribs poking through tightly stretched flesh. He'd lost body mass—perhaps as much as five percent.

No wonder I feel lighter . . . and light-headed.

The sight of water awakened his thirst, and Logan drank deeply. When he was finished, he shook the water from his face and hair. Then he wrapped a supple swath of deer hide around his flanks.

Clad in little more than an improvised loincloth, Logan rolled the boulder aside and stepped into the new day.

The morning was bright and cloudless, so cold his breath turned to frost each time he exhaled. Lifting his chin, Logan sniffed the frigid air. He walked in a circle, stalking the area around the cave. Finally, he paused and sniffed again.

Then he took off in a run, descending a winding trail that led to the foothills, the forest—and prey.

19

THE NOISE OF THE BOISTEROUS, IMPROMPTU TOWN meeting in the Librarian's cabin kept Thomas awake for what he thought was half the night. As the subject of said gathering, he was not invited to attend the proceedings. Unfortunately, he lived close enough to hear the racket as the meeting went on.

Thomas lay in his bunk, eyes closed, pillow over his head, trying to shut out the loud and incoherent voices. Finally, long past midnight, he heard a whole bunch of yeas and not too many nays. Things got quiet after that, and Thomas dropped into a dreamless sleep.

A sharp pounding on his door woke him a minute later—or, at least, that's what it felt like. When Thomas opened his eyes, he saw the morning sun shining dully through the frosted window and realized he'd been asleep for many hours.

The pounding resumed. Thomas rolled into a sitting position and winced when his bare feet hit the cold hardwood floor. He pulled trousers off the hook and slipped them on. Then he tugged a wool sweater over his head.

More pounding, insistent now.

"I'm coming. Hold your freaking horses," Thomas cried.

He unbolted the door and opened it. The crowd at his doorstep surprised him, and Thomas took a step backward. At least a third of the town was there—maybe forty people. The Librarian. Old Herman, the town drunk. Waldo Parsons, the unofficial mayor and the other town drunk.

Thomas noted that nobody from the doomsday cult was present, but most of the men and all of the women from the old hippie commune were there, a parade of gray hair and bandanas.

Leading the pack, Marvin the Zen Naturalist.

"Can I help you?" Thomas said.

"You can help everyone in this town, Swimming Horse," Marvin said. "You can help by leaving, and taking your instruments of war with you."

Thomas blinked. "Excuse me?"

"You violated the town law," Marvin said. "No weapons except for hunting. So we held a vote, and the people spoke. The citizens of Second Chance have banished you. We want you gone by sunset."

Thomas stepped out of the cabin in his bare feet.

The ground was so frozen it burned like fire. Thomas ignored the pain and moved forward until he was face-to-face with Marvin.

"You folks came unprepared."

Marvin smirked. "What are you talking about?"

Thomas folded his muscled arms. "You should have brought torches and pitchforks. No self-respecting mob can run the monster out of town without waving a lot of pitchforks around. It's not good form."

The Librarian laughed once. Marvin shot the old man an angry look.

"We're not a mob," Marvin insisted. "I told you. We voted you out, that's all."

Thomas scanned the crowd. "And was this vote unanimous?"

"That question's irrelevant," Marvin said. "Everyone agreed to abide by the vote, whatever the results. Majority rules."

Several of the others, including Ben and Jerry, and Jesse Lee, a grizzled Vietnam vet, avoided Thomas's gaze, which told him where they stood. Even the Librarian glanced away.

Thomas squared his shoulders. "Seems to me it's the mob that's ruling. Well, just to let you know: I've done nothing wrong, and I'm not going anywhere. This is my home, too."

Marvin's face flushed. "Don't be difficult, Swimming Horse. You're not the only one with a gun around here!" The man spun and faced Ben and Jerry.

"Tell him," Marvin commanded. "Tell him what will happen if he doesn't leave today. *Now*."

Jerry looked away. After a moment's hesitation, Ben stepped forward.

"Look, Thomas," Ben began in a reasonable tone. "Bringing an automatic weapon here . . . it just wasn't cool, man. You're scaring folks and breaking the rules. Not even the doomsday settlers have combat weapons."

"Maybe they ought to," Thomas replied. "Because something is going on up in the mountains. Something bad. What I saw yesterday was only the beginning—"

A woman screamed. Everyone turned when Big Rita appeared in the clearing, yelling and gesturing wildly. But the Native American woman was mingling words in French Canadian and her native Inuit, so Thomas failed to understand her. At last, she pointed and shouted in English, "Look! The mountain! The mountain is on fire!"

The crowd that had assembled in front of Thomas's log cabin acted in pretty much the same way he imagined the folks of Pompeii did when they saw Mount Vesuvius blow its top.

They panicked.

In less than ten seconds, the mob dispersed. With shouts, screams, and curses, the townspeople headed for the dubious safety of their homes.

Thomas went inside, too. But not to hide.

He dropped onto his bunk and tugged heavy, insulated socks over his feet. Then he dug out fresh boots—the pair he'd worn yesterday was still drying by the fire, and he didn't want to risk frostbite.

After adding another layer of clothing under his sweater, Thomas took his canteen off the hook on the wall and dipped it into the bucket. When the container was full, he strapped it to his belt, along with a survival knife, a compass, and a half-dozen clips of ammunition.

Thomas stuffed his army-issue backpack full of dry socks, shirts, trousers, and spare gloves. He added matches, army MREs for food, and more clips of ammunition. Then he pulled on his warmest parka, waterproof gloves, a hat, and several scarves.

He donned the backpack and reached for a weapon. He ignored the Remington Arms Model Seven Alaska Wilderness rifle, grabbed the Colt Commando instead. He squeezed the trigger on an empty chamber, thrust a loaded clip into the breech, and slung the automatic weapon over his shoulder. At this point, Thomas didn't give a damn who saw it.

He exited his cabin and glanced upward. Orange fires washed across the top of the mountain, then appeared to recede like waves on a shore. It was strange behavior for a fire, and Thomas was convinced the conflagration was not natural. Again he watched as a fiery ball flowed across the mountainside and then ebbed like a burning tide.

Looks like a flamethrower.

"Tommy boy, where are you going?" a voice called.

Thomas glanced over his shoulder and saw the Librarian standing in front of his long house.

"I'm going up the hill," Thomas replied. "I'm gonna find out what's happening."

The old man's face was pale. He glanced at the blazing mountain, then looked away. "Look. The fire's not spreading," the Librarian said. "You can see that the danger is contained. We're safe down here. You don't have to go up there."

"Fires spread, Librarian, unless they're put out," Thomas replied. "Somebody has to go up there. It might as well be me."

"We don't want trouble, Tommy boy. Don't bring it down on us."

Thomas ignored the old man's warning and took off in a run. He reached the edge of town in less than a minute and followed the steep trail up the mountainside, toward the burning summit.

"I'm sorry the glitch in your bionic vision system prevents you from seeing this, Dr. Vigil," the Matron said, her eyes locked on the satellite surveillance monitor. "In just three minutes, Blowtorch has blanketed the entire western face of the mountain in fire."

Dr. Vigil ignored the monitor, scanning the room to find that everyone else was watching the screen. Technicians in orange suits. Corporal MacKenzie and his small unit, the only regular Canadian troops who remained after the recall. Even Major Sallow's scarred and pockmarked face was directed at the monitor.

"I was under the impression you wanted to avoid a conflagration," Megan said. "That is government-protected land."

"Never fear," the Matron replied. "Blowtorch is merely putting on a show to attract the attention of Weapon X and flush the creature out into the open. I assure you, he is *not* going to burn down half the Canadian wilderness."

Corporal MacKenzie stood tall and straight, hands behind his back. "With all due respect, ma'am, he looks like he's going to burn it all down to me."

"Blowtorch is perfectly capable of controlling the fires he generates," the Matron said. "He can extinguish them within seconds, if he chooses. Power without control is useless—the proof is Weapon X."

"How does he do that, ma'am?" MacKenzie asked. "Control the fires, I mean."

"You're a soldier, Corporal. You're familiar with the composition and properties of napalm, correct?"

MacKenzie nodded. "Napalm is a highly flammable petroleum-based jelly used in bombs and munitions. When a napalm canister bursts, it disperses the burning viscous material over a wide area; the jelly clings to objects and personnel for maximum destructive effect, because napalm is nearly impossible to extinguish."

"A concise and accurate description," the Matron said. "And one that highlights the difference between a standard incendiary device and Blowtorch, who does not use napalm or any type of jelly or liquid to generate fire. Instead, he utilizes a highly flammable methane gas produced in three auxiliary stomachs—"

The Corporal blinked. "Did you say stomachs, Matron?"

"Blowtorch actually has *four* stomachs," the Matron said. "One is perfectly normal—the one he was born with. The other three digestive tracts were harvested from Angus bulls and grafted onto his lungs, using advanced antirejection drugs to facilitate tissue merging at the cellular level."

MacKenzie stared, jaw slack. "He's got bellies in his lungs, ma'am?"

Megan turned her head to hide her amusement. She'd studied Blowtorch's unique anatomy and metabolism and understood the basic concepts. Corporal MacKenzie had not been briefed, so the details about Blowtorch's curious physiology obviously had come as a shock to the soldier.

"Yes, Corporal, the stomachs have been grafted onto his lungs," Megan said. Then she smiled. "And by the way, Blowtorch has extra lungs, too. Four in all."

"And these produce fire?" MacKenzie asked.

"The lungs provide propulsion only. The flammable gases are actually produced in the auxiliary stomachs, via a process of methanogenesis—"

"Excuse me?"

"Methanogenesis is the formation of methane through the use of tiny microbes. In this case, the microbes are located in Blowtorch's auxiliary stomachs. Gas production is enhanced by the addition of generating substances like oligosaccharides, wheat gluten, cellulose, and raw nitrates. The flammable gas is then expelled from the ancillary lungs through his mouth, riding on a jet of pure oxygen processed in the man's lungs." The Matron nodded. "You see, when Blowtorch inhales, his chest and abdomen can expand up to ten times its normal size. To accommodate this action, his rib cage has been severed, then reconnected with strips of an expanding plastic."

"But how do the gases ignite?"

"A series of mandibles similar to a crab's mouth line the walls of Blowtorch's throat. These mandibles click together to create sparks, which ignite the methane as it passes through the esophagus." The Matron paused. "Our agent quite literally blows fire, which gave rise to his code name."

"Those mandibles must make talking difficult," MacKenzie observed. "The little guy didn't say much while your technicians were prepping him."

"Yes, Blowtorch is mute, I'm afraid," the Matron replied. "His larynx was shattered by a mortar shell while he served with the Canadian Army on a United Nations police action in Africa."

"With all that gas, it's a wonder he doesn't blow himself up."

"Blowtorch sweats a viscous substance that retards flame." Megan stepped forward. "His perspiration is actually flame-proof."

"And you claim your man can put the fires out, too?"

"There is a trio of bony projections rising from Blowtorch's shoulders and smaller spikes running along either side of the man's spine. They are actually funnels that collect and store various gases and compounds from the atmosphere. Blowtorch can create fire in his belly and intensify the blaze by fanning it with pure oxygen collected and stored in his spines. Or he can smother the fire as effortlessly as a child blows out the candles on his birthday cake—by spewing pure nitrogen, just like a fire extinguisher."

Corporal MacKenzie exhaled. "This Blowtorch is a frightful creation, no doubt about it."

The man's words were not meant as a compliment. The Matron failed to notice. "Thank you, Corporal," she replied. "But the credit goes to Professor Thorton and his team of specialists. Those dedicated men performed miracles in the early programs and here in this lab."

The mission specialist cried out from his command station. "Matron! Look at the screen. Weapon X is approaching the combat zone."

"Yes," the woman said. "I see it. They should make contact in a few minutes."

The Matron faced her staff. "All personnel report to your action stations," she commanded. "I want every recorder on and as many satellites as we can reposition over this section of the wilderness."

Features taut, the woman stared at the monitor again.

"Now, let's see who wins *this* round."

20

LOGAN HAD BEEN STALKING DEER WHEN THE strange fires began scorching the mountain.

It started with a peculiar hissing sound, like the working of some bizarre blacksmith's bellows. Suddenly, a red-orange cloud rolled over his head, blotting out the sky and turning the landscape a sickly scarlet hue. The tops of pine trees exploded in flames; burning embers fell from branches, sizzling as they hit the snow.

Then came the thunder of hooves. Logan lurched off the trail and flattened himself against the rocks as a huge stag bolted past, followed by six long-legged fawns.

When the stampede was clear, Logan pushed away from the rocks. He knew immediately that the flames were unnatural, a weapon, and the people who'd sent

Slammer gunning for him were back for a second round, this time with a new contender.

He was tempted to run down toward the valley, right behind the deer, to hide until the burning stopped and those who hunted him went away and left him alone. But Logan knew they would never stop.

It was simple economics. Somebody—probably these same bastards—had gone to an awful lot of time, trouble, and expense to turn a freak of nature into a freak of science. Now they wanted their double-down freak back.

He knew they would come at him, again and again, until they defeated him or he beat the crap out of them. Either way, Logan figured it was better to face the flames now, rather than awaken from a deep sleep one morning to find his cave had been turned into a crematorium while he'd been dreaming.

He soon regretted his decision.

The hissing came again from above, and fire filled the sky, descending right on him this time. With his hide and hair badly seared, Logan ran for cover, diving into a drift of fast-melting snow. He sucked in air—and breathed fire instead. Lungs scorched, he coughed, spat blood. Blisters erupted on his skin; his flesh puckered and cracked.

As icicles dropped from the trees, staking the snow around him, Logan dug with his hands, burrowing deeper into the snow. The ball of fire receded, leaving only a few burning trees in its wake. Smoke wafted through the forest, along with a chemical stink that stung Logan's nostrils. Glowing embers hovered in the air like burning fireflies.

Logan stumbled to his feet and shook the slush from his shoulders. The skin twitched on his back, arms, and legs as the suppurating burns healed.

Then came another whooshing roar—but the fire burned in another direction. Logan could see the source of this searing carnage was the plateau near the top of the mountain, a broad swath of rocks and trees just under the shadow of the summit.

Whoever's after me, they're firing blind. Trying to flush me out like a crazy-scared deer. Why can't they just leave me alone? Haven't they done enough?

A low rumble emerged from his throat.

Fine. If the bastards want me, let 'em come.

Snarling, Logan dashed through the burning snow, toward the noise and heat. He reached the rocky plateau a moment later, scrambled to the top of a heap of ice-covered boulders.

Logan was not sure what he was going to find—a squad of men with flamethrowers; that decrepit old World War II hero, the Human Torch; maybe a fire-breathing, prehistoric dragon. None of those would have surprised him. What Logan found certainly did.

A lone man stood in the middle of the fire-swept clearing. He was bald and shirtless, his ample love handles a mushroom bulge that draped over tight black briefs made of shiny fire-proof asbestos. Standing with short, chubby legs braced, the man's skin shone wetly, as if he'd just climbed out of the bathtub.

While Logan watched, the stranger trampled around the clearing in ill-fitting black boots made of the same fireproof material as his shorts. By far the most bizarre thing about his outlandish appearance were the irregularly shaped, bone-white spikes that projected from the man's shoulders and the two rows of shorter spikes that ran in parallel lines down the center of his flabby pink back.

The man must have sensed Logan's presence, because he turned to face him. Logan saw close-set gray eyes over a bulbous nose; otherwise, the intruder's features were bland and eminently forgettable.

"Who the hell are you?" Logan yelled.

The man did not reply. Instead, he grinned and stepped forward, his eyes locked on Logan's. For a moment, the pair stared silently at each other.

"Say something?" Logan demanded. "What's the matter, Smokey the Bear got your tongue?"

The stranger opened his mouth as if to speak, but his reply was a loud, whooshing sound that filled Logan's ears. The tiny hairs on his arms prickled as the air around Logan began to stir. A swirling breeze sprang up, rustling the pine branches and kicking up snow.

The little man's eyes bulged in their sockets, and his cheeks puffed cherry red. His mouth stretched wider, and the sucking roar continued, until a terrible wind swept through the clearing. A blast of air slammed Logan's spine and nearly uprooted him from his perch.

Legs braced, Logan watched as the little man began to expand, his torso and abdomen swelling like a grotesque human balloon. The *snikt* of Logan's claws extending was lost in the howl of cyclonic winds that were being sucked into the stranger's lungs. Finally, Logan heard a strange piping sound and realized the noise was coming from the peculiar projections on the man's back.

The stranger continued to expand like a spiked blowfish, until his corpulent, inflated body tottered unsteadily on chubby, dimpled legs. All of a sudden, the stranger's glazed eyes focused—on Logan. A ball of fire burst from his throat and shot across the clearing like a sizzling cannonball.

Logan tried to dodge the missile, but he moved too late. The burning ball of roiling gas struck his chest and exploded outward. Tentacles of blue-white fire wrapped themselves around his body. Flames scorched his eyes, and Logan cried out.

In the searing blast of volcanic heat, the icy cluster of boulders gave way under Logan's feet. As the hillock crumbled, he was tossed backward. Burned and blinded, Logan tumbled over the edge of the high plateau.

• • •

Waddling on thick legs, Blowtorch hurried across the clearing. When he reached the spot where Weapon X had fallen, he crouched on one knee, gazed over the edge of the precipice. Blowtorch saw scorched marks and a hole in the snow where his prey had landed far below.

Grinning again, Blowtorch inhaled for a full thirty seconds. Then he opened his mouth and vomited another fireball.

The snowdrift exploded into sizzling steam on impact. He reeled backward, blinking as a scalding cloud reached his perch. The fog cleared in a few seconds, and the man peered over the cliff.

The snowdrift had completely evaporated. In its place was a naked patch of smoldering trees and scorched earth the size of a small lawn. Warily, the fat man scanned the area below the plateau. He saw nothing but rocks and pine trees and snow. Blowtorch frowned when he realized there was no sign of an adamantium steel skeleton. Weapon X had gotten away.

Logan blindly crawled through clouds of spitting steam. When he reached a copse of pine trees, he groped and dug into a pile of drifted snow under dipping branches. Hidden—or so he hoped—Logan rubbed snow on his stinging face, into his scorched and tearing eyes.

Logan waited for his vision to clear. He listened

warily, fearing a sneak attack. But none came. All he heard was the wailing wind and the whisper of swaying pine branches.

Logan tried to open his eyes. His left eyelid remained stuck closed for a moment, then separated with a ripping sting. The right eye stubbornly refused to open, so he ignored it. With one good eye, he scanned the cliffs. There was no sign of his attacker, which probably meant the man was stalking him right now.

He tried his right eye again. This time it opened, but the world was a blur. It would have to do, he decided, but before he could move again, he heard crunching footsteps. Someone was approaching his position. He cautiously lifted his head out of the snow pit.

The tree above Logan blew apart in a burst of yellow fire. Leaping out of hiding, he was showered with burning needles and flaming splinters. He took off across icy rocks, blue jets of fire tracing his path like machine-gun bullets. The tiny fireballs spit and crackled when they struck snow, or exploded in a shower of white sparks against the rocks.

Logan jinxed as he ran, right, left, always one step ahead of the blasts until he reached the end of the line. Without hesitating, he leaped over the edge of the mountain, falling several feet before stabbing his claws into the side of the cliff. The jolt nearly yanked him free, but he managed to hang on. Suspended once again like a spider on a wall, Logan scrambled along the vertical cliff, claws digging into the rocks.

Above him, the fat man's whooshing lungs expelled another time. A blast of fiery gases rolled over the side of the plateau, a waterfall of molten lava that scorched rocks and sent icicles plunging to the foothills.

Logan swung precariously from one claw, narrowly avoiding the torrent of burning incandescent gases. He shifted direction, moving along the sheer cliff to a spot behind his attacker.

While a second burning blast rolled over the ledge, Logan darted onto the plateau, dove behind a stand of tall oaks, and searched for a means to strike back at the fat little bugger before he burned every regenerating molecule from his frame.

Logan glanced up at the tall branches over his head, then at the thick tree trunk in front of him. With a quick double slash, he severed the trunk of the massive oak. The oak separated with a loud snap, then toppled toward the fire-breathing asshole.

The pudgy man whirled at the sound, saw the oak tree falling, and opened his mouth. Logan heard a loud burp; then a blast of fiery gas slammed into the falling tree.

The mighty oak exploded like a lit stick of dynamite.

The concussion washed over Logan. He threw up his hands to shield his eyes from shards of wood, chunks of burning bark, and fiery branches. Gashed, burned, and punctured with dozens of jagged splinters, he reeled as a second burst of fire struck his chest and threw him backward. Logan flipped end over end and tumbled into a shallow ravine. The debris from the falling tree continued to rain down on him.

Bleeding from a hundred wounds, he pressed his back against a boulder the size of a bus. He felt fire scorching his lungs and gasped as the creature sucked the oxygen out of the atmosphere.

Logan tried to rise but was pinned by the heavy trunk of the shattered oak crashing down on his legs. As he struggled to free himself, the little man dashed toward him. Suddenly, the living blowtorch was standing in front of him, eyes glowing in triumph, a lopsided grin plastered across his chubby face.

Blinking against the heat, Logan growled a curse, stopped struggling, and slumped against the rocks. "Go on. What are you waiting for? Finish it."

Blowtorch inhaled. Logan's ears popped as the air swirled around them. The loud whoosh became an ear-battering roar. Then the man's bulging eyes focused on Logan. Thrusting his head forward, Blowtorch spat a steady stream of blue fire.

As the flames engulfed Logan, agony traced every nerve in his tortured body. Cells boiled, flesh burned, organs burst. Muscles melted away and reappeared, only to melt anew. His phenomenal metabolism sped up to compensate for the magnitude of the physical damage.

Finally, some unknown tipping point was reached; the regenerative process hit critical mass. Logan's flesh vanished, only to reappear, phoenixlike, a microsecond later.

Flesh disintegrated and reformed again and again. Through it all, the only constant was the pain—an anguish so intense it seemed impossible for Logan to bear.

Logan opened his mouth, but his tongue burned away before he could shout. The raging trauma turned every microsecond into an aeon of torment. His jaws stretched wide, his mouth gaping, the sound that emerged seemed to spring from the primal core of Logan's being.

Soon, his screams filled the blasted clearing. His tortured howls echoed across the mountainside and drifted down, into the valley and the settlement far below.

21

THOMAS STRUGGLED TO REACH THE SUMMIT. Because the old trail had been shattered by the avalanche, he was forced to find a new way up.

His search was difficult and frustrating. Several times, he was confronted with a dead end and had to double back and find another path. Fires continued to roar above him, and the mountain was rocked by strange winds and eerie piping sounds.

Near the end of his ascent, Thomas had to navigate a vertical cliff without proper equipment. At last, he found a section of the old trail still intact and began the final leg of the climb.

As Thomas neared a plateau, he witnessed an oak tree waver and topple, followed by a deafening explosion that rocked the mountain. Minutes later, he followed a narrow path that led to the broad plateau under the shadow of the mountain's jutting peak.

Battered by wind, Thomas slipped the Colt Commando off his shoulder and threw the safety. Clutching the assault rifle, he moved through the trees until he encountered a wall of black smoke. Half-blind and gasping, he crested a ridge—then stopped dead in his tracks.

You've got to be kidding me.

Thomas blinked. But when he opened his eyes, the obscenely obese man in swimming trunks was still there. And—impossibly—he was still spitting fire at what appeared to be the shattered trunk of a tree.

The fat man did not see Thomas; he was too intent on his target. Suddenly, above the incessant roar of the burning gas, Thomas heard agonized screams. Human screams. He rushed forward, and finally saw the fat man's victim.

The wild man.

Thomas watched the man's flesh blacken and burn, watched him writhe in the agony of the damned.

Thomas had no reason to take a side in this fight. He really didn't know who was right or wrong; he couldn't even understand what was really happening. But one thing he could see: a man was suffering, and another man was causing that pain. Thomas acted out of instinct.

He raised the rifle.

The first bullet tore a meaty chunk out of the fat man's neck. His eyes widened in shock, and the jet of fire streaming through his lips sputtered. The second struck lower, taking him in the armpit.

The fat man detonated in a flash of blue flame and pulverized flesh.

The blast was the loudest sound Thomas had ever heard. The shock wave struck him with sledgehammer force, and he was swept away like a twig in a gale.

Thomas heard nothing after that.

The concussion flattened trees and blasted snow and debris from the plateau. In a flash, the fires were extinguished as chunks of wood, pine needles, and human flesh were blown skyward. They soon fluttered down again, to pelt the ground in a gore-soaked rain.

As the last echoes of the blast faded, the violent winds stilled. In the center of the blast zone, two fat legs teetered in smoldering boots, then toppled to the scorched ground. Smoke rose from the blackened earth, and an eerie silence descended over the plateau.

Under the shadow of a massive boulder, someone cursed a blue streak.

Then a ropy, muscular arm emerged from a pile of smoking rubble, followed by another. With a final roar, Logan burst out of the wreckage. He stood, legs firm, drinking in the fresh, cool air that swept across the blasted clearing.

He ignored the bleeding limbs in the center of the plateau and scanned the area for a sign of the stranger who'd saved him. He'd searched for less than a minute when, faintly, Logan heard a strange clicking sound. He followed the noise until he came upon a gruesome discovery.

The fat man's head and upper torso were sprawled on the rocks. The head was still alive, eyes moving side to side, mouth opening and closing spasmodically.

Logan choked when he realized the clicking sound was coming from the man's throat. Then he saw the weird, sparking claws through the bullet hole in the neck.

"Stinking freak."

The fat man looked up at him and tried to grin. Logan snarled, and in a silver flash, the claws popped out of his wrists. He crossed his arms in a double slash, and the man's head leaped from its shoulders.

Logan grunted when the cranium landed at his feet, dying eyes staring up at him. With an angry curse, he kicked the grisly trophy over the side of the mountain.

Shuddering, Logan turned his back on the twitching carcass. He carefully circled the area, until he spied the shattered remains of a Colt Commando. The barrel was twisted like a pretzel, and from the condition of the gun, Logan figured finding the owner was a lost cause—so he was surprised to hear a moan coming from a shallow depression in the earth.

He hurried to the scene and found a man there— the one who'd shot him over the deer. His coat was in tatters, but a military-style backpack was still draped over his limp shoulders. Logan placed his ear against the man's chest and heard a pulse. He also heard the grinding of bones that indicated a broken rib.

Next he checked the man for wounds, and his superficial search came up with nothing mortal. The man moaned again but did not open his eyes. Under the scorch marks, Logan could see he was in his thirties and a Native American. There was bright blood flecking his lips, and that was not a good sign.

He's probably dying right now.

The man moaned again, but it was clear to Logan that he wasn't conscious.

Best to leave him here. Nothing I can do for him. Might as well die in peace.

Dark clouds rolled across the sun, casting a grim shadow over the landscape. Logan shivered as a gust of frigid arctic air swept across the plateau.

Storm's coming, but this poor bastard will probably freeze to death long before that. Not such a bad way to go, either.

But to Logan's surprise, the man on the ground opened his eyes, coughed, and cried out in pain.

"Whoa, settle down," Logan warned. "You've got a busted rib. Maybe internal injuries."

The man moved his mouth, but no sound came out.

"Don't try to talk," Logan said.

Gently, he slipped his arms under the fallen man and lifted him off the ground. Thomas groaned again.

"I know it hurts, but you're gonna die if I leave you here."

Thomas nodded, as if he understood. Then his eyes rolled back, and he seemed to pass out.

"That's good. You should rest," Logan said. "I'll get you to a nice warm cave and patch you up. Who knows, you might even live."

22

"You're telling me that you lost track of Weapon X?" the Director raged.

"I lost track of nothing, sir," the Voice replied, its tone defensive. "I'm telling you that the surveillance satellites have not yet located its current position."

"But how can that be? I ordered continuous surveillance—"

"And I warned you that was not possible," the Voice insisted. "One satellite drifted out of range while another came on station. In the seven-minute-and-twenty-two-second lag time in coverage, Weapon X vanished."

"It . . . it can't have gone far," sputtered the Director.

"Most likely, Weapon X is holed up in a cave," the Voice replied. "Underground, especially under several feet of granite or heavy metal, his adamantium skeleton is less detectable to orbital sensors. Plus, there are many iron ore deposits in the region, which further interfere with our instruments—"

"Enough excuses," the Director said, frowning. "We have other issues to deal with."

"The civilian."

"The *witness*. The local *idiot* who interfered in the battle and altered the outcome."

"But sir, surely the man saved Weapon X from destruction," the Voice protested.

"Ridiculous," the Director cried. "You saw the biological monitors. Weapon X's metabolism was off the charts. Review the tapes for yourself. Weapon X regenerated faster than the Matron's oversized Zippo lighter could inflict damage. In another few minutes, Weapon X would have recovered, then struck down his opponent."

"Blowtorch died in any case," the Voice said.

The Director snorted. "*Blowtorch*. The Matron's code names are not particularly original."

"You mentioned the civilian?" the Voice prodded.

"Ah, yes," the Director replied. "The population of that town must be isolated until they can be dealt with. They've already seen too much and interfered too many times. If some of them flee the valley, they may tell the world what they saw."

"What do you propose?" the Voice asked.

"According to our satellite map, the only way in or out of that valley is on a trail that leads through a narrow canyon. I want Major Sallow to dynamite that passage, seal it up."

"If they realize they are under assault, trapped, the citizens may react," the Voice warned.

"A storm is coming. It doesn't appear severe, but it will help hide our activities," the Director declared. "Tell Sallow to make his demolition appear natural. Like an avalanche, perhaps."

"Consider it done, sir."

"And keep looking for Weapon X. I want it located within twenty-four hours, or I shall activate another advanced AI program to take your place."

Logan laid the man on the deer-hide bed. Then he stoked the smoldering fire until it roared to life. He added some wood and the blaze filled the cave with warmth and flickering light.

The man was still out, so Logan took the backpack off his shoulders and rummaged through it. He found MREs, tore a pouch of beef stew open with his teeth, and swallowed the contents in a single gulp. He devoured three more Meals Ready to Eat, then tossed the backpack into the corner.

Next, Logan stripped away the man's shredded parka, then his wool sweater and olive drab undershirt. He finally located a wound—a nine-inch splinter of wood was embedded in the man's rib cage. The man writhed and cried out in his sleep as Logan carefully pulled the stake out.

He sanitized one steel claw in the fire, then used it to probe the wound. Logan dug out a handful of smaller splinters before he washed the puncture with fresh water drawn from his trough. He dressed the wound with rags torn from the man's parka.

Logan noted that the man had other scars crisscrossing his torso. Old wounds, including a nasty knife slash across his chest and shrapnel scars on his arms and shoulders. Logan wasn't surprised to find tarnished dog tags hanging around the man's thick neck.

"Thomas Swimming Horse, Lieutenant, United States Army," Logan read. "Blood Type, O. Religion, none. Born in Red Canyon, Arizona. A citizen of the Cherokee Nation—and I'll bet you've seen your share of action, too, by the look of you."

Tamboor, West Africa
Six years ago

The crowd in the center of town had become a mob. The warlords were working overtime to stir up tribal hatred, while the imams were denouncing the infidels in their midst. The anger boiled over into arson, and smoke from burning tires hung in the air over the markets, mosques, and minarets of Tamboor's capital city.

Things were worse on the edge of town, far from the United Nations peacekeeping forces. There were gunshots and looting. Homes, businesses, and the tiny Roman Catholic church had been set on fire, too.

If the situation continued to deteriorate, members of the despised Hutsu minority would soon be dragged into the streets and set alight beside the tires. It didn't help that the United Nations grain shipment had been delayed by red tape and tribal enmity. The IPs—indigenous peoples—were difficult enough to deal with when their bellies were full.

Captain Bob Howard stepped out of the concrete metal shop the UN peacekeepers were using as a field command during Operation Breadline. Like his men, Howard wore chocolate-chip-patterned desert camouflage BDUs and a Kevlar helmet, along with eighty pounds of gear, including weapons and ammunition. All that equipment was scorching hot under the tropical sun, but that was the least of their worries.

Captain Howard glanced at the nearly deserted marketplace, the trucks lined up waiting to drive away. Then he scanned the shouting, angry mob straining against the ropes to enter and loot the area as soon as the UN left with its charges.

So far, the peacekeeping troops from the Indian Army had kept the citizens of Tamboor out while the minority Hutsus packed up and left their urban ghettos under the protection of UN escorts. The central Hutsu marketplace was the point of assembly—not a wise choice, considering that section of the city was surrounded by hostile forces. But that wasn't Captain Howard's call. His orders were to escort the Hutsus out of the city. They should have been gone already, but the minority tribesmen were taking their own sweet time packing into the trucks.

Meanwhile, the mob was getting rowdier by the minute.

"Corporal Miller!" the captain bellowed over the noise of the crowd.

"Yes, sir," the other man replied.

"Tell those people driving the Red Cross trucks to pick up the pace. Things are going to get ugly here, real fast."

The corporal took off in a run for the lead truck.

"Lieutenant Hanley! I need to see you now."

But it was Sergeant Thomas Swimming Horse who appeared at the captain's side.

"Sir, the lieutenant headed across the market to talk with the Indian commander," he reported.

"Why didn't Hanley use the com?"

Thomas shrugged. "We're having trouble coordinating with the Indians using radios, Captain. All communications with foreign forces have to be channeled through JOC. There's been a lot of delays."

Captain Howard swore. "I'm going to ream those pukes at Joint Operation Command a new hole if they don't correct the problem, ASAP," he growled. "In the meantime, I want you to establish a second perimeter, position some heavy machine guns and RPGs around the trucks until we move out."

"Smell trouble, sir?" Thomas asked.

"Let's just say that this fight, and these people, are

not worth dying for. I want to make sure my men are covered in case the Indians cave." He unrolled a map. "I want three fire points. Here, here, and one right here." The captain wanted to triangulate the area, trap any potential aggressors inside the marketplace, where they could be gunned down with relative ease. "That post near the gate will be a real hot spot, so I want you to go there with a fire team."

Thomas nodded. "Yes, sir."

"Be careful, Sergeant. My daughter would be very upset with me if I didn't bring you home in one piece."

Thomas blinked. "Excuse me, sir?"

"Give your brain a chance, son. You can't keep something like that a secret. For one thing, the incoming mail crosses my desk before it gets to you. I should know my own daughter's handwriting by now. She's been writing you two or three times a week."

Thomas looked sheepish. "I was gonna say something, sir. We'd been seeing each other. Then this deployment came along and—"

"This little fiasco messed up all of our lives, Sergeant. I'm particularly sorry about that spot with Special Forces Command you sacrificed to come here with the unit."

Thomas grinned. "Are you kidding, Captain? Tamboor is a real gas. I wouldn't miss this for the world."

Captain Howard grinned and dismissed him.

Thomas went off to select his men, then divided them up into fire teams. He shouldered a heavy machine gun and was about to move out, when Thomas spotted Lieutenant Hanley and two Rangers at the end of a narrow side street.

"Yo, Captain! Here comes the lieutenant," Thomas called, pointing.

Captain Howard nodded and stepped into the middle of the street. Hands on hips, he waited for his second-in-command.

Lieutenant Hanley had almost reached the captain's side when Thomas heard the squeal of tires. A technical appeared at the end of the street, wheels kicking up dust. This one was a GM pickup truck with dappled camouflage paint covering the steel plates welded to its body. A fifty-caliber machine gun was mounted on the bed of the truck. A ragged banner waved from the antenna—the star and crescent flag of the warlord Abu Kahlil.

The gunner spied the officers in the street and fumbled with his weapon. Meanwhile, the truck kept on coming.

Thomas slipped the rifle off his shoulder and grabbed the man next to him. "Fire the RPG!" he commanded.

The private dropped to one knee and aimed the rocket-propelled grenade at the oncoming vehicle. Thomas was close enough to feel the hot blast and watch the grenade streak an unwavering path past the shocked officers and into the speeding truck.

The missile punched through the windshield, then

exploded inside the cab. Both doors blew off, and the driver vanished in a red mist. Fire engulfed the machine gunner. The screaming man tumbled off the flatbed, and his skull cracked open on the pavement.

The truck kept on coming.

Captain Howard and the two Rangers scattered. Lieutenant Hanley was rooted to his spot, transfixed while death rolled toward him.

Suddenly, strong hands closed on the lieutenant's collar. "Get out of here!" Captain Howard roared, shoving him against a building. Hanley's helmet slammed into the concrete wall. Captain Howard was still in the street when the technical struck him. The officer was knocked down by the truck, which continued forward, rolling over him.

At that moment, flames reached the ammunition box, and the pickup truck blew apart. The blast shattered windows and rocked soldiers off their feet. The truck flipped over onto its side and burned.

Thomas ran to the crash. The fire still raged, but behind the wreckage, he found Lieutenant Hanley, bleeding through a shattered nose. Thomas assisted the man to his feet and moved him away from the flames. Medics rushed forward to help. They grabbed the lieutenant under his arms and carried him to a stretcher.

There was no helping their commander, however. Captain Bob Howard was dead.

THOMAS CRIED OUT AND OPENED HIS EYES. HE found himself in a cave, surrounded by cold stone walls. He was lying on a deerskin hide, beside a flickering fire. And he wasn't alone.

The wild man eyed him from the center of the cave. His meal had been interrupted, one hand still clutched an MRE pouch. He wiped his lips with the other.

"You're awake," he said.

Thomas blinked, not sure he'd heard what he thought he'd heard. "You can talk?"

"Only if I want to, Lieutenant."

"I'm not a lieutenant," Thomas protested weakly. "I'm . . . retired."

The wild man grunted. "Figured as much. You wouldn't be here if you still had the army."

"In this cave, you mean?"

"Living in the wilderness," the other man replied. "Not a place for conventional folk."

"Who are you?" Thomas asked.

"Call me Logan."

"Logan? Is that a first name or last? Should I call you *Mister* Logan, since you're big on titles?"

"Just Logan."

Thomas tried to sit up—and the cave lurched. He slumped back down on the hide, panting.

"Calm down, Thomas Swimming Horse," Logan said. "You had a chunk of wood in your gut. I pulled it out and cleaned the wound, but the puncture is pretty deep, and you need professional help."

"Then why don't you get me some?" Thomas demanded.

"Testy, aren't you, considering I saved your life."

"Unless I was hallucinating, the last time I looked, you were on fire," Thomas replied. "Some guy in rubber briefs was cooking you, till I shot him."

"You shot me once, too. Is it time for payback?"

Suddenly, Thomas's eyes went wide, as he thrashed on the bed and fumbled around with his hands. "Where's my gun?"

"Don't worry, kid," Logan said. "I was joking about the payback."

"My gun!"

"It's ruined, soldier. You survived the blast. Your assault rifle didn't."

Thomas settled down. "Blast? What blast?"

"You're loopy, kid." Logan moved across the cave to the man's side. "Here, eat this," he said, thrusting an MRE at him.

Thomas took the pouch but didn't try to eat.

"What? You think it's poisoned?" Logan asked. "This is *your* food. I got it out of your backpack. When the storm clears, I'll hunt us some fresh meat."

Thomas noticed the wind whistling outside for the first time. "How long have I been out?"

"Maybe half a day. I brought you here because I didn't have time to take you back to your settlement. The storm was coming—it started a few hours ago—and I didn't want to get stuck in your fair city."

"Smart move," Thomas said. "The folks in Second Chance preach tolerance and acceptance, but they don't always practice either."

Logan snorted. "That's why I live alone."

The hunger gnawed at Thomas's insides, and without thinking, he opened the MRE. "What brings you to these parts?"

"Target fixation. I was stalking the bluebird of happiness and got lost."

Thomas smiled weakly. "You bagged the bird, though, right?"

Logan grunted. "No comment."

They sat in silence for a time, the only sounds the fire's crackle and the howl of the wind. Thomas took a bite of food, then another. Logan brought him a stone cup filled with fresh water, and he drank deeply.

Finally, Thomas finished his meal, wiped his lips with the back of his hand. Then he spoke.

"What are you, Logan, some kind of experiment or something?"

Logan looked away. "That's a loaded question."

"Okay," Thomas said. "Then who are the people after you? The guys in the orange suits with the black helicopters?"

"They're a bunch of mad scientists and government pukes who think they own me," Logan replied, his body tensing. "To them, I'm property, bought and paid for. Needless to say, I don't see it that way."

Thomas tried to sit up and gasped, clutching his side.

"I told you to settle down," Logan commanded. "I think you're bleeding again."

Logan pulled back Thomas's shredded parka, which he'd been using for a blanket. "Damn, you *are* bleeding. And I think you have a fever, too."

Thomas began to shiver. "How can I have a fever when I feel so cold?" he moaned, teeth chattering.

Logan wrapped the coat around Thomas's neck and upper body. "You're going into shock. I'll get you more water."

On the way to the trough, Logan tossed more wood into the fire. When he returned, cup in hand, Thomas was unconscious. The Native American's swarthy face was flushed and sweaty, his hair matted. Even worse, the flesh around his puncture wound was hot and puffy. Logan cleaned the area, then squeezed out some of the infection.

He used a firebrand to cauterize the wound, maybe to burn out the infection. Finally, he used part of a clean shirt he found in the backpack to make a new dressing.

Nothing more I can do for the kid now, he mused. *He's got a fever, I have no medicines, and we're stuck in this cave until the storm passes. The poor bastard will either make it through the night, or he won't. . . .*

Six years ago

Thomas had wanted to travel back to the States with his commander's body. He'd wanted to go to Maryland to attend the funeral of the finest man he'd ever known. He'd wanted to help his girl, Abigail, and her mother get through a terrible tragedy that he felt as deeply as they.

Unfortunately, the army didn't observe such niceties. Thomas was, after all, just another sergeant under Captain Howard's command. The deployment to Tamboor didn't end with the captain's life, nor did his own duties with the regiment. So Thomas remained behind.

Hours after the captain's death, Thomas had written a long, rambling letter to Abigail, asking her to forgive him for not being there. He'd sent the letter the very next morning. He'd written another letter that afternoon, another one that night, and one more after he'd stood at attention and saluted the Hummer bearing their commander's body as it passed them on the way to General Mbele International Airport.

Meanwhile, the hunt for the warlord Abu Kahlil intensified, as did Thomas's duties. Newly promoted, Captain Hanley took over the unit. One of his first acts was to bump Thomas up to lieutenant, with twenty men under his command. Disillusioned with the mission, Thomas had vowed to do what the captain wanted and keep his men alive. He'd succeeded, mostly.

His vow became more difficult to keep when his unit was paired with a squad of Delta Force commandos. Reconnaissance missions deep into Abu Kahlil's turf and snatch-and-grab raids replaced grain distribution duties.

For two months after Captain Bob's death, Thomas continued to write letters to Abigail. Dozens of them. But no reply ever came. Finally, he worked up enough courage to go to the call center and phone Abigail's college dorm. Her roommate answered and told him Abigail had never returned to school after her father's funeral.

Thomas tried Captain Howard's home next, and several times after that. Mrs. Howard never seemed to be home, and he always got an answering machine. He never left a message. He didn't know what to say.

Another two months passed, and Thomas accompanied Delta on a raid at one of Abu Kahlil's bomb factories. The tribesmen guarding the place were quickly dispatched by Thomas and his men. While Delta grabbed the bomb maker and several computers, Thomas chased a pair of Kahlil's uniformed officers into a bunker filled with contraband weapons, ammunition, and a cache of stolen UN grain.

Thomas hardly had time to adjust to the gloomy interior before one tribesman came at him. He dodged the man's pistol shot. Then Thomas cut him in half with a long burst from his M-16.

Suddenly, the second man jumped out from behind a pile of crates. He threw down an AK-47 and waved his arms in the air. Thomas recognized the man immediately. It was Abu Kahlil himself.

"Do not shoot," said the man. "I want to speak with your commanding officer or a United Nations representative."

He spoke perfect English; according to the Delta Force profile on Abu Kahlil, he'd attended Harvard. The UN secretary general wanted to make a deal with him, convince the man to turn diplomat and "negotiate" a peace with the provisional government, stop slaughtering minority Hutsus—for a price, of course. It was the very reason Delta Force had been tasked with kidnapping the warlord.

"You can see I am unarmed," said the man who was directly responsible for Captain Howard's death.

Thomas's rifle never wavered. He pulled the trigger, killing Abu Kahlil on the spot.

After that, "the fit hit the shan," as Captain Howard used to say.

The UN commander blew his top, or so Thomas was told by Captain Hanley, who expressed "disappointment" before they both faced Hanley's superior.

Thomas never lied. He told anyone who asked what he did and why he did it. After he was done telling the regular army, Delta dragged Thomas off for a "debriefing" that lasted forty-eight hours straight.

In the end, his commanders didn't press charges or even hand him a dishonorable discharge. The army just quietly let Thomas know that his career in the United States military was effectively over. Captain Hanley advised him to file early discharge papers. Two days later, Thomas was sent back to the States.

Two MPs accompanied Thomas from headquarters to the airport. They didn't let him get his kit or say good-bye to the men he once commanded. They just threw him in a Hummer and took off. When a female transport officer handed him his transfer papers at the terminal, she asked Thomas for a final destination.

"Maryland," he told the woman.

Fourteen hours later, Thomas was there. He arrived on a Friday afternoon. He'd been thinking about what to say, what to do, for the past ten hours. So when the plane landed, he didn't wait. He called Mrs. Howard on a pay phone at Dulles International Airport.

She answered on the second ring. Thomas recognized her voice at once. He heard others, too, talking and laughing.

"Mrs. Howard? My name is Thomas Swimming Horse. I knew your late husband, Captain Bob . . ."

"Of course, Sergeant. I remember you—"

"It's Lieutenant now, ma'am."

"Good for you. Are you in town for the wedding?"

"Excuse me?"

"I sent out so many invitations, I'm not sure who's coming," the woman said, talking over him. "I invited most of Bob's friends, of course, but with the deployment and all, many of them are in Tamboor. Are you calling from overseas, Lieutenant?"

"No, I'm right here in D.C. I was wondering about Abigail—"

"Oh, she'll make such a beautiful bride. The rehearsal is in a few hours, and the wedding is tomorrow. Do you have an invitation?"

"No, ma'am."

"I'm sure we could squeeze you in, if you want to come. I'm sure Abigail would love to see you. You can meet Edward—"

"Edward?"

"Edward Jameson Billings, of the Georgetown Billingses. He's a lawyer, of course. Just like his father. Edward works for the United Nations Human Rights Commission in New York City—"

"Please deposit twenty-five cents to continue this call," an electronic voice interrupted.

Thomas looked down at the coins in his hand, frowned, and hung up. There was no point in continuing the conversation. He'd found out all he needed to know.

That evening, Thomas returned to his original billet at Fort McHenry, collected his effects from his personal storage bin, and delivered his discharge papers to the local commanding officer.

"Tom! Come on, Tom. Wake up, man!"

Thomas opened his eyes, squinted against the sun. He was on the ground, outside, wrapped in an untreated deerskin. A fire blazed beside him. Someone touched his arm, and Thomas looked up into the grizzled face of Jesse Lee.

"Hey, man, he's alive," Jessie called. "I can't believe it, but Tommy's alive."

Thomas heard footsteps clomping in the snow. Then Ben and Jerry appeared. Both men were swaddled in down from head to toe. Ben lugged a shotgun, Jerry a hunting rifle with an oversized scope. Their expressions were etched with concern.

Thomas tried to sit up, and a dizzy spell washed over him.

"Steady, dude," Jesse said, placing his gloved hand on Thomas's chest.

"How . . . how did you find me?" Thomas asked.

The man grinned toothlessly. "It was easy, man," he said. "We could see the smoke from the center of town. The Librarian said it was you, but after three days—"

"I've been gone three days?" Thomas cried.

Jerry nodded. "After the storm ended, we figured you'd turn up. But a day went by, then two. Marvin said you probably died in the explosion."

Ben leaned close. "Yeah, what happened up there, anyway?"

Thomas sat up, scratched his head, and played for time. There was so much he could say, and so much he'd rather keep to himself.

"I don't know what happened," Thomas said at last. "I was close to the summit, on the big plateau, when the whole place just . . . blew up. I woke up in the storm. Trees were flattened. There was no sign of anyone. I caught some shrapnel, so I holed up until conditions got better and I could move again."

It was all a lie, and his story was full of holes. Thomas watched anxiously as the others processed his words.

"What happened to your assault rifle?" Jerry asked.

Thomas shrugged. "Lost it in the explosion. My coat got shredded, too. But I brought some MREs, lived off them."

"Where did you get that deerskin?"

"Snared a doe, after the storm," Thomas replied quickly.

Ben's eyes narrowed with suspicion. "Without a gun?"

Thomas ran his hand along his forearm, a tribal signal. "Cherokee tracking skills," he said. "Best in the world. If you're a Cherokee, you don't need a gun."

"Why did you sack out here?" Jesse Lee asked.

"What do you mean?"

The man stood and gestured with his thumb. "When we saw the fire, the Librarian said it was you. But you were so close that none of us could figure out why you didn't sleep in your own cabin."

"Guess I got weak," Thomas said. "Anyway, it's not my cabin anymore. I got booted out, remember?"

"Nobody's going anywhere," Jesse said. "Not until the spring thaw. It wasn't much of a storm, but it caused an avalanche at the pass. The trail's under tons of snow. Not even the Cat can get out."

Thomas absorbed the news, and it troubled him. *The pass doesn't have avalanches, not even in the worst weather.*

Jesse touched his arm. "Think you can get up, man?"

Thomas nodded. But when he stood, his head spun. He remembered something Logan said in the cave. Something about a fever, a possible infection. Logan must have nursed him through the worst of it, then carried him down the mountain and lit the fire to signal Second Chance. Thomas couldn't remember a thing, except that maybe he was dreaming. . . .

"Can you make it?" Ben asked.

"I'll need help," Thomas replied.

Jerry shouldered his hunting rifle and took Thomas by the arm. Jesse Lee wrapped his other arm around his own broad shoulders. With Ben on point, the men half carried Thomas back to Second Chance.

24

LOGAN REMAINED NEAR, WATCHING FROM A PLACE among the rocks, until the trio of rescuers led Thomas back to their village. When he was certain the wounded man was in good hands, Logan headed back to the solitude of his cave.

He was pleased Thomas didn't tell the others about the "wild man in the hills" or the fracas he'd stumbled upon. So far, anyway,

Shows good sense. The less people know, the better off they are. No point in dragging a whole town full of innocents into this war.

Logan suspected it might already be too late to worry about that. He'd listened to the discussion among Thomas and his rescuers, heard one man mention an avalanche that had trapped the townsfolk in their valley. Logan found that to be a tad coincidental, and more than a bit suspicious.

The ones hunting me . . . they must know what happened to their matchstick. That Swimming Horse interfered with their plan. Saved my life.

It was possible they might decide to go after Thomas, just to get even with him for messing up their plans.

Or they might decide to go after the whole town, just to keep my existence, and their little war in the mountains, a secret.

Logan couldn't let that happen.

"Director. The Matron has requested a moment of your time."

"What does that harridan want?"

"I believe she wishes to discuss a resumption of operations against Weapon X, now that the weather has improved."

"No," the Director said. "Absolutely not."

"She's quite insistent. I fear the Matron won't accept a negative answer from me. She will have to hear it from your own lips."

"Don't bother me with—"

Another voice filled the office. "Director," the Matron began, "thank you for taking the time to speak with me."

The man behind the desk tugged at his white hair with both hands, face pained. "Yes. What is it?"

"Now that the storm has broken, I believe it is time to resume Weapon Null's operations."

"No."

"Sir?"

"I said no," the Director replied. "Your team's theatrics have attracted too much attention already. I was forced to isolate the settlement in the valley. If those people witness any more of your antics, I may have to permanently neutralize them."

"I understand the need for secrecy, but surely—"

"As it stands now, isolating them was a futile gesture. The damage has already been done by that armed interloper who destroyed your firestarter and ruined my carefully crafted plan."

"With all due respect, Director. Plans can be recast. Death is permanent, and it was *my* agent who died. Despite our losses, my team is eager to continue the—"

"You've had your chance. Now it's my turn."

The Matron's tone was wary. "What are you planning?"

"I've alerted START. The response team and a support aircraft will be on station in five hours. I expect a strike against Weapon X by oh-three-hundred."

"My God, Director, you can't be serious," the Matron cried. "The Special Threat Action Response Team hasn't a chance against Weapon X."

"They are specialists, Matron. All of them are highly trained and in possession of advanced devices to counter Weapon X's abilities."

"It's hopeless," the Matron insisted.

"I beg to differ. START has trained for more than

a decade to neutralize extraordinary threats, beings of great power—"

"They are specialists, and they are no doubt well equipped," the Matron said. "But START has never faced a real menace before. They may be trained, but they are untested."

"Everyone must start somewhere."

"Not with Weapon X," the Matron countered. "No amount of training could have prepared them for the force they are about to face."

"My decision is final," the Director proclaimed.

"Then you are sentencing those men to death."

The Director chuckled. "You always were melodramatic."

"And you always were cold, distant. Your concern is for numbers, statistics, *results*. Not human beings—"

"Enough," the Director said, waving a dismissive hand. "Let's not relive the past. The present is painful enough."

"Give my team one more chance," the Matron pleaded. "I'll prove their worth to you."

"Request denied. You and your team are to remain on-site, in the event your services are required to perform minor support duties."

"Gideon, listen to me. Surely—"

"No!" The Director's eyes flashed with anger. "I forbid you from initiating any further action against Weapon X. Stand down at once."

"But—"

"End of discussion."

• • •

The Matron punched the com button, breaking the connection.

Request denied. That's all the Director has to say to me? After one of my team was seriously injured, another killed?

She sat alone at her command station, inside the shattered ruins of the Professor's laboratory. It was long past midnight, and the only other signs of activity were the real-time satellite images of the mountain playing on the high-definition monitor. Night-vision filters tinted the picture a bright lime green.

I shouldn't be surprised at the Director's rebuff. Gideon always was a calculating schemer. Always weighed his options, even when . . .

The Matron let that train of thought lie. *No point in reliving the past . . . and he's not wrong about that. The present is painful enough.*

She called up the files she had on the Special Threat Action Response Team. The database was extensive, because nothing about START was classified—and that was the point. In the Matron's estimation, START was nothing more than an elaborate public relations stunt devised to make normal Canadians feel safe in a world that was increasingly populated by supervillains, powerful mutants, and other preternatural threats.

Every decision concerning the Special Threat Action Response Team was made with the public's opinion in mind. In Canada, the original five members were nearly as famous as the original seven astronauts in the America of the 1960s. And why not? Like the original astronauts, they were the perfect team, selected as much for their photogenic qualities as for their undeniably impressive skills.

The choice of stalwart, square-jawed Commander Angus Trent as leader lent the team a futuristic air. Recruited out of the government's Lilliputian astronaut corps, Trent was one of the first Canadians into space, which made him the closest thing Canada had to a rocket-riding hero.

Marcel Le Quont, START's second-in-command, punched the French-Canadian ticket. The little man was a bit of a rogue, with a checkered past that included a stint in the French Foreign Legion and several very public love affairs with starlets, recording artists, and celebrities. He hung out with a famous Australian film star, and the two men were often spotted drinking to excess at parties and pubs. Despite his chaotic personal life, Le Quont was loved and admired in his native Quebec.

Sarah Blake was the obligatory female member of the team, but she was far from merely a politically correct choice. As a liaison between the Canadian Royal Navy and the U.S. Navy, she became the first woman to complete Navy SEALs training. The grueling course was only the beginning. Blake climbed Everest, swam the Amazon and the English Channel, and ran with the bulls in Spain.

Willi Von Trakker was a twice-decorated member of Joint Task Force Two, Canada's equivalent of the U.S. Special Forces Command. Before that, he served in the Royal Canadian Mounted Police's Special Emergency Response Team. A counterterrorism expert, Willi was named START's chief of intelligence.

The youngest member of the team was also recruited from JTF-2. Before joining the military, Charles Drum was a championship martial artist. During testing, it was discovered that Drum was also a mutant who possessed phenomenal speed and an almost supernatural reaction time. Research data suggested that Drum actually could anticipate an attack on some unconscious level. In training missions, he'd repeatedly sensed missile attacks in time to dodge every last projectile.

Impressive. But not nearly enough to defeat Weapon X.

The intercom buzzed, and she punched the button. "Matron here."

"This is Corporal MacKenzie, ma'am. I've returned from the mountain. Along with my flight crew, I've conducted a thorough sweep of the plateau. We've recovered several remains of your man. . . ."

"I see."

"The mission commander suggested they be placed in Blowtorch's hibernation chamber, then frozen."

"An excellent idea," the Matron replied. "We shall conduct funeral services for Blowtorch just as soon as we return to CCRC headquarters. He'll be laid to rest beside his brave and noble brethren in the cemetery at Shroud Lake."

"I was not aware the facility had its own cemetery."

"Not everyone who comes to the Combat Casualty Rehabilitation Center is rehabilitated, Corporal MacKenzie. We've had our share of failures."

"I see."

"One more thing, Corporal. Please inform the mission commander that it's time to activate Thorne."

"I'll get on it right away, ma'am."

The Matron settled back at her command station, called up the digital files on Mr. Thorne, and replayed them on the big monitor. She'd watched the demonstration a hundred times, marveling at the man's phenomenal physical abilities and the way he'd mastered his bizarre condition.

Yet even as she watched, the Matron realized that Thorne would be no match for Professor Thorton's creation, any more than START. In a one-on-one face-off with Weapon X, Mr. Thorne would perish.

I really couldn't bear to lose another agent. Fortunately, Mr. Thorne will never have to face Weapon X. . . . I have a very different mission in mind for this next operation.

The woman beamed as the plan crystallized in her mind.

The Director had ordered her not to take action against Weapon X, and she would obey his command; but he never said anything about the people from that town, the men and woman who'd unwittingly allied themselves with the Professor's creation.

*If I can**not** strike at Weapon X, then I will strike at those aiding him. And after START's spectacular failure, the Director will turn to me, begging for help—*

The Matron's intercom buzzed again. This time, it was the mission commander.

"Matron. I've just received a puzzling communiqué from the Department. I've been told that an AC-130 will enter our airspace within the next three hours."

"Our instructions in this matter?"

"We are not to interfere, or even attempt to make contact with that aircraft or its passengers," the man reported.

"Listen carefully," the Matron said. "I've just spoken with the Director, who informed me that he's dispatched the Special Threat Action Response Team to deal with Weapon X."

"Does this mean our mission has ended?" the man asked.

"No. Our orders are to observe the operation from here, and provide follow-up support if necessary. I want everyone to assemble in the laboratory in fifteen minutes."

"Very well, ma'am."

"Please awaken Dr. Vigil and notify her of the impending conflict," the Matron commanded. "I'm sure the doctor will be most interested in the outcome."

25

Combat Casualty Rehabilitation Center
Shroud Lake, Ontario

THE FOUR LARGE TURBINE ENGINES IDLED, FILLING the aircraft with an incessant, ear-splitting din. Inside the cockpit, the noise was reduced to a quiet, constant whine that formed little waves on the surface of the pilot's cooling coffee.

Captain Peter Mondello drained the Styrofoam cup and tossed it into a paper bag next to his seat. He'd been running flight checks with his copilot when they received a call from the tower.

"Your aircraft has been refueled and reprovisioned. Your passengers are crossing the tarmac now, Captain Mondello," Lieutenant Benteen reported.

Mondello glanced through his windshield. "I see them, Lieutenant. Thanks for the heads up."

"As the CCRC's head of operations and security, let me add that it's been an honor to serve members of the United States Air Force."

"Thanks again, Lieutenant," Mondello replied. "And let me say I'm mighty impressed with your fully automated airstrip. Refueling and deicing services are fast and efficient, and you stowed START's gear in record time."

"Efficiency is my religion," Benteen said.

"After this mission is over, maybe I can convert you."

"Pardon me?"

"We'll get together. Visit the local pub. Meet a few local ladies."

"That would be . . . interesting," Benteen replied.

Captain Mondello signed off. He stood and stretched and placed his clipboard on the pilot seat.

"I'd better go down and greet our honored guests," he told his copilot.

The other man laughed. "I think Mary Pat, Lisa, and Radar Ruth beat you to the punch, sir. They're on the tarmac now, waiting. They want to meet Canada's heroes."

Mondello shook his head, exited the cockpit, and climbed down the metal stairs to join the three female officers from his twelve-person air crew. They hardly noticed his arrival. Their eyes were glued to the five black-clad figures striding across the snow-swept air-field under glaring runway lights.

Captain Mondello spied the rank on one man's

uniform, stepped forward and saluted. "Captain Peter Mondello, United States Air Force Special Operations Command."

"Commander Trent," the man replied, returning the salute and offering his hand.

After the introductions were made, Mondello's passengers joined him on his exterior preflight check. As they circled the massive, sprawling aircraft, he got a chance to observe the Canadians.

He decided that the commander of START was the biggest disappointment. With a name like Angus Trent, Mondello expected a big, burly guy with the expansive, blustery personality of a lumberjack.

But Commander Trent was not particularly tall or broad-shouldered, and he possessed delicate, almost patrician features. His closely trimmed mustache made him seem a bit effete. While the women gushed, Commander Trent remained aloof—more concerned with the mission at hand than socializing, Mondello guessed.

Marcel Le Quont was even shorter than his commander, and his features were much more rugged, with a pronounced chin, a nose that had been broken several times, thick, muscular arms, and a barrel chest. He was openly flirtatious with the airwomen, watching them with dark, intense eyes.

Sarah Blake was taller than all of the men on her team, and taller than Mondello, too. Slim-hipped and small-breasted, she had long and gangly arms under black overalls. She possessed bony features and bright green, penetrating eyes. Mondello heard the woman had passed Navy SEAL training, so he wasn't surprised to see that her head was completely shorn of hair.

Willi Von Trakker was blond and blandly aloof, a man who seldom met anyone's gaze directly. Mondello pegged him as an intelligence officer the moment they met. No matter the service, intel pukes were all the same.

Small and compact, Charles Drum was a nervous ball of energy. His movements were graceful and controlled, yet the man's muscles seemed like tightly wound springs, waiting impatiently to uncoil.

Captain Mondello thought that Lieutenant Drum was the most charismatic individual of the bunch and couldn't understand why the ladies continued to gush over the coolly indifferent Commander Trent.

Guess it's the same now as it always was, he thought, shaking his head. *Women wet their pants over an astronaut.*

At forty-four, Mondello had twenty years on the rest of his crew, but this was the first time he had felt like an old man in their presence. Clearing his throat, he directed his heroic guests toward the front crew hatch.

"Let's board, shall we?" he called, suddenly eager to take off.

He led them up the steel steps and into a crowded compartment the size of a small room. "This gunship is a modified version of the C-130 Hercules, the most versatile and widely flown cargo aircraft in the world," Mondello explained. "On your right you'll find your twenty-five-millimeter Gatling cannon that can lay down eighteen hundred rounds of ammunition from an attitude of twelve thousand feet in under a minute."

Mondello led them through a long corridor. "Your gear is stowed here," he said, pointing to a neat stack of crates. "You can prepare for the mission in this compartment. You'll find everything you need, MREs, the head."

Le Quont and Von Trakker grabbed several cases and carried them into the prep area.

"Positioned at the rear of the aircraft are the forty-millimeter Bofors gun, and a hundred and five-millimeter Howitzer that fires out of the side of the fuselage." Captain Mondello grinned. "Your government requested a bird with firepower, and I think the air force delivered."

"Your aircraft is perfect for the mission, and your crew is ready, by the look of them," Commander Trent said. "If all goes well, we won't need any fire support. We'll know soon after we bail out, either way."

The commander glanced at the frantic activity around him. "I'm going to have to cut the rest of the tour short and help my men prepare for the operation."

"Very good," Captain Mondello replied. "We'll take

off in five minutes. Estimated time of arrival over the drop zone, oh-three-hundred hours."

Radar Ruth followed Captain Mondello back to the cockpit. "Pretty amazing, huh, Captain?"

"What . . . those guys?"

"Commander Trent especially," Ruth gushed. "But they all look so rugged. I'd hate to be the poor slob going up against them. Whoever it is, the dude hasn't got a chance."

Mondello raised an eyebrow. "That's probably what the Philistines said about Goliath, until David came along and finished him off."

Radar Ruth frowned. "With all due respect, Captain, I remember that show, too. The kid's name was *Davey,* and Goliath was his talking dog. Frankly, I don't get your point at all."

"Just forget it, Ruth," Mondello called as he headed for the cockpit. "Get back to your station, and prepare for takeoff."

"His name is Phillip Thorne." The Matron stood beside Dr. Megan Vigil on the high platform overlooking the Professor's half-ruined lab. Beneath them, a team of orange-clad technicians lifted a tall, blocky man out of a metal cylinder and placed him on the biomonitoring table.

Dr. Vigil watched with interest as they fitted electrodes on the unconscious man's head, wrists and thighs, and over his heart.

Meanwhile, on the other side of the massive space, Corporal MacKenzie and the Matron's mission commander watched the radar screen for the approach of the Special Threat Action Response Team, due to arrive at any moment.

Because she was blind to the images on the screen, Dr. Vigil had been drawn to the activity inside the operating theater. She climbed the platform and stood with the Matron as her staff rolled the cryogenic cylinder out on a wheeled gurney, then broke the hermetic seal.

"Mr. Thorne came to us from a Canadian Royal Navy research ship that had been cruising near the Galapagos Islands," the Matron continued. "He was deep-sea diving with two other sailors when they were stung by a species of prehistoric jellyfish never encountered before or since. The other men died— unpleasantly—within a few minutes. But not Mr. Thorne. No, Ensign Thorne somehow survived."

Dr. Vigil lifted her dark glasses to study the man on the table. Thorne looked like a sailor, with close-cropped blond hair, a bull neck, ropy muscles on his arms, legs, thighs. He had a tattoo on his well-developed chest—a fouled anchor with a smiling mermaid perched on top.

"Why was he brought to the CCRC?" Megan asked.

"Soon after he recovered from the poison sting, Thorne began exhibiting symptoms of what first appeared to be a debilitating skin disease mimicking leprosy," the Matron explained. "First, lesions appeared on his torso, arms, and legs. Then the epidermis began to swell in some spots, recede or grow brittle in others. Then something curious occurred."

Megan lowered her glasses over her eyes and faced the Matron. "What was it?"

"According to the files of Dr. Anton Snyder, the CCRC's chief psychiatrist at the time, Thorne experienced what researchers call a lucid dream. In his vision, he saw himself as a kind of human porcupine. When he woke up, that's exactly what he'd turned into."

"A metamorphosis. Shades of Gregor Samsa," Megan said.

"And like Kafka's protagonist, Mr. Thorne was stuck, in more ways than one. His spikes ranged from one inch to three feet long—the man was impaled to his bed. The spikes were made of razor-sharp bits of cartilage, as hard as bone, sharp as diamond points."

"As grotesque as Kafka's bug," said Megan.

"You have no idea, Dr. Vigil. Thorne could not move. It was difficult for the medical staff even to approach him, to feed him, provide sanitary care. . . . At first, there was panic, but eventually cooler heads prevailed. Dr. Snyder was summoned, and he deduced that Thorne's subconscious mind had actually guided the restructuring process of his flesh. That realization led to the breakthrough."

Megan frowned. "You mean a psychological breakthrough?"

"I mean a complete physical and mental breakthrough, Dr. Vigil. Eventually, with hypnosis and therapy, Dr. Snyder brought Thorne's subconscious ability to the level of conscious thought. Within days, this simple, moderately educated sailor learned to control the shape and appearance of his epidermal tissue."

"An amazing talent, it's true," Megan said. "But I fail to see how Thorne can defeat Weapon X. Unless you have conceived a strategy I have not yet gleaned."

The Matron became guarded, which instantly aroused Megan's suspicion. But before she could press the woman, alarms sounded.

"An aircraft has just entered our airspace," Corporal MacKenzie called from his command station.

Megan glanced at her watch. It was 0259 hundred hours. The Special Threat Action Response Team was here. And START was right on time.

26

Battle Management Center
AC-130U Spectre Gunship
10,000 feet over Second Chance

"ANY SIGN OF WEAPON X, WILLI?"

Von Trakker heard his commander's question on his headset and glanced at the woman beside him. Airwoman "Radar Ruth" Rayburn shook her head, her eyes glued to the ground radar screen.

"Nothing but trees, Commander," Von Trakker replied. He activated his spectrometer, along with the ultraviolet and thermal sensors.

"Negative . . . no sign of Weapon X on any band."

Commander Trent cursed. "It's holed up in a cave, protected from our sensors by granite and iron ore deposits."

"Should I lay down a field of fire on that mountain?" Von Trakker asked. "That might flush it out."

"Not yet," Trent replied. "Tell the pilot to drop altitude, down to six or seven thousand feet. Weapon X might pop out of hiding, just to see what all the noise is about."

A few moments later, Willi Von Trakker's ears began to pop as the aircraft descended in a circular pattern centered on the mountain.

"Let's give it a few minutes, then we'll think about shooting," Commander Trent said. "Meanwhile, keep your eyes open, Willi."

"Roger that," Von Trakker replied.

Inside their overcrowded preparation area, Commander Trent signed off and faced the other members of his team. He was pleased to see they were battle-ready and prepared to make a combat jump in seconds. Once their target was pinpointed, all they had to do was close their visors, pressurize their Stark Industries Flex-Shield combat survival suits, and activate the optical head-up displays inside their helmets

Over their armor, Le Quont, Blake, and Drum each wore a night-black High Altitude Wing Kite. Commander Trent wore one, too, but his "wings" were made of opaque plastic, filled with fluorescent gases, and wired with "flash" circuitry.

The HAWK harness was a highly specialized piece of "personal aerodynamic hardware" developed for use by the Strategic Hazard Intervention Espionage Logistics Division, better known as SHIELD.

START members cut their teeth on the HAWK, because the device was the most advanced and versatile means of insertion into a hot LZ. The device could be launched from any altitude; the HAWK was also stealthy, and the user had complete control of his speed and angle of descent.

Strapped to their forearms or on their backs, the START members wielded a variety of specialized weapons, specifically chosen for each mission to counter the threat they faced. For Weapon X, they broke out their entire arsenal.

Commander Trent scanned the expectant faces and shook his head. "Nothing yet." The others visibly relaxed, but Trent still read nervousness in their manners. "Okay, people. Let's run down the plan again."

Everyone groaned, and some of their nervousness dissipated as soon as they focused on the task at hand.

"We descend on Weapon X from four angles," Le Quont began.

Trent nodded. "Then I'll hit it with a flash attack that won't do much harm but should disorient the target long enough—"

"For me to fire," Le Quont declared, hand on his holstered weapon.

"And then I open fire," Sarah Blake said, raising the gun in her gloved hand.

"We both hit Weapon X with chemical heat. Two darts, three if we can nail him dead-on," said Le Quont. "But we are not to fire carelessly."

"Right," Commander Trent said. "I can't stress this part enough. The boiler's way too nasty to fire wild. If any one of us gets hit with a dart, it's tomato soup time . . . okay, what's next?"

"Next I swoop in and lay the variable-frequency stun net on the sucker," Charles Drum declared. "The restraint should live up to its name and stun Weapon X."

"With four to six darts in it, even Weapon X's phenomenal healing abilities will be overburdened, if not overwhelmed," Trent said. "Either way, the combination of the darts and the variable stun net should be enough to make the target docile, perhaps even render it unconscious."

"Unconscious would be nice," said Le Quont.

"Real nice," Drum agreed.

"If it doesn't go down, what's our next option?" asked Sarah Blake.

Commander Trent stared through the tiny window at the purple night sky.

"You each have secondary weapons of choice. I suggest you resort to them," Trent said. "If that fails, call Willi. Whoever is left standing will paint the target with lasers. The gunship will do the rest." He faced his team. "I promise you that Willi will rain hell down on Weapon X, until there's not enough left of it to regenerate a hangnail—"

Alarms sounded inside the cramped compartment. The main lights went dim until only a soft scarlet glow filled the chamber. Then Willi Von Trakker spoke to the team through their headsets.

"We've located the target," he declared. "Weapon X is moving along the western face of the mountain."

They all heard the excitement in the intelligence officer's voice. They all felt it, too, along with the surge of adrenaline, as the same realization hit them.

This time, it's real.

"Weapon X is out in the open," Willi continued. "It's moving toward the plateau where it fought its last battle. I'm forwarding the precise coordinates to your HUDs. You should have it now."

"Pressurize," Trent commanded.

The team members closed their visors, and a hissing sound filled their ears. Inside their helmets, tiny digital display boxes lit up. A GPS navigational system provided a map of the terrain and a blip to mark Weapon X's position.

"Open up the belly," Trent commanded.

With a hissing pop, a hatch in the floor opened. Air rushed into the compartment, battering the black-suited warriors as they gave one another a final equipment check.

"Everybody ready?"

The team faced their commander, gave him a thumbs up. Through her visor, Sarah Blake smiled weakly.

"See you on the ground," Trent said. Then he dropped through the opening and vanished in the darkness.

One by one, the Special Threat Action Response Team members jumped through the hatch, following their leader into the frozen night.

Logan was on the move as soon as he heard the throbbing engines overhead. So far, the enemy had not located his little mountain sanctuary. Logan wanted to keep it that way. The moment he heard evidence of his persecutors' return, he hiked quickly away from his cave.

Outside, the night was still, the landscape in the grip of a blast of arctic cold. There was no moon, and the mantle of stars was obscured by low-hanging clouds.

Logan moved through the darkness using his other senses, and his instincts, more than his eyes. Occasionally, he would pause on the icy trail and listen to the wax and wane of engine noise as the aircraft made passes over the mountains. Logan knew the aircraft was circling, but so far, it had remained invisible, no doubt flying without running lights.

Sometimes, Logan would sniff the air for the stink of men, but tonight, all he could detect was the smell of scorched wood wafting down from the burned-out plateau. The warbling whine of the engine continued to reverberate off the mountains as Logan continued to climb.

It took ten minutes for him to reach the plateau. Despite a blanket of fresh snow that covered most of the damage, the place appeared more ravaged than Logan remembered. Parts of the mountain came down in several places, and most of the oak and pine trees had been leveled.

Logan smiled. *At least there's no place for the enemy to hide. The next SOB who wants a piece of me can try to take it right here, out in the open.*

The clouds broke unexpectedly, and Logan scrambled to the top of a low rise. Under the dull glow of stars, he carefully surveyed the area.

Nothing. No sign of intruders. I'm alone.

Suddenly, the wind kicked up, hissing across the powdered snow like an angry serpent. Logan felt eyes on his back, and his hairs prickled. He turned to find a winged demon diving down on him out of the night sky.

Claws extended, Logan raised his arms to fend off the batlike creature's attack.

Commander Treat saw Weapon X deploy its claws, and he wheeled to the side. He used the sensors in his right glove to activate the HAWK's twin repulsion engines, which slowed, then halted his descent. Simultaneously, ridged wings unfurled right before Weapon X's startled eyes. He snarled, claws swiping, but Trent was just out of reach.

For a split second, Commander Trent seemed to hover on wings of opaque plastic. Those wings, which were filled with fluorescent gases, exploded in a burst of blazing light, bright as burning phosphorus.

As if illuminated by a giant flashbulb, the plateau was bathed in white luminescence. The snow twinkled like a jeweled shroud over the blasted landscape.

The fluorescent wings faded to black in a few seconds, but the damage had been done. Logan's night vision was obliterated, and he was effectively blind. Through tearing eyes, he saw nothing but motes of throbbing light roiling behind his retinas.

But Logan's ears still worked. He heard his attacker's wings cutting the air, the whine of tiny jet engines that powered the HAWK harness as they glided over his head.

Rage began to rise in Logan, but he beat it back, forced his mind to focus on strategy, make it a sport, a hunt. Still blinded, he ripped the air—once, twice.

His attacker had been steering his harness with his right arm extended. Logan's claws caught the man's forearm, severing flesh, muscle, and bone as easily as a hand cutting water. The dismembered limb tumbled to the icy ground in a gush of arterial blood.

Logan's second slash cut through the hollow wings. With a popping hiss, the pressurized fluorescent gases rushed through the rupture, and the wing collapsed. Shrieking, his waving stump gushing steaming gore, the winged man slammed into a snowdrift.

Logan listened, heard the sound of more wings cutting the night.

He whirled in time to hear a metallic thud. Then he felt the sting as a dart stuck his biceps. Another thud, and a second needle pierced his neck, just above the collarbone. Logan felt air as a third missile whizzed past his ear.

At first, it was nothing more than a tiny sting, an insect bite. Then Logan cried out, and his body was wracked with tremors. Absolute torment washed over him, a gut-churning agony that he had never experienced before—not in the mad Professor's lab, not under the vivisectionist's brutal knife, not even when he was burned by the Blowtorch's withering fire.

He tried to scream, but bubbling hot blood filled his lungs. Gasping, Logan dropped to his knees, felt the wonderfully cold snow sizzle under his simmering flesh.

The darts contained a chemical compound that, once introduced into the victim's bloodstream, caused human hemoglobin to come to a fast boil inside the arteries, veins, heart, and organs. The unstable compound was the product of years of intensive research by several of the most brilliant biochemists on the planet.

Though the "boiler" was instantaneously fatal to a normal man, START was never so optimistic concerning Weapon X. They did harbor hopes that the device would debilitate the Professor's creature, perhaps even knock him out. They could never have been more wrong.

Logan's agony began to subside as his phenomenal recuperative powers overwhelmed the poison in his system. Within a few seconds, his blood cooled, and his cells repaired themselves.

When another pair of darts struck him a moment later, Logan's system had already learned to compensate for the chemicals. This time, he felt no more than a slight burning sensation at the site of the wound, a discomfort that almost immediately passed. In the end, the powerful chemical darts didn't do much more to Logan than make him angry. Again, he fought the Weapon X blood tide and struggled for control.

The jet engines on Marcel Le Quont's harness sputtered and died—not unexpected, because the HAWK harness had limited fuel capacity. But it was the French-Canadian's bad luck to land directly in front of a pissed-off Weapon X, just when its pain subsided and its vision finally cleared.

Le Quont hit the snow in a fighting crouch, his discarded harness fluttering to earth behind him. The man aimed a dart gun at Weapon X's chest, but before he could squeeze the trigger, Weapon X snatched Le Quont's forearm and bent it upward until the limb snapped like a dry branch. Le Quont moaned, and his fingers went into a spasm, squeezing off several rounds.

At that moment, Sarah Blake soared over their heads, and a dart struck the woman's thigh. She yelped in surprise. A split second later, shrill screams boomed inside her teammates' helmets. The howls ended soon after, when the woman's face dissolved into a bubbling red mist behind the Plexiglas visor. The battle suit collapsed in on itself, now nothing more than a bag of hot liquid.

Like a burning moth, what remained of Sarah Blake fluttered to earth.

Le Quont roared, trying to tear his broken arm free from Weapon X's crushing grip. While the man struggled, Weapon X plunged its claws into the French-Canadian's midsection. Le Quont wheezed as black blood stained his lips. Weapon X twisted the claws, ripping the man's guts, then yanked the blades free and stepped back.

Marcel Le Quont tumbled to the cold ground.

Panting, legs braced, Weapon X was unaware of Charlie Drum's descent. Then the stun net dropped over its broad shoulders, and its body jerked spasmodically as a thousand volts of electricity coursed through it.

Battling against the paralyzing shock, Weapon X thrust its clawed arms upward and outward. With a ripping noise, it severed the titanium-reinforced metal net like wet tissue. Sparks exploded in the night, then sizzled in the snow, sending up clouds of steam. Shaking its torso like a wet dog, it flung off the last bits of the net, eyes casting about for its attacker through the artificial mist.

Less than fifty feet away from Weapon X, Charles Drum slipped out of his harness and landed in a battle-ready crouch. Then the steam clouds parted, and the two eyed each other across a shadowy expanse of charred trees and drifting snow.

27

LOGAN WAS SURPRISED WHEN THE MAN HE FACED yanked a bizarre handgun out of its holster and tossed it onto the ground. Then the stranger pulled his helmet off and shook sweat out of his hair.

He eyed Logan as plates of shorn Kevlar plopped onto the snow. Next, the man released the clasp on his utility belt, which was heavy with gear. It clattered to the rocks.

Finally, his opponent stepped away from the pile on the ground and thrust his arms out. With a sharp click, two twenty-four-inch gravity blades dropped from their hidden housing—one from each of the man's forearms. He raised each arm and struck the two blades together as if he were sharpening them. Then he dropped into a crouch and approached Logan, the blades gleaming silver in the starlight.

Logan's growl became a chuckle.

"You're coming at me with those things?" he shouted.

His opponent blinked and stepped back. Logan figured the man was surprised that Professor Thorton's monster could actually speak a coherent sentence.

"Yeah," Logan called. "I can talk. And I can fight even better."

He lunged, a clawed arm lashing out.

The other man moved with a preternatural speed that took Logan by surprise. The man dodged his blow and delivered a slashing cut of his own—right across Logan's face. Logan grunted and reeled back. Then he tasted his own blood and his eyes narrowed.

He launched into a spinning attack that sent his foe scurrying. The attack was fast enough to surprise a leaping panther, but his foe managed to avoid a pair of slashing blows, move in behind his defenses, and stab Logan in the chest.

Another chuckle echoed across the frozen expanse. This time, it was the stranger who laughed.

Logan felt his skin tingle as the puncture wound closed. He *wanted* to roar, let the blood tide wash over him, charge, slash, stab, and obliterate his opponent, but he refused to give in to the Weapon within. Though it was the most difficult thing he'd ever done, Logan continued to resist the urge to strike out in anger.

The two men stalked each other. Logan used the time to center his thoughts, force the blood rage out of his mind, replace it with cold, calculating reason.

A quiet stillness settled over the plateau. The winds faded, the clouds vanished, and the two men stood opposed, eyes locked in a soundless struggle as aggressive as the physical combat that preceded it.

Then the man sprang at Logan, lunging with both bladed arms thrusting. His furious attack pushed Logan backward. Steel crashed against steel, and the plateau rang with the terrible clamor of a medieval battlefield.

At first, his opponent's astounding speed overwhelmed Logan, but he managed to hold his own and found openings to push back. Soon he was pressing his own attack with lunges, parries, feints, and thrusts, drawing upon martial skills he never knew he'd possessed.

Now his every slash drew blood, until his foe bled from a dozen wounds. Logan became more aggressive, even as his opponent weakened. He pushed the man backward, until finally he was teetering on the edge of the high plateau.

In desperation, the man attempted a descending chop meant to split Logan's adamantium skull with one arm's blade. But the attack was telegraphed, and Logan raised both arms to parry the blow. The quick move trapped the man's blade in between Logan's claws.

Logan dropped to one knee. A quick twist, and the blade shattered. Another twist, and the bones in the man's forearm snapped. His foe cried out and stumbled backward until he nearly toppled over the edge of the cliff.

Logan spun and kicked. With a grunt, the man hurled sideways, away from the ledge. He flew across the clearing until his spine slammed against the shattered stump of a fallen oak.

Somehow, his attacker remained conscious. Logan charged forward, and the man managed to roll aside, just ahead of a descending slash that splintered the tree trunk. Then the man was back on his feet—just in time to parry another swipe with his remaining blade. Logan kept up the attack, lashing out with both clawed hands, wearing the other man down.

Finally, the man's boots slipped on the snow. He stumbled.

A sweep of Logan's right arm shattered his opponent's final weapon. Ruined steel clanged to earth as the force of Logan's blow drove the man to one knee. Clutching his broken arm, the man looked up in time to see the silver arc of adamantium steel that severed his head from his body.

The headless corpse pitched forward, spilling gore onto the frozen rocks. Logan stepped back and watched as death spasms wracked the body. His nostrils flared as he sniffed the coppery tang of fresh blood. Finally, the corpse stilled, and Logan sheathed his blades.

In the quiet aftermath of the battle, Logan's keen

ears detected another sound: the electronic crackle of
a radio headset.

Logan whirled and spied a gore-streaked figure
crawling out of a snowdrift on the opposite end of the
plateau. The dying warrior clutched an object in his
remaining hand. The device resembled a flashlight,
but Logan blinked in surprise when a laser dot appeared in the center of his chest, just over his pounding heart.

"Willi, fire on my target . . . fire now," the man
gasped in a pain-wracked voice.

The reply was faint, but Logan could just make out
the words.

"Commander," a frenzied voice said, "you're too
close to the target. I'll hit you, too."

"You heard my order. Open fire!"

Logan heard the roar of the aircraft directly over his
head, then a long string of small explosions. From the
sky, he saw the hail of fire descending upon him, and
he ran like hell.

The citizens of Second Chance were shaken from
their beds by the crackling sound of gunfire rolling
through the valley. They hurried out of their cabins,
wrapped in blankets, robes, even furs. They collected
on their porches and in the clearing beside the well,
muttering fearfully. Necks craned, the townspeople
watched as arcs of red fire descended from the purple
sky to pound the mountaintop.

Explosions soon followed the gunshots. Loud bursts illuminated the mountain in flashes of orange, yellow, and red. Sometimes an incendiary bomb would burst, and a mushroom of rolling fire would rise above the summit.

A short lull in the violence was followed by another sustained stream of gunfire that chewed up the cliffs, stirred up clouds of snow and dust, and sent an avalanche of debris tumbling all the way down to the foothills.

At first, Thomas ignored the sounds. Stubbornly, he remained in his bunk, even when he heard excited voices outside his cabin, then cries of alarm and fear.

But as the shooting continued long after he thought it would end, Thomas's curiosity was roused at last. He sat up, slipped on his boots, and stumbled to his feet. Groaning from the pain in his side, he wrapped his Mexican blanket around his shoulders and went to the door.

Though it was a little past four in the morning, just about everyone in town was outside, even the bikers' children. The kids laughed in delight at each burst, thinking it all great fun—save for Mrs. Lyons's new baby, who was wailing with good sense at the noise.

When the people saw Thomas come through his door, a few of them stared. He pretended not to notice, fixing his eyes on the firefight as he limped across his porch and stepped onto the hard-packed snow. He spotted the Librarian in his overcoat, standing outside his long house next door, stroking his long beard. Gathered around him were the paunchy middle-aged mountain men Ben and Jerry and the old grizzled vet Jesse Lee. The big tattooed biker Bill Lyons was there, too, beside his wife. She cradled the bawling baby; he cradled his shotgun.

Finally, Thomas spotted slender, loud-mouthed Marvin in his bright yellow J. Crew parka. The little lawyer-turned-Zen-Naturalist was openly glaring at him.

"Do . . . do you think it's some kind of military maneuvers?" Jerry asked his neighbors.

Jesse Lee snorted. "It's military, all right, but it ain't no maneuvers. Those're live rounds we're hearing."

"Are you sure, old man?" Bill Lyons demanded.

"Sure I'm sure!" Jesse Lee's thumb jabbed his chest. "I had interdiction duty on the Ho Chi Minh Trail. That's Puff the Magic Dragon!"

Marvin squinted. "Have you been drinking?"

Jesse Lee smirked. "Puff the Magic Dragon is slang for a C-130 gunship, Marvin. That's what we used to call them back in Nam."

Bill Lyons faced the mountain again. Another loud explosion sent trees into the air. "So what the hell is a gunship doing shooting up our mountain in the middle of the freakin' night?"

"We came to live here for the peace and quiet! To be

left alone!" Mrs. Lyons cried as she rocked her sobbing baby. "Someone should make them stop!"

Thomas snorted to himself. *First sensible words I've heard in days.*

Ben and Jerry both looked at Thomas. The Librarian faced him, too, along with Jesse Lee. Thomas felt their eyes on him, but he continued to keep his focus on the mountain.

Another long burst of machine-gun fire arced into the cliffs, starting several miniature avalanches. Then the gunfire sputtered and died. In the abrupt silence, everyone heard the throb of aircraft engines.

Soon the avalanches ceased their rumble, and the engine noise faded. Thomas turned and headed back to his cabin, only to find his way blocked by several men, including Marvin, Jesse Lee, Ben and Jerry, Bill Lyons, and the Librarian.

"So. Have I been booted out again?" Thomas asked.

"Nothing like that," the Librarian firmly assured him. "It's just that—"

"You know more than you're telling us!" Marvin cried, shaking his finger like an angry schoolteacher entitled to answers. "You went up the mountain the other day. Then the whole place blew up. Now you're back, and you told Ben and Jerry that you didn't see a thing. Well, I don't believe you—"

The Librarian raised his hand. "Calm down, Marvin."

"What do you mean, calm down? He probably had something to do with this mess. Him and his guns. But like a good soldier, it's top-secret. That's right, isn't it, Swimming Horse? Your lips are sealed—"

"Enough!" the Librarian barked.

Heads turned, as other people who'd gathered outside heard the loud voices. Thomas spotted Big Rita in the crowd, and she offered him a friendly smile. He didn't see the little yellow owl—as he'd come to think of twelve-year-old Rachel.

The Librarian touched his arm. Thomas met the older man's gaze.

"We're stuck here, Thomas," he said softly. "And something's going on that none of us likes. Now, if you don't know what's going on, that's fine. That just means you're as much in the dark as the rest of us." The Librarian paused. When he spoke again, his voice was nearly a whisper. "But if you do know something—*anything*—then you've got no right to withhold information. Good news or bad, we live here, too, and we have a right to know what's threatening us."

Thomas shifted uncomfortably.

"I know you know something," the Librarian pressed. Then he glanced at the horizon. "It's nearly dawn. Why don't I brew some coffee and rustle up some breakfast over at the long house? Then you can sit down with the rest of us and tell us what you saw up there."

Thomas sighed. "Lead the way," he said. "And you

better serve up some eggs and bacon. *American* bacon. Not that crappy Canadian stuff."

Rachel stood on her Aunt Ellie's front porch, beside Mrs. Carlyle. The woman had been nursing the girl's elderly guardian when the noise and commotion woke everyone up.

Soon the pyrotechnics faded, and the folks of Second Chance headed for home.

"Time for bed, child," Mrs. Carlyle insisted, pushing Rachel toward the door. But the girl had spied her friend Thomas, who'd returned after some bad things had happened to him. Rachel wasn't sure of all the details, and she wanted to talk to Thomas and find out all that happened.

"Come on, girl, get inside."

Rachel hung her head. "Yes, Mrs. Carlyle."

A weak voice called from inside the log cabin. "Your aunt's calling me, Rachel. I've got to go see what she wants," the woman said. "Make sure you bar the door behind you. Who knows what kind of crazy things are going on in these hills."

"Yes, ma'am."

Rachel watched the woman enter the cabin. Then the little girl whirled to watch Thomas across the clearing. She noticed that he was now surrounded by some of the other men, so she crept off the porch and cautiously approached the group. She got close enough to hear the Librarian say that he was going to make them all breakfast and that Thomas was going to tell them all about what happened to him.

This I've got to hear! Rachel decided.

While the others were still talking, the twelve-year-old slipped through the door of Henry the Librarian's long house. She tucked herself in a hiding place where no one would see her and where the Librarian would never look—between the shelves that held old, musty copies of *Reader's Digest* Condensed Books and a yellowing stack of a periodical called *People*.

Rachel pushed up her large, horn-rimmed glasses and curiously leafed through the magazine on top of the stack. It was full of pictures and not many words. The photographs were of people she'd never heard of, doing things she didn't understand.

Then Rachel heard the men enter the long house. She peeked between the books and saw Thomas was with them. One of the other men looked in her direction, and Rachel quickly ducked—she didn't want anyone to catch her before she got a chance to hear Thomas's story.

28

THOMAS DRAINED THE TIN CUP OF ITS LAST DREGS of coffee and set it on the table. He leaned back in his chair, gazed through the grimy windows. Outside, the sun was rising on a clear, cold morning.

"Okay," Thomas said, facing the others. "So now you know what happened on the mountain. Any questions?"

The men all stared at Thomas as if he'd gone crazy. Jesse Lee's jaws gaped in open befuddlement. Ben and Jerry, who thrived on conspiracy theories and tales of alien encounters, seemed to be wavering between skepticism and stark panic. Bill Lyons simply stared at the coffee left in his cup; then the big, tattooed biker sighed and shook his shaggy head. The Librarian scratched his beard while he processed the particulars of Thomas's incredible tale.

Finally, Marvin broke the silence. "You shot the guy?"

Thomas nodded. "Once or twice. Then he blew up." He mimed an explosion with his hand. "Poof! The fat, little fire-breathing dude was gone."

Marvin squinted with disapproval. "But why did you shoot? What was he doing to you?"

"Nothing. But that's not the point," Thomas said. "He was burning the wild man, trying to kill the person who saved my life."

"So you took a side in a fight you don't even understand?" Marvin threw up his hands. "You're completely reckless. Out of control!"

"Hell, Marvin, any one of us would have done the same thing," Ben countered. The paunchy mountain man had shed his sealskin coat but kept his Russian-style fur hat on his bald head. "If I met a fellow in the woods wearing leather briefs and breathing fire, I'd shoot him on the spot, just for being freakin' weird."

"*You're* weird, Ben. You and your brother Jerry," Marvin said. "How about that? Does that mean I should shoot you?"

Jerry narrowed his gaze. "You could try."

"Ah, this is just nuts!" Bill Lyons declared. "The whole damned story is *loco*." He pointed at Thomas. "Dude, you probably slipped on the ice and hit your head, then dreamed everything."

"Then how do you explain the firefight last night?" Jesse Lee pointed his own finger at Bill. "Not to mention that fireball the other day? We all saw it. *You* saw it, too, Bill. It wasn't no dream."

The grizzled vet shifted his gaze to Thomas. "I think I believe him." He folded his arms and sat back in his chair. "Thomas never lied to me, to any one of us."

"No," Marvin said. "Our soldier boy here just hid an illegal gun—"

"Oh, come on. This ain't exactly San Francisco, Marvin," Bill pointed out.

The Librarian had remained quiet, listening to his neighbors. Finally, he spoke up. "So what about this wild man?" he asked Thomas. "You said he helped you, saved your life. Did you actually talk to him? What did he say?"

Thomas rose and began to pace the room. *I've got to be careful here . . .* "Look . . . I didn't say we talked, exactly," he lied. "I said we *communicated,* like the first time I met him. We could have ended up feuding over the deer I shot. Instead, we split the venison between us, sort of by mutual consent."

"Without a word spoken?" the Librarian asked skeptically.

"You saw the wound in my side." Thomas rubbed the back of his neck. "I was feverish, maybe delirious. I can't remember if we talked. I just know the wild man helped me survive; then he dragged my sorry butt down the mountain so you guys could find me."

"But this wild man. He must be some kind of threat, or maybe a fugitive," Marvin insisted. "I mean, the government and the military wouldn't be after him if he hadn't done something really bad. And you said yourself the guy has metal claws that come out of his hands. What are those for, opening beer cans?"

Jerry grunted. "Yeah, we all know that governments never persecute innocent people."

Ben, Bill Lyons, Jesse Lee, and Thomas all laughed. Only Marvin missed the joke. "What's so funny?" he demanded. "There's a wild man fugitive with metal claws wandering the mountain, and half the Canadian military gunning for him. And we're stuck right here, between a rock and a hard place."

Thomas blew out air. "Come on, Marvin."

"I'm not exaggerating. We're trapped here!" Marvin cried. "The trail is buried. The only other road out is on the other side of that mountain, and none of us dares to go there!"

"Let's not panic," insisted Jesse Lee. "After what happened last night, I doubt there's much left of that wild man. Who could survive a pounding like that?"

Yeah. That's the million-dollar question, isn't it: Who?

Though he'd told the others about Logan's incredible healing powers, Thomas was the only one who'd actually witnessed the process, watched while Logan's flesh burned and reformed, again and again. The others might be able to convince themselves the "wild man" was dead meat, but Thomas very much doubted it. Wisely, he kept that opinion to himself.

"Jesse's right," Bill Lyons said, rising. "If there was a wild man—and I ain't saying there was—but *if* there was, he's pretty much a goner now."

The Librarian nodded. "You might be right. . . ."

"Sure he's right," said Jesse. "I saw close up what one of those gunships can do, on the Ho Chi Minh trail. Saw a whole convoy of armed men shot up. Must've been a hundred dead Viet Cong there, none of them in one piece—"

"Enough," Marvin interrupted. "I've had enough of your barbaric war stories."

"Maybe we should go up the mountain and have a look around," Ben suggested.

Jerry rolled his eyes. "Now, that's just asking for trouble, ain't it?"

"We have a right to know what happened," said Ben.

"No, we don't," Marvin insisted. "It's none of our business."

Ben pointed to the window. "It is *our* business because it's happening right next door to us!"

"Stay off that mountain!" Marvin warned. "Bad enough Thomas chose to shoot instead of staying out of a war that was none of his business. Let's not bring more trouble down on our heads by tempting fate."

"Amen," grunted Bill Lyons. Then the tattooed biker hefted his shotgun and moved toward the exit. "Thanks for breakfast, Bookworm," the big man called over his shoulder as he went out the door.

While the others filed out of the long house, Thomas remained behind, rocking back and forth on his chair. Soon he was lost in thought.

Thomas knew that physically, he was still pretty messed up. Too fatigued to handle a climb or any trouble if he ran into it. But in a couple more days, he knew he'd be just fine. After that, Thomas vowed to go back up the mountain and find out what really happened to the "wild man." To Logan.

"I've never seen a device like this before."

Dr. Vigil stepped past the Matron, for a closer examination of the complex machine. She ran her hand along the burnt-out control panel and touched the cold power conduits hooked to the main system hub. As she circled the device, her booted feet trampled bits of glass and circuitry, the debris from a half-dozen shattered monitors that surrounded the central control station—still shining, jewel-like, despite layers of dust and neglect.

The women stood in a dark, forgotten chamber just off the main lab. Here scorch marks blackened the walls, loose wires dangled from broken ceiling panels, and ominous brown stains were everywhere.

"It's called a Reifying Encephalographic Monitor," the Matron said. "The REM is a powerful device for probing the human mind."

Megan ran her hand along the smooth metal of the mainframe sheath. "I presume this device was used during the creation of Weapon X."

The Matron was surprised by the other woman's observation. "Why would you conclude that, Doctor? Weapon X is not supposed to have a mind, you know."

"But it does . . . I mean, *he* does," Megan replied. "And to answer your question, it was very simple. The REM is here, in this place, so it was used on Weapon X. From what I could glean, this entire facility—its staff, and all it contained—was dedicated to a solitary goal, the creation of the ultimate human weapon."

"It was Professor Thorton's dream," the Matron said.

"In that case, I'll offer another observation. Professor Thorton was a driven man. One might even say *obsessed*."

Dr. Vigil turned her back on the Matron, fingered the control panel. Then she turned a switch. "There's no power."

The Matron nodded. "When it was operational, the REM required almost ten percent of the facility's energy to run. Were we to restart it, the machine would need its own backup generator just to maintain normal power levels."

Megan looked up from the control panel to stare at the shattered monitors. "You want me to restart this . . . this machine."

"Of course," the Matron replied. "This device, used in conjunction with a certain member of my Weapon Null team, will ensure our success, and the ultimate defeat of Weapon X."

Megan lifted her dark glasses. She used the ultraviolet spectrum to detect cracks or flaws in the power conduits, the mainframe. There was damage, but no critical components were compromised. While she studied the machine, her artificial eyes glowed red in the dim chamber.

"Is there anyone here who's worked with this device?" Megan asked. "Or perhaps there's someone on your technical staff familiar with these components?"

"I have the schematics," the Matron replied. "I've printed them out for you. But that's the best I can do—"

"No one is available?"

"This device is very special," the Matron explained. "As far as I know, there are only three REM devices in the world besides this one. One is at Kennedy Space Center, another at Central Intelligence Agency headquarters in Langley, Virginia. SHIELD owns the third one. And God knows what they've done with it."

Megan absorbed the information. "I'll have to restart another backup generator, but that shouldn't be a problem, beyond the time it will take," she said. "Not everything can be salvaged. You'll have to replace these monitors—"

"I've already contacted Lieutenant Benteen. You will have six new plasma screens on-site by this afternoon."

Megan frowned. "You were that sure I would help you?"

"I *hoped* you would help me, that's all," the Matron

replied. "If you refused, I would have found another way to move forward. I'm not giving up. Not after all the losses my team has suffered."

Megan folded her hands behind her back. "You seem certain the Director will revoke his command forbidding you to act."

"What choice does he have now? His Special Threat Action Response Team lies defeated, dead on the top of that mountain. There's no one else who can bring that experiment down, short of the entire Canadian Army—and maybe not even them." The Matron shook her head. "The only way the Director will give up is if he no longer believes Weapon X is worth his trouble. That's why I've taken steps to ensure that will never happen. . . ."

The Voice spoke, cutting the silence. "Director? We must speak."

"Leave me alone." The words were uttered like a sustained moan. The Director remained slumped in his chair, chin on his chest, eyes closed.

"The C-130 has returned to Shroud Lake," the Voice said, ignoring the Director's request. "Willi Von Trakker has filed his report. He is eager to resume operations against Weapon X, using the backup team. Though he feels they will need several weeks to develop a new strategy, Von Trakker is confident that—"

"There will be no further operations against Weapon X," the Director murmured.

"But sir, START still has resources. They are willing to strike again—"

"And Major Sallow contacted me earlier, offering his services and the services of his men." The Director rubbed his temples. "He's a gallant fool but a fool nonetheless. The Special Threat Action Response Team failed. What chance do Sallow and his men have?"

"If you don't want to lose more personnel, there's always the Matron's team," the Voice said. "I'm absolutely certain that she's eager for another chance."

"I'm sure she is," said the Director. "But it's not worth the trouble."

"I beg to differ, sir."

"*What?*" the Director roared with some of his old fire. "You question my decision? My authority? How dare you?"

"I only meant to say that there are new data on the value of Weapon X," the Voice said in an apologetic tone.

The Director frowned doubtfully. "You'll have to explain."

"I have received several back-channel communiqués," the Voice explained. "Certain institutions and government agencies have expressed . . . *interest* in Weapon X."

The Director's eyes narrowed with suspicion. "How do they know the creature even exists?"

"That I cannot answer," the Voice replied. "But the fate of Professor Thorton is not the best-kept secret in the intelligence community. And the Matron has not been particularly discreet in the way she conducted her operations, either. I have observed humans for many years, and sir, people do talk."

"Indeed," the Director replied. "And who are these institutions and agencies?"

"DARPA was the first to express an interest. Their director contacted me two days ago—"

"Two days ago? Why was I not informed?"

"You were distracted by START's ongoing operations. I thought it best to await the results of their action, while your energies remained focused on the task at hand."

"I see . . ."

"Later, Dr. Felix Coupland contacted me—"

"From Oak Ridge?" The Director snorted derisively. "I didn't know that dullard was still working in the defense field. I thought a man of his limited talents would have found a suitable position in the food additive business by now."

"He's *very* interested in Weapon X," the Voice said. "He offered quite a substantial fee if—"

"Turning Weapon X over to Felix would be like giving an infant a loaded shotgun. Amusing, perhaps, but it's bound to end badly."

"SHIELD has also made contact," the Voice continued. "They seem very interested in the creature's true identity. The Russians have also made contact. And the Saudis—"

"Your point?"

"That this exercise has actually increased the value of the commodity called Weapon X. If you abandon the creature, sooner or later, one of these agencies—or perhaps all of them—will continue the hunt for it themselves. Sooner or later, someone will succeed in capturing it."

The Director tugged on his snow-white hair. "That would be bad, wouldn't it? I'm happy to sell Weapon X to the highest bidder, but I won't simply give it up."

"I thought as much."

"Well, this certainly changes things. Contact the Matron," the Director said, his eyes burning with a new fire. "Inform her that my ban is lifted, and she may initiate action against Weapon X. Tell her that I shall provide every resource at my disposal, at least for the time being."

"Anything else, Director?"

"Yes. Tell that insufferably annoying harridan that this is her last chance."

29

FOR SIX DAYS, MEGAN VIGIL WORKED TO REPAIR the Reifying Encephalographic Monitor. She shunned sleep, skipped meals, and generally pushed herself to her physical and mental limit.

Already thin and pale, she soon became emaciated, her complexion so pallid and sickly Corporal MacKenzie suggested she be checked out by a medical officer. But along with food and sleep, Megan brushed aside the corporal's concerns, and brushed him aside, too.

"If I want your help, I'll ask for it, Corporal. Now leave me alone," she told him on the morning of the fifth day, when MacKenzie not only brought her a warm meal but insisted she eat it.

"I'll go," MacKenzie replied. "But I think something is wrong with you. You're troubled, Miss Vigil, and if you get any worse, I'm going to drag you away from this horrid place myself. That's a promise."

Megan eyed the man through her dark glasses. "Corporal, you're being ridiculous."

"You're so possessed you don't see it," MacKenzie replied. "But I swear, if you get too crazy, I'll carry you out of this facility myself."

Corporal MacKenzie stormed out after that. Megan didn't see the man again that day, or the next. She hardly noticed the corporal's absence, though without MacKenzie to take care of her, Megan skipped more meals and more sleep.

Yet if anyone had asked Megan why she was working so determinedly on the Matron's behalf, beyond her inherent fascination with the technology, she wouldn't have been able to form a coherent reply.

Maybe it's just that I feel a kinship with her. . . .

The accident that took Megan's eyes had also taken her far away from the world of normalcy, diverted her from the life she'd wanted, expected. Likewise, the Matron's love of her freak-show menagerie had made her something of a misfit, too.

She wondered if the Matron had suffered a terrible loss as well.

That was one explanation for why the woman was so driven, why she worked so tirelessly for a cause that seemed so hopeless. In any case, Megan felt there was something noble about the Matron's concern for her grotesque technological orphans.

It was something close to love.

Megan continued her work until the morning

of the sixth day. While two of the Matron's technicians loaded software into the REM's mainframe—programs that would enable the device to interface with the new monitors—Megan finally finished connecting the advanced plasma screens to the rebooted power generator. She opened several floor panels and was about to climb down into the power ducts when the Matron paid her a visit.

"I'm eager to hear about your progress," the woman said. "The operation is proceeding well on my end. We should be ready to go as soon as the REM is up and running."

Megan nodded. "It's up and running right now. The problem is power. I've had to reboot two emergency generators in order to provide enough juice to fully activate the REM. That meant a lot of rewiring."

"How much?"

"Relax," Megan replied, wiping soot from her pale hand. "The work is finished. All that's left is to test the variable resistors I've installed."

"Was that necessary?" the Matron asked.

Megan shrugged and fished a galvanometer out of her tool kit. "The sliding contacts on the original potentiometers were corroded, so I had to start from scratch."

"And you'll finish today?"

"In an hour or so, if all goes well," Megan replied. "Two hours at the outside."

The Matron smiled. "Oh, very good."

A technician appeared at the woman's shoulder. "Matron, the plasma screens are functional. We're running a final diagnostic check now."

While the Matron watched, Megan returned to her task. As she worked, Megan began to wonder exactly how the Matron was planning to utilize the Reifying Encephalographic Monitor.

The device was used to plumb the human mind while the subject was in a tranceike state. But she didn't understand or so far question how the REM could help the Matron defeat Weapon X, and the Matron had not offered an explanation.

"This device uses a phenomenal amount of power," Megan said, her tone conversational. "The multiple plasma screens suck up juice, too. Makes me wonder what all that power is used for."

"The REM performs two critical tasks," the Matron explained. "First, the device induces a realistic trance—so realistic the users are not aware they are dreaming while in tune with the device."

Megan stopped working, her interest suddenly piqued. "Are we talking virtual reality?"

"Indeed we are," the Matron replied. "It's virtual reality without clumsy screens or monitors, and with a full range of senses—sight, sound, touch, smell, taste. In an REM trance, reality exists inside the head of the user."

"Virtual reality without monitors," Megan repeated. "Then why all the plasma screens?"

"The second task of the Reifying Encephalographic Monitor is to turn brain waves—human thoughts—into digital images. What the user experiences in VR is projected onto the screen for observers to watch and interpret . . . and *control,* if necessary."

Megan glanced at the flickering needle on the galvanometer, saw that it tested normal, and moved quickly to the last potentiometer.

"You say the REM trance feels real?" Megan asked. "How real?"

"So real that use of the device was restricted," the Matron confessed. "NASA was using it as a virtual learning tool and mission simulator. But continued use apparently caused delusional behavior among a small group of subjects. Now the REM is not even being utilized as a teaching aid."

"And yet the technology shows so much promise," Megan said. She climbed out of the power duct and closed the floor panels. She had to step around a group of technicians who'd entered the restricted chamber. There were two cyberspecialists and a medical officer.

Perhaps they're here to witness the first test of the device.

She quickly forgot about them as she connected the power coupler and activated the twin generators. In a few moments, the REM was powered up.

"System normal," the technician at the control panel said. "One hundred percent functional."

With a satisfied sigh, Megan faced the Matron.

"Thank you, Megan," the woman said.

"I'm glad to be of service," Megan replied, wondering why so many people were crowding her. "If there's anything else I can do—"

"There is," the Matron said.

Megan felt a sting on her forearm. She whirled and saw the medical officer beside her, a hypodermic gun in his gloved hand.

"What—" she began, but her voice died in her throat. Suddenly, Megan stumbled and felt strong hands seize her. Then her vision faded to black.

Logan's belly rumbled. He was so hungry he actually considered eating raw one of the rabbits he'd snared. But he knew it would taste much better properly cooked over a hardwood fire. Better yet, he still had several salt and pepper packs from Thomas's MREs in his cave to spice things up.

The morning had been cold and gray, the afternoon blustery. Now it was near dusk, and he'd been hunting all day. Logan's mind was focused on one thing: supper. His mouth watering, he trudged through knee-deep drifts until he reached the edge of a winding, snow-covered road wide enough to accommodate a vehicle.

It took Logan several days to find a new way down the mountain. The path he eked out was on the opposite side of the peak, far from Second Chance and its citizens. Unfortunately, he also found the snow-bound road, which had obviously been used in better weather.

Logan didn't like being near the road any more than he liked living close to the town. But since he'd started hunting in this region two weeks before, he'd never seen a vehicle or found any tracks, so he figured the place was safe enough until spring.

Anyway, he had no choice—not if he wanted to eat.

The wildlife that fled the mountain during the two firefights had not returned in the intervening days. As time passed, Logan was forced to range farther afield to hunt for meat. Deer were scarce, so he started hunting rabbits, which he devoured at a rate of six or seven at a sitting.

He'd caught twenty today, in snares he'd set all over the forest. Bundled in deerskin, the meat tied together by a leather rope and slung over his shoulder, Logan headed back to the mountain, whistling tunelessly.

When he reached the road, he carefully crossed it, using the same footprints he'd made when he came down that morning. That way, anyone who tried to follow his tracks up the mountain would soon lose the trail. Logan saw to that, by crossing a wide expanse of blasted rock too windswept to hold snow—or a footprint.

He'd just stepped onto the trail that led to the foothills, when the mountain range echoed with the staccato sound of machine-gun fire.

Logan groaned. *Not again.*

At the report of the first shot, he'd ducked instinctively, even though he knew the fire was not directed at him. Fearing another attack—and eager to deal with it quickly—Logan hung his catch over the limb of a tall tree and followed the road in the direction of the firefight.

The machine-gun fire ceased, only to be answered with a few shots from what sounded to Logan's trained ears like a military-style weapon firing NATO regulation nine-millimeter rounds.

Soldiers fighting soldiers, in the middle of Canada? This should be interesting. . . .

Logan increased his pace. As he neared a bend in the road, the shots became louder. Soon the nine-millimeter was answered by another burst of machine-gun fire. Then an explosion, and Logan saw an orange ball of fire rise above the snow-draped forest.

He ducked into the trees, moving in a shallow ravine that ran parallel with the road. Soon he spied smoke and fire. Slipping behind the thick trunk of a century-old oak, Logan watched five snowmobiles run circles around a burning snowcat stalled in the middle of the road.

Logan had almost no time to process the scene before a vivid memory image exploded in his mind, stunning him. The scene mimicked the violence in front of him. Real as life, Logan saw wild Indians on horseback, whooping as they circled a blazing Conestoga wagon.

The dreamscape was so vivid it felt as if he were in two places—or two times—at the same moment. The memory—or hallucination—was so powerful Logan reeled from its impact, clutching at the oak tree to steady himself.

In a moment, another gunshot cut the frigid dusk and snapped him back to reality. Logan heard a wet smack; then someone howled. He looked up to see one of the men in orange jumpsuits drop off the back of a snowmobile and land facedown in the snow.

More gunfire erupted from the snowmobiles, pinging off the snowcat's tough hull and spider-webbing the safety glass.

Cautiously, Logan advanced, using the terrain to camouflage his movements. At the edge of the road, he paused. Over the sounds of roaring snowmobiles, Logan heard a man's voice inside the shattered snowcat.

"Stay down, Miss," he said.

Suddenly, the door popped open. A tall, lanky corporal in Canadian Army olive drab leaped out of the cab, leading with a USP Tactical. The nine-millimeter jerked in his hand, and another orange-suited man tumbled into the snow.

The corporal jumped to the ground and sank calf deep in the powdery snow. Grunting as a bullet grazed him, the soldier dropped to one knee and fired again. Another man cried out, and a snowmobile sped out of range.

Exposed now, the corporal was an easy target. Three machine guns opened up on him simultaneously. His body contorted as a dozen bullets tore through flesh and bone. The USP flew from his grip and bounced off the snowcat's hull. Then the dead man pitched forward.

Inside the cab, Logan heard a sob. A snowmobile pulled up beside the smoldering snowcat, and a gunman stepped off the back. He pointed the barrel of his G36 Commando short carbine at the man on the ground and pulled the trigger, firing into the fallen man's back until he emptied his clip.

Logan heard a woman scream. The gunman turned to face the snowcat.

Without conscious thought, Logan dropped his claws to fighting position. He rose and dashed across the road.

Logan was beside the armed man before he had a chance to reload. He plunged his claws into the man's guts, then whipped the machine gun from the dying gunman's hand. He tossed the corpse to the ground, ripped the empty clip free, and tossed it away.

Astride the snowmobile, the driver was gaping in shock. Logan spun and slashed through the man's neck. As the headless torso pitched from the snowmobile, Logan ripped an ammunition clip from the dead man's belt and snapped it into place. Before the others could react, Logan opened fire on them.

His first burst struck a snowmobile's fuel tank, and it exploded in a ball of oily fire. The driver was blown skyward, his corpse landing in a tree, where it dangled, burning.

The other vehicles quickly fled the scene, following the snowcat's tracks back the way they came, leaving dead men in orange suits behind.

Logan's claws withdrew. He glanced at the machine gun in his hand, then tossed it aside. He ignored the corpses in orange while he gingerly turned the corporal over. The dead man was older than Logan expected. There was gray in his light brown hair, and he wore no ring on his finger.

A lifer. This guy's whole world was the army. . . .

Logan found a name tag on his uniform. Mac-Kenzie.

"Hard way to go, MacKenzie. But at least you died fighting," Logan muttered. "Fighting who, I couldn't say."

Logan heard a sound and tensed.

The woman.

In the thrill of the kill, Logan had forgotten the reason he'd intervened in the first place. Cautiously, he approached the burning snowcat. The cab's door was ajar. Logan opened it wide.

"Don't hurt me," a sweet voice pleaded.

She was so small that Logan didn't see her at first. Finally, he spotted her cowering on the floor, underneath a wool blanket covered with shards of glass. Logan took a closer look, saw pale skin and red hair behind a pair of oversized dark glasses.

"I won't hurt you," he said. "But we have to go."

"Where's Corporal MacKenzie?" she demanded.

"He's gone," Logan replied. "They killed him."

She gasped.

"Come on."

"No!" she cried.

"If you don't come with me now, I'll leave you here."

"Go," she sobbed.

"If I go, those guys on the fun-mobiles will come back here and kill you. Or you'll freeze to death. Either way, you'll be dead." Logan extended his hand. "Come on," he whispered.

Tentatively, the woman reached out and gripped his proffered hand. Logan grasped hers and dragged her gently out of the shot-up snowcat.

The woman was thin, almost emaciated. Lifting her, Logan doubted she weighted more than ninety pounds, even in her winter gear.

Gently, he set her down. She touched the ground so lightly, her booted feet barely sank into the snow. He reached into the snowcat and pulled out the wool blanket, shook the glass off it, and wrapped it around the woman's skinny shoulders.

"Can you stand?" Logan asked, one arm still clutching her waist.

She seemed dazed but nodded.

"Who are you?" Logan asked. "Why were those men trying to kill you and your friend?"

The woman blinked behind her dark glasses. Logan reached up to take them off, but she stopped him.

"What's your name?" Logan asked softly.

"Megan . . . Dr. Megan Vigil."

"Do you think you can walk?"

She nodded again. Logan was about to let Megan Vigil go when she went limp in his arms.

"Sonofa—"

Logan threw the woman's body over his shoulder. Then he dashed down the road until he reached his bundle of rabbits. With his meat hanging over one shoulder and the woman draped over the other, Logan began the long trek back to his cave.

30

IN THE FLICKERING FIRELIGHT, MEGAN WATCHED the man for a long time. Behind her dark glasses, her eyes followed him while he moved about the cave, turned the meat over the fire, stitched something together using tendons for thread and a sharpened bone for a needle.

The man filled a cup made from a hollow log with water from a trough. He shook off the excess liquid, then crossed the chamber and set the cup down next to her makeshift deerskin bed.

"You've been watching me for an hour," he said. "Are you going to say something, or are we going to pretend to be an old married couple and dine in silence?"

"You can speak," Megan said. "I wasn't dreaming."

"I can cook, too," he replied with a smile. He lifted a spit with bits of smoking meat. "Hasenpfeffer, anyone?"

"You're Weapon X."

The man grunted, set the spit next to the cup. Then he crossed the cave and sat down on a rock, facing the crackling blaze inside a ring of stones.

"Please," he said, gazing into the fire. "Call me Logan."

"That's your name?"

He shrugged. "It's as good a name as any."

Megan sat up, and the wool blanket fell away. Her coat was gone, and she blushed and clutched at her clothing, until she realized she was still fully dressed.

"I'm not that kind of a guy," Logan said. "Though I'll have to admit you're a damn sight better-looking than my last houseguest." He chuckled at his own joke.

Megan took the cup and drank. The water was cold and fresh, and she gulped more. Then she reached for the grilled rabbit, bit a piece off, and chewed.

"They told me you were a monster," Megan said.

Logan turned his head to face her. "Who told you that?"

"They call you Weapon X. They say you're Professor Thorton's greatest creation. To them, you're a living legend . . . or a nightmare."

"Who the hell is *they*?"

"The Director. Everyone at Department K."

"Yeah? Why Weapon X, anyhow? What happened to A through W?"

"Technically, you're Weapon *Ten,* but the Roman

numeral tends to confuse people. Anyway, Number Ten doesn't quite communicate the awesome power you represent." Megan took another bite of meat. "Does any of this come as a shock?" she asked between chews.

"Lady, to be honest, I don't know what the hell you're talking about."

Behind her glasses, Megan registered surprise. Then she nodded. "Of course, how could you know what they call you? What they turned you into?"

Logan crossed the cave and stood over her. "Why don't you tell me?"

And so Megan did.

She told him about Department K and the Director. How DARPA, the Pentagon, and Canadian military intelligence got together with the goal of creating the ultimate soldier, the perfect living weapon.

She told him about Professor Thorton, the brilliant, twisted genius who conceived of the Weapon Program and oversaw its development, from Weapon Null to Weapon Ten—Logan—which turned out to be the Professor's ultimate creation, and his assassin.

She told him about Dr. Abraham Cornelius, the man whose technology made the adamantium bonding process possible. And about Carol Hines, the dysfunctional, haunted woman who used her technology to invade Logan's mind and obliterate his personality.

"Only they failed," Logan said at last. "I still know who I am. Or at least I think I know." He stood and began to pace. "There are aftereffects. Headaches. Nightmares. For a long time after I escaped, I had blackouts. Bouts of . . . violent tendencies. Whatever you want to call the behavior, I couldn't control it. Something would turn the aggression on, and I'd be rampaging for days, killing. Then I'd just snap out of it."

Logan grinned, his sharp teeth gleaming white in the dim cave. "That doesn't happen much anymore, so don't be scared. Looks like a lot of stuff they did to me is permanent. But I think I've pretty much beaten those urges—maybe for good." He frowned. "Sometimes, though . . ." His voice trailed off.

"Tell me," Megan said after a moment.

"Sometimes I have these memories," Logan continued. "Impossible memories. I see myself as a samurai, or as a paratrooper commando with the Canadian Army in World War Two. Sometimes I'm on the frontier, fighting *Indians,* if you can believe it."

Logan lashed out in frustration, struck the wall of the cave with his fist.

"I know it sounds insane. When I say it out loud I *know* it's insane. Yet the memories keep coming and coming and I don't know what's real and what's some kind of hallucination . . . or implant."

His expression darkened and he shook his head. "These . . . scenes . . . they are so vivid, right down to the tiniest detail—a brand of soap, an elaborate design on a samurai sword handle, a craps game in an army barracks before D-Day."

Logan faced her. "Is that possible? Could I really be more than a century old?"

Megan sighed. "I'm sorry. I don't know anything about who you were before they turned you into Weapon X. Only that . . ."

"That I'm a mutant?" Logan snorted. "No surprise, doll. I figured that one out way before the maniacs in lab coats ever got hold of me." Unexpectedly, he threw back his head, and his laugh bounced off the walls. "Hell, I figured that's why they wanted me in the first place."

Hours later, they were sitting side by side on the deer-skin. Megan had pulled off her boots, and the wool blanket was tucked tightly around her slim form. It was close to midnight, the night cold and still. The hearth flames flickered, and their wavering light danced along the cavern's walls.

"Why did those men try to kill you?" Logan asked.

Megan folded her hands on her lap and looked at Logan through tinted lenses. "I won't lie to you. I was part of the group that's hunting you."

"Who? Department K?"

Megan nodded. "They want you. *Badly*. They regard Weapon X as an investment that escaped them. Now they want to recoup their losses."

"How are they going to do that? I'll never do any-one's bidding again. I'm nobody's meat puppet. Not anymore."

"The Director wants to capture you. Sell you to the highest bidder," Megan confided. "He and a woman called the Matron have set up a new headquarters in the Professor's lab, he place where they created you."

Logan's jaw dropped. "It's close?"

"Fifty miles away. Maybe less. That road, where you found me. It leads to the facility."

"So why did they turn against you?" Logan demanded.

Megan shifted uncomfortably. No matter how hard she concentrated, she could only recall vague and contradictory images.

"I think . . . I think I must have been drugged or something, because I can't recall too much," she said softly, her gaze fixed on the wavering shadows. "I remember I was helping them repair a machine. I worked on it for, I think, days . . . and when it was done . . ." Her voice trailed off, and Megan shook her head. "They did something to me. I'm pretty sure Corporal MacKenzie warned me about the danger. Said he'd get me out of that place if things got too rough. I guess they did." She faced him again. "Anyway, I finished my work, and then they surrounded me."

"Who?"

"Those men in orange suits," Megan cried. "Then someone stabbed a needle into my arm, and I don't remember anything else, until Corporal MacKenzie woke me up. I was lying on a lab table of some kind. I was restrained, hooked up to a machine. MacKenzie freed me, helped me dress, then bundled me into the snowcat. We took off after that . . . just drove away."

Megan trembled at the memory. "That's right," she cried, a note of hysteria creeping into her voice. "I remember he threw me in the backseat and covered me with a blanket. Warned me to keep still and quiet. Somehow he got past base security."

"What happened next?"

A shadow crossed Megan's face. "We drove all night and all the next day, but the snow was deep, and the snowcat didn't get very far. Then they found us on the road. There was a lot of shooting. The corporal told me to stay put, then he took off . . . then you showed up—"

Megan began to cry. Logan folded her small, frail body in his arms and held her close. She sobbed for a long time, tears streaming down her cheeks. Finally, she lifted her chin and looked up at him.

"They're going to come back, you know. They're not going to stop until they get both of us."

"Don't worry," Logan said softly. "I won't let that happen."

Megan nodded, her wet cheeks pressed against his flesh, her warm breath tickling the hairs on his chest.

"You're not a monster," she said softly.

Logan chuckled. "How do you know? I doubt you can even see me with those silly glasses on."

Before Megan could protest, Logan slipped them

off her face. She threw up her hands to cover her eyes.

"Hey, it's okay," Logan said, pulling her hands away. "You've got beautiful eyes—"

"Don't . . . don't tease," Megan said.

"Who's teasing? Red hair and green eyes. It's a killer combination."

Megan faced the fire and blinked her eyes. "It's not very bright in here."

"I can throw some more wood on the fire, if you're cold."

"It's not that," Megan said, pulling away from him. The blanket draped around her, Megan rose and hurried to the water trough.

Logan watched, puzzled, while she stared at her reflection in the water. She touched her cheeks, her eyes.

"They're gone," she breathed.

"What?" Logan asked, rising. "What's gone?"

Megan looked at him, puzzlement etched on her pale face. "I . . . I don't remember now. Something about my eyes . . ." She rubbed her eyes and then stared at her hands. "It must have been a nightmare," she said at last. "A horrible, horrible nightmare . . ."

"You're still confused," Logan said, touching her shoulders. "Maybe you're suffering from shock."

Together, they crossed the cave and sat down again. He kept one hand around her waist, and she touched his arm, looked up at him from under long eyelashes.

"Logan, I want to thank you—"

"Forget it." He pulled his arm away and waved dismissively.

"No, I can't forget it, Logan." Megan moved closer. The wool blanket slipped down. "You saved my life. . . ." She captured his hand and pulled it to her breast.

"Wait," Logan said hoarsely. "This might not be such a good idea."

"You're wrong. This is the first smart move I've made in a long time."

Their eyes met and then their mouths, tentatively at first. When her tongue parted his lips, human need overrode Logan's rational concerns. He pulled her to him, pressing her small form against his hard-muscled frame.

His touches were rough at first, but Megan didn't mind. In fact, she was soon reveling in his bruising caresses, eager to help him tear at her clothing. She was feeling something wholly new now, a pleasure she'd never before experienced.

Laughing, she used her lips and teeth to trace a pattern down Logan's body; then she trembled with anticipation when Logan laid her down, rained kisses on her neck, breasts, belly, thighs. When it finally came, their coupling was frenzied, almost fierce. For a few minutes, they rested. Then Logan took her again—this time more slowly, gently.

Their lovemaking continued into the night. Megan's rapturous cries filled the cave. They continued until the fire burned low, until the morning sun rose in a violet sky, until they both fell into a deep sleep, their bodies intertwined on the soft deerskin bed.

The Matron watched the monitors. She was on her feet, white knuckles gripping the back of her chair. The tiny chamber was jammed with personnel and additional equipment, moved there from the command center for the duration of the current operation.

"We've got the satellite positioned directly over the cave and another one lined up to take its place in a few hours," the mission commander declared. "Now that we know where it lives, and we have a homing device within proximity of Weapon X, we will never lose track of it again."

"Are you recording this?" she asked, eyes glued to the monitors.

"Every second," the man at tech com replied. "Audio *and* visual. We're even getting biological readings on Weapon X. It's all being dumped into the mainframe's memory cache for future reference."

"Should I begin forwarding these data to Department K?" the mission commander asked.

"Absolutely not!" replied the Matron. "The Director gave me complete discretion during this operation, and I intend to use it. We will evaluate all the data from here and decide our next move. The Director is to remain out of the loop. Do I make myself clear?"

"Affirmative, ma'am."

The Matron's eyes moved from screen to screen. She could not believe what she was seeing, hearing.

Weapon X is not a monster. It's not some killing machine, not even a Super-Soldier. Weapon X is a man.

The Matron placed her hand in the pocket of her lab smock and felt something there. She pulled out Dr. Vigil's dark glasses and stared at the object in her hand.

This has become complicated . . . very complicated. . . .

The medical technician looked up from her instruments, eyes wide.

"My God," she cried. "These readings are off the chart. All the previous data we had on Weapon X are outdated now."

"Something . . . unexpected occurred," the mission commander said as he studied the readout. "Back when Blowtorch was burning Weapon X, I think there was a biological cascade of some kind."

The Matron slipped the glasses back into her pocket. "Explain."

"The violence that was done to Weapon X actually kickstarted certain biological processes . . . systems that were in place but latent. The attack pushed the creature's metabolism to its limit—which somehow initiated a higher level of biological activity—its immune system, its regenerative abilities, even its strength, speed, and endurance, have all increased exponentially."

The Matron nodded. "Then Weapon X has adapted to the stresses of its environment."

"Precisely," the mission commander replied. "It's

actually functioning much better now than it was when Dr. Thorton first created it."

In more ways than the merely physical, the Matron realized. *He's mastered his violent urges, he's using psychological tools, communicating with his fellow human beings . . . in more ways than one.*

She sighed heavily.

Weapon X is human again—more than human. Which means he has to be isolated immediately, before he becomes fully socialized, perhaps even forges an alliance with the people in the valley.

The woman turned away from the monitor. "Major Sallow?"

The soldier stepped forward, spine rigid, shoulders squared, his scarred hands folded behind his back.

"Yes, ma'am."

"Alert Mr. Thorne. Tell him he's going into action immediately. He has his instructions. He knows what he has to do."

"Yes, ma'am," Sallow replied, a half smile etched across his pockmarked face.

"Operations will commence immediately," the Matron continued. "I want Thorne on site *now*."

31

RACHEL WAS AWAKENED AT THE CRACK OF DAWN by Mrs. Carlyle's rooster. She covered her ears with a pillow to shut out the noise, but it didn't help. The rooster wouldn't shut up and the chickens began to cluck, too, so Rachel gave up trying to sleep and sat up.

Rubbing sleep from her eyes, Rachel rose from her narrow bunk. She yelped when her bare feet touched the chilly floor, and she quickly plunged her icicle toes into furry slippers. Huffing against the cold, she hurried across the cabin to the hearth.

She furiously stoked the fire, until sparks flew up the chimney. Then she tossed more wood onto the blaze to heat the room up.

When the cabin was finally warm again, Rachel crept to the bedroom and looked in on her aunt. Ellie was sleeping peacefully in her bed. Big Rita was on the chair beside the nightstand, also snoring, her knitting sprawled across her lap. Rachel didn't have the heart to wake them up.

She tried to brew tea but discovered that Big Rita had finished off the fresh water the night before.

That meant a trip to the well, so she slipped on her jeans and oversized work boots. Then Rachel dug a clean sweater out of her cedar chest, tugged it over her nightshirt. Finally she donned her parka and a wool hat.

On the way out the door, she grabbed both buckets—the one at the hearth and the metal canister Aunt Ellie kept on the rough wooden table.

The morning was colder than normal, and Rachel dropped her pails to zip up her coat. While the chickens clucked across the way, the girl made the short walk to the stone well in the center of the village square.

The sky was gray, with low-hanging clouds that obscured the top of the distant mountain. No birds sang. No one else was awake. The only sound Rachel heard was the crunch of her boots on the hard-packed snow.

When she arrived at the well—which was really a stone platform with two pumps side by side, spouts facing in opposite directions—Rachel dropped the buckets and knocked the ice off one spout with a hammer chained to the pipe for just that purpose.

When she was satisfied the spout was clear, Rachel pumped the rusty metal handle. It took only a few strokes before fresh water gushed out of the spout.

She filled the open bucket first, then placed the metal container under the flow and filled it, too.

A shadow fell over her, and Rachel looked up. She gasped, startled to see a stranger.

"Don't be afraid," the man said, offering her a smile.

"I'm not afraid," Rachel replied. "Just surprised, that's all."

"Do you need help with those buckets?"

Rachel shook her head. "I can handle it." Meanwhile, she studied the man from head to toe.

The stranger was tall and broad-shouldered, with a stubble of black hair on his scalp. He wore moccasins and crude leather pants stitched together with dirty white twine. His upper body was swathed in a riot of different furs—Rachel recognized gray wolf, wild rabbit, beaver, mountain lion, and wolverine pelts on the intruder. She drew the logical conclusion.

"Are you the wild man from the mountain?" Rachel asked.

The stranger widened his eyes in mock surprise. "So you know about me? I guess the whole town knows about me by now, eh?"

"Of course," Rachel replied.

In truth, most people in Second Chance didn't believe the wild man existed, or they didn't care. Rachel believed because Thomas told the Librarian that he saw the man with his own eyes, and Thomas never lied.

She only knew about the wild man because she'd spied on the meeting several days ago. Things had been quiet on the mountain since then, and even the people who thought the wild man was real figured he was either dead or gone.

Rachel smiled, excited to be the first person actually to speak to the mysterious stranger.

"What's your name?" the man asked.

"Rachel," she replied. "What's yours?"

The man moved closer to the girl, until his form blotted out the wan sunlight.

"Call me Mr. Thorne," he purred. "Everybody does. . . ."

Big Rita's screams shattered the morning stillness. Her anguished howls brought most of the citizens out of their cabins.

Jesse Lee was strolling to the well for fresh water. He heard the cries and rushed to the pumps, the second person to arrive on the scene.

He choked and dropped to his knees in the snow when he saw the broken buckets and the blood.

"Why? Why?" Rita sobbed over and over again, when she wasn't shouting at the heavens in her native Inuit.

Others crowded around. Cries of horror and of rage echoed through the tiny community.

Thomas arrived on the scene with the Librarian. The two had been drinking coffee together when they heard the commotion.

"What's wrong?" Thomas demanded, pushing his way to the front of the crowd. He smacked right into Ben.

"It's Rachel," Ben wailed, snot running down his beard. "The wild man killed her."

Thomas pushed past the big man, saw the carnage. He stifled a curse, then looked away.

Ben was inconsolable. Jerry supported his brother.

"Ben's right," muttered Jerry. "It was the freakin' wild man what did this. Something's gotta be done."

Ben's hasty accusation was repeated by more onlookers, until it spread like wildfire through the crowd.

"You don't know that," Thomas said, first to Ben and Jerry, then raising his voice to everyone else. "None of you knows that, because nobody was here to see who did this."

Marvin pointed an accusing finger at Thomas. "Who else would have done it? It was the wild man, and you know it." He gestured to the girl's terrible wounds. "Her throat cut. Three parallel slashes down her body, from her neck to her legs. You said the wild man had claws on his hands."

"You can't jump to conclusions," Thomas argued. "The wild man ain't the only stranger to show up in these parts of late."

Bill Lyons clutched his sobbing wife in his tattooed arms. "The army's shooting up the mountain. But why would they come down here and butcher a little girl? There's no reason for it."

"Why would the wild man do it?" Thomas demanded.

"'Cause he's a freaking monster, and I say we kill him," Ben cried, spit flecking his lips.

Voices clamored in agreement. Thomas could see that the crowd was fast turning into an angry mob.

Another voice was heard, loud enough to drown the noise of the townspeople. "Shut up, all of you! Have some respect for the dead!"

It was Jesse Lee. He removed his army-surplus jacket and covered Rachel's corpse with it. Carefully, he lifted the dead girl in his skinny arms.

"Come on," the Librarian said softly. "Let's take her to the long house."

"What about the wild man?" Marvin demanded.

Thomas squared off with the little man. "What about him?"

"Aren't we going after him?"

It was Ben who spoke. "Damn right we are," he declared, wiping his eyes.

Hunched over her command station, the Matron scrolled through the data on her main screen. The suspicions she'd had for the past several hours had been confirmed by the data her team had gathered.

Weapon X is human again. There's no other way to

categorize his actions. Everything we've observed in the past twelve hours points to that conclusion.

The Matron knew there was more evidence than the information stored in the mainframe. In his after-action report, Major Sallow described the Weapon X attack on her technicians as "methodical and well conceived," his race to rescue Dr. Vigil "noble."

If that wasn't enough, Weapon X used a captured machine gun against his attackers, displaying "superior marksmanship skills," according to the Major.

He fought with strategy instead of brutish instinct, and Weapon X used a conventional weapon instead of tearing his enemies apart with his bare hands. He's still a killer, but not a messy one.

And he fired a gun. You can't get much more human than that.

Suddenly, the woman frowned. *In the process, he and the late Corporal MacKenzie killed six members of my security staff. All good men . . .*

The Matron pushed aside her grief and continued to absorb the data on her screen.

But it's almost worth the cost in blood, to see, to quantify and measure this remarkable being the Professor created. As an instrument, Weapon X is nearly perfect. But he is no longer the savage beast the Professor wanted him to be.

She dialed back through the digital recordings stored in the REM's mainframe, until she found the images she wanted. The Matron played back the event several times.

Even after Dr. Vigil unleashed his long-sublimated libido—the human psyche's most dark and dangerous territory—Weapon X did not act on the violent urges programmed into him.

The Matron dimmed her screen.

Weapon X has reached a level of humanity not many civilized men achieve. Yet the Professor and the Director both deemed the creature a failure—and perhaps they are right.

As a savage, remote-controlled killing machine, Weapon X is a disaster. A failure of such magnitude, he could have been placed with the other failures in the Weapon Null Program.

That thought came as a revelation. The Matron clutched the control panel to steady herself.

Could that be the solution? Could we reason with him? Could Weapon X be convinced to join Weapon Null?

The Matron pulled the dark glasses from her lab smock, clutching them like a talisman.

Megan has already gained his trust—and perhaps more than that. Could she convince Weapon X to make that final step and return to civilization?

Her intercom buzzed. "Yes?"

"This is mission command. Major Sallow and Mr. Thorne have returned. They report that their operation was successful. The major is convinced that the people of the town will no longer aid Weapon X in any way."

"Good. Very good," she replied.

"Major Sallow has also requested permission to forward a copy of his after-action reports to the Director," the man continued.

"No, absolutely not," the Matron replied. "Tell the major his request is denied."

"Yes, ma'am."

The Matron ended the call.

So Weapon X is effectively isolated. Perhaps Megan can persuade him to come down from the mountain and rejoin the world of men—to become a member of Weapon Null.

Excited by the thought, the Matron immediately reactivated her command center. Then she interfaced her control board with the Reifying Encephalographic Monitor's system. When the interface was achieved, the Matron went to work.

After several hours of programming, the Matron pressed the EXE command key. Within the next several minutes, the REM device would communicate a new set of subliminal commands to Megan Vigil.

After she launched the data bundle, the Matron experienced a sense of helplessness that she found extremely unpleasant. She preferred to control all aspects of an operation, yet as of now, her hands were tied. She'd done all she could. The rest was up to the physical charms and persuasive powers of Dr. Megan Vigil.

It's just like the fairy tale. Only beauty can tame the beast.

Major Sallow exited the facility with his copilot. Together, the two men followed the snowy path to the airfield under cloudy gray skies.

Before they reached the tarmac, they were challenged by a pair of armed men in bright orange snow suits.

"Excuse me, Major," the older one said. "What's your business on the flight deck? No sorties have been authorized."

"We're not going anywhere," the major replied with an innocent smile. "Had some trouble with the ground radar this morning. Coming through this cloud cover, things got pretty hairy. Next time, I don't want to smack into a mountain range, so Cody and I are going to run a diagnostic test."

The man's eyes narrowed suspiciously. "Are you sure that's necessary, sir?"

The major's smile vanished. "Who are you to ask?"

The man puffed out his chest. "I'm a security officer for the CCRC, Major Sallow."

Sallow placed his hands on his hips. "Then shouldn't you be prowling around Shroud Lake, intimidating the local caribou population?"

His copilot snickered.

"Security goes where the team goes, Major." He stepped aside. "Go ahead, run your test. But no flights for any reason."

"I hear you," Sallow said over his shoulder while he and his copilot continued down the path.

The copilot waited to speak until they were out of earshot. "Is it me, or are there more and more of these little suckers in orange suits running around?"

"You're not wrong," Sallow replied, his gray eyes

fixed on his command ship parked in the middle of the snow-swept tarmac. "I suspect the Matron has been using secret back-channel communications with Lieutenant Benteen back at the Combat Casualty Rehabilitation Center. She's adding personnel, but I haven't figured out her endgame yet."

The copilot nodded. "I wondered what the Chinook was doing here day before yesterday."

"The woman flew eight more security personnel and technicians in from Shroud Lake," Sallow said. "Add to that the ten who came in last week. They're starting to outnumber us."

The pair reached the night-black MH-60L Direct Action Penetrator, an armed version of the Blackhawk designed for special operations over enemy territory and low-level attacks on ground targets.

Sallow popped the cabin door, and they climbed inside.

"You think the Matron is bucking the Director?" the copilot asked, activating the battery-powered systems.

"No doubt of that," Sallow replied. "I think maybe she's also bucking to *become* Director."

The copilot shook his head sadly. "Next thing you know, a woman will be running for prime minister."

While the copilot pretended to repair a perfectly functional ground radar system, Major Sallow strapped on his radio headset and powered up the wireless data transmission system he'd had secretly installed in his ship before the mission began.

When the transmitter was up and running, Sallow plugged in a powerful stick drive that contained a compressed copy of all the data and digital files on Weapon X and the current operation gathered by the Matron and her team over the past fifteen hours.

"G-dash-eight. G-dash-eight, this is A-O-LYS fourteen umbra, prepare to receive an urgent transmission, Director's eyes only."

A moment passed before a faint voice replied to their radio message. "A-O-LYS fourteen umbra, this is G-dash-eight. We are ready for your transmission, over."

Major Sallow pressed the send button. Then he removed his headset and stowed it away. When the data transmission ended, he disconnected the stick drive and tucked it into the pocket of his battle dress uniform.

Sallow wore a self-satisfied smirk when he spoke again.

"That witch isn't the only one with back-channel communications capabilities. It'll be interesting to see how the Director reacts to this news."

32

THE LONG HOUSE WAS PACKED TO THE GILLS WITH
the concerned citizens of Second Chance. Men and
women sat at tables or on the floor. They leaned
against the shelves, piled up books to create additional seating, and generally messed up the Librarian's
stacks.

Henry is going to be pissed about that, Thomas mused.

The big meeting had been called for sunset. Most
folks who lived in the center of town showed up or
sent someone to represent them. Even the town's unofficial mayor, Waldo Parsons, made an appearance. As
usual, he was drunk as a skunk, slouched on a chair at
the end of the table.

Thomas noted that no one from the commune
over the hill had bothered to show up. The old hip-
pies made it clear to the Librarian that they didn't
think what happened was any of their business—but

of course, they lived a mile or two from the mountain, not under its shadow. And no one in their settlement had been murdered—yet.

No one from the survivalist camp showed up, either. Jesse Lee had headed up to their concrete bunker to invite them to send a representative, but they wouldn't let him in, wouldn't even come out and talk to him face-to-face. They just wiggled a shotgun under his nose through a steel gun port and ordered him off their compound. That left pretty much everyone else in Second Chance to deal with the problem.

While the Librarian spoke, Thomas scanned faces, speculating where each man or woman stood on tonight's business. It was a pointless exercise, but it kept his mind occupied.

Better this than brooding about poor Rachel.

A jolt of helpless rage welled up inside him. Thomas wanted to kill the filthy bastard who did this just as much as everyone else in town. He just didn't think Logan had anything to do with Rachel's murder.

"I want to conclude the opening statement by informing you that little Rachel will be laid to rest beside her mother, tomorrow noon, up on the hillside. I hope you'll show up and say a few words."

The Librarian looked up from his notes. "Next order of business?"

Ben slammed his meaty fist on the table. "I move we form a posse and hunt down the wild man."

"I second the motion," Jerry bellowed over the chatter that erupted as soon as Ben stated his proposal.

"I move we take a vote on the matter," Marvin said.

The Librarian opened his mouth to speak, but everyone was talking so loudly that he couldn't shout over them. He snatched a ball-peen hammer from his hearth and banged it on the table.

"Order. Order!"

The room quieted.

"I object," said Thomas. "You're not forming a posse; you're putting together a lynch mob."

The long house exploded with angry voices, while others—a minority—called for calm.

"What are you objecting to?" Bill Lyons yelled. "We haven't voted on anything yet."

"You're making a mistake. The wild man didn't do this—"

Marvin cut Thomas off. "You can read minds?"

"No, I can't," Thomas said, facing him. "But I *can* predict the future. If you make him mad, the wild man will wipe you out. All of you."

Bill Lyons snorted. "If I get him in my sights, he's a *dead* wild man."

"Oh, yeah? What do you think you can do with a few guns, when an army and a human flamethrower couldn't stop him?"

"We can run him off," Ben said.

"But you don't even know where he is," Thomas cried.

"He's somewhere on that mountain," Jerry said. "If he's up there, I can track him."

Thomas knew the big man was not bluffing. Both Ben and Jerry were as good as his grandfather used to be.

"I move we vote!" Marvin shouted.

"Second," said Ben, folding his arms and staring straight ahead.

"Motion passed," the Librarian said, punctuating his declaration with a bang of his hammer. "So, do we form a posse? Ayes?"

The rafters shook with cries. The nays were a whisper.

"The ayes have it, by a landslide," the Librarian declared, banging the hammer again.

"This is a mistake," Thomas said. "The wild man didn't do this. He doesn't even keep a weapon in his cave."

Jesse Lee grunted. "With claws sticking out of his arms, he doesn't need one."

"Wait a minute." Ben stood up and pushed through the crowd to stand before Thomas. "Did you say you were in a *cave* with this guy?"

Thomas bit his lip. "Maybe."

Ben whirled to face the others. "I know where that damn cave is," he told them. "It's between the ledge and the plateau near the summit."

"Yeah, that's right," said Jesse. "That cave used to be a cat den."

"Sonofab—"

"What's the matter, Ben?" Jerry cried.

"We know where he is, but we can't get to him. The trail's gone. Obliterated," Ben replied.

"Maybe not," Jerry said. "The wild man got down here. If he can come here, we can get to him—"

Bill Lyons lifted his hand. "What if we follow the road—"

"The avalanche blocked the pass," the Librarian said. "We can't get out until the spring thaw. Figure late April, early May."

"But we don't have to get out," Bill said. "We just have to follow the road to the other side of the mountain, then climb up to the cave from there. I know a couple of trails."

"Damn," said Jesse Lee with a stupid grin, "that sounds like a plan."

"Then it's done," said Ben. "We'll leave at dawn. First light."

"Don't do it," Thomas pleaded.

"You're outvoted," said Marvin. "Drop the subject."

Thomas threw up his hands. "Fine. You win, but you're still wrong. Oh, and by the way? Just keep in mind that you're all committing suicide." He headed for the door.

Old Herman and Ray Creighton stepped forward and blocked his escape. Ray clutched a gnarled shillelagh with both hands. Herman grinned at him, exposing yellow teeth.

"What the hell is this?" Thomas demanded.

"We're not going to let you go up there and warn your pal we're coming," Herman said.

Thomas was outraged—though they were right to suspect him, for he was planning to do exactly that.

"Let me out of here." Thomas pushed Herman aside and lunged for the door.

"Stop him!" Marvin yelled.

Ray Creighton whacked Thomas on the back of his head with his club. Thomas pitched forward, too stunned to cry out. Voices yelled in protest, but another blow followed the first, and Thomas hit the hardwood floor.

A third blow came, but he barely felt it. As darkness closed around him, Thomas heard the bang of the gavel and the Librarian's voice.

"Meeting adjourned."

Megan slept until late afternoon. When she woke up, she was thirsty and ravenous. She and Logan shared what was left of the cooked rabbit, saving the uncooked meat for their evening meal.

After lunch, Megan told Logan she was feeling much better and wanted to go outside to see the sun. He helped wrap her in layers of deerskin and wolf hides. Then he led her to a ledge that overlooked the valley and the mountain range beyond. They curled up under the furs and watched the sun set over the mountains.

"Logan, what are you going to do next?"

He blinked. "Go back to the cave. Cook up the rabbits. Eat dinner, then maybe . . ." He ended his thought by pulling her close.

She gently pushed him away.

"I'm talking about the future. When the spring comes," Megan said.

Logan shrugged. "Honestly? Never gave it much thought. I'm fine up here. There's food, shelter. I thought I'd stay awhile."

"But you can't," Megan insisted. "They're going to come for you, again and again, until they take you down. Put you in a cage."

Logan chuckled. "That's never gonna happen."

"Well, what about me? You've got a steel skeleton, superior strength, healing powers. You don't feel the cold, or hunger, or pain the way I do. This world might be fine for you, but I could very easily slip on the ice and fall off the mountain or get eaten by a wolf."

Logan seemed suddenly uncomfortable.

Megan knew she should shut up now, but a voice inside her head compelled her to speak.

"You're not alone anymore," she told him.

"Whoa," Logan said. "I don't remember proposing."

Megan was silent for a long time, careful not to let Logan know how his words cut her. Those emotions further confused Megan.

What is wrong with me? I'm behaving like a possessive schoolgirl in the throes of a crush.

The silence continued, while the sun slowly sank behind the mountain, until only its light illuminated the sky in hues of red, pink, and orange.

"Forget about us, then," Megan said at last, struggling to keep the bitterness out of her voice. "Think about *your* future. The Department is never going to stop hounding you. Unless maybe you—"

"What?" Logan growled. She sensed his irritation—and his suspicions. Eager to make things right again, she babbled on uncontrollably.

"Maybe I know someone we can trust," she said. "Someone who's stationed back at the facility."

"Are you nuts?"

"Listen," she pleaded. "There's a woman who runs a special hospital for people . . . people like you. She's an important member of Department K, too."

"Those butchers—"

"She's not like the others. The Matron cares about people, and she's powerful enough to stand up to the Director, protect us both."

Even as she spoke the words, Megan doubted them. Deep down in her heart, she really didn't trust the Matron, because Megan knew the woman was as driven and obsessive in her own right as the Director himself.

But despite her misgivings, soothing words poured out of her mouth, as if a tiny voice was in the back of her mind, speaking the words she should speak, pushing her to pressure Logan.

To Megan's surprise, Logan threw back his head and laughed at her argument.

"You're not thinking straight, doll face," he told her. "They'll have us both down for mandatory vivisection as soon as we're brought in."

He stood up, seized Megan's waist, and lifted her off the rock. She laughed, too, as he tossed her around as if she were a feather. Finally, Logan set her on her feet.

"It's getting dark, and you're cold and hungry," Logan said, taking her hand. "Let's head back to that nice warm cave. I'll cook supper, and in the morning I need to go hunting."

"Do you have to go? I don't want you to leave me alone," Megan said, suddenly nervous.

"Don't sweat it, doll. You'll be safe inside the cave. No one ever comes up here."

"Except the bad guys."

"Yeah, you got a point. But so far, they've been a bunch of pushovers. Anyway, they don't have a clue where I live."

33

WEAPON X AND THE WOMAN WERE MAKING LOVE. Again. The Matron turned her back on the plasma-screen images.

"Keep recording, but cut the visuals," she commanded.

The data manager nodded, and the screens went black.

"She was so close."

The DM looked up from his control station. "You said something, Matron?"

"I was only thinking aloud. Sorry to interrupt."

The Matron sat down at her own command station, thoughts swirling.

Twice Dr. Vigil brought up the possibility of surrender. Once on the ledge and again just now. But for some reason, there's been resistance. Not only from Weapon X but also from Dr. Vigil herself.

The Matron rose again and paced across the cramped chamber to the REM's main control station.

I can dial up the emotions, but the woman already suspects she's being manipulated. Megan's libido is quite high, so she's responded well to Weapon X's advances, but perhaps the good doctor lacks the nesting gene.

Her intercom buzzed, snapping the Matron back to reality. She punched the button. "Yes, what is it now?"

"Sorry to interrupt, Matron, but this is a matter of security. We have a dozen helicopters arriving right now. Major Sallow and his staff are on the tarmac to greet them."

"Why is this a problem?"

"The flight has not been authorized by you, Matron. No landing permits have been issued."

"Major Sallow has my full confidence. Obey him as you would me," she said, ending the conversation.

The Matron approached the mission commander. "What are they doing now?"

He glanced at the miniature plasma screen at his station. "They're sleeping."

"There won't be any more conversation tonight," the Matron said. Rubbing her eyes, she stifled a yawn. "Perhaps I should sleep for a few hours. I'm sure nothing will happen before dawn—"

The sound of boots tramping in the corridor outside were suddenly heard over the whirring of the mainframe computers. The steel blast door burst open with a loud clang. A brace of armed men in black uniforms entered and circled the occupants of the REM chamber.

"What's the meaning of this?" the Matron cried.

Major Sallow strode through the door and met the Matron in the middle of the room.

"I have the unfortunate duty of informing you that you have been relieved of command," Sallow said.

The Matron was stunned. Her lips moved, but no sound emerged.

"Hold on a minute, Major," the mission commander said.

Major Sallow turned to his subordinate. "Sergeant, arrest that man."

The mission commander stepped away from his control panel. "This is mutiny, Sallow. I'll see that—"

The sergeant's gun butt ended the man's protestations. Two soldiers gripped the unconscious mission commander by his arms and dragged him from the room.

Sallow pointed to a young officer. "Lieutenant Pierce, take over the command console."

The man saluted crisply. "Yes, sir."

Major Sallow scanned the shocked faces inside the chamber. "If anyone else has a problem with the change in command, speak now, and you will be relieved of duty."

No one spoke, not until the Matron found her voice. "Major, this ridiculous mutiny will not give you

Weapon X. You endanger everything we've worked for with this fascist display."

"It's *you* who've endangered the mission, Matron. The Director has countermanded your orders with instructions of his own." Sallow faced the communications technician. "Which member of the Weapon Null team is in the queue for activation?"

"That would be Bipolar, Major."

"You wouldn't dare!" the Matron cried.

"Begin activation procedures. I want Bipolar up and running by morning."

The Matron lunged at the major. Two soldiers grabbed her, slamming the woman against the steel wall.

"I protest this inhuman treatment," she said, struggling.

"Take her away. Lock her up in the zoo compound with her mission commander," Sallow said.

"There's a problem, Major," said Lieutenant Pierce.

Major Sallow fixed his gaze on the communications technician. "What problem?"

"Unless you've brought a qualified psychiatrist and REM technician with you, the Matron is the only person in this facility who knows how to operate the Reifying Encephalographic Monitor," Pierce stated.

"Is this true?" Sallow demanded.

Several technicians nodded.

"I can maintain the link between the subjects," the chief medical technician said. "But I have no knowledge of how to manipulate the subjects, or issue sub-liminal commands."

The com tech nodded. "She's right. If you want to go forward with the mission, Major, then the Matron must remain at her post."

Major Sallow's face contorted.

"Very well. Let her go. But I want that woman kept on a tight leash. She's not to make a move without my express permission or issue any commands to her agent in the field."

Thomas felt hands on his body, and he opened his eyes. Big Rita stood over him, her index finger cov-ering her lips. He was in his own bunk, bound. He struggled, then heard a loud snore. Thomas lifted his head.

Old Herman was slumped in the chair beside his bed, an empty mason jar in his lap. The man had passed out. Thomas could smell the stink of moon-shine in the stifling room.

Then he felt tugging on his arms. Rita had his hunting knife in her tiny hands and was sawing away at the thick ropes around his wrist.

Thomas snatched the knife from her as soon as his hands were free. With a quick swipe, he freed his feet and sat up.

The room lurched suddenly, and a throbbing ache bounced around inside his skull. Despite the woman's plea for silence, he began to mutter.

"Ray Creighton, I'm gonna shove that shillelagh up your—"

Big Rita shushed him. Thomas knew there was no danger of Herman waking up. But after Thomas stood up, the first thing he did was tie the sleeping man to the chair just to be sure.

Thomas glanced out the window. The sun had just risen. In the valley, the morning was gray and foggy. "When did they leave?"

"About an hour ago. It was still dark," Rita replied. "Here, take these."

The woman slipped a rusty old .38 Police Special into his hand, along with a box of shells. He opened the chamber, spun it, and peered through the barrel. It was clean, at least, but Thomas was still afraid the antique would blow up in his hand when he tried to fire it.

Thomas loaded the revolver and slipped it under his waistband anyway. Next, he slid his hunting knife into a sheath on his belt. Then Thomas took his Remington down off the rack and loaded it, too.

"You're not gonna hurt anybody?" Rita asked, wringing her hands.

"I'm going to save those crazy fools from themselves, if I can," Thomas replied. "Then I'm going to talk with the wild man, find out if he knows anything about Rachel."

"Why don't you just leave this place?" Rita said. "You don't need to go through the pass to get out of here. You're an Indian and a tracker. You can go over the mountain. Why do you stay?"

"Because this is my home, and I'm through running."

Thomas tugged on his boots and stomped his feet.

He crossed to his pantry, found a bottle of generic aspirin, and swallowed three of them without water. He hoped that would take care of the pain in his head.

"Thanks, Rita."

Thomas opened the door—to find the Librarian standing on the threshold. The old man clutched a knife in one hand, his iron skillet in the other.

"I was just coming here to knock Herman out and set you free," he said.

Thomas jerked his head in the woman's direction. "Too late, hero. Big Rita beat you to it."

The Librarian looked at him with wide eyes. "Do you need any help?"

"You'll only slow me down."

Thomas pushed past the man and vanished in the cold.

Major Sallow watched technicians attach radiation-proof panels to the black, formfitting suit of a tall man standing in the middle of the laboratory. Though his back was turned, Sallow could see that the subject's physical appearance had been altered.

Sallow stood on the metal platform in Professor Thorton's old lab, overlooking the command center.

The major had moved operations back to the lab and away from the cramped and confining REM chamber because of the shift in mission priorities.

The focus was on Bipolar now, and a direct frontal assault on Weapon X. Not on the Matron's secret plots or her magic mind machine.

The chief medical officer appeared at Sallow's side, a frown on her elfin face.

"Report," Sallow commanded.

"As you can see, Bipolar has been activated. Once his shielding is in place, your helicopters can put him on the mountain within the hour."

Sallow faced the woman. "Tell me about this freak," he said.

The doctor winced at the soldier's choice of words. Sallow's faint smile told her it was his intent to offend, and he was pleased that he had.

"His name is Lieutenant Kenneth Biggs. He was a communications specialist in Tamboor."

Sallow grunted. "Biggs and I chewed some of the same ground, then."

"Lieutenant Biggs was helping to build a state-of-the-art telephone system for the people of Tamboor when he was severely injured in a car bombing."

Down on the floor, technicians were placing a domed helmet over the man's shaved head.

"His skull was shattered; his jaw, tongue, and nose were burned away," the doctor continued. "There was permanent damage to his larynx and vocal cords, as well.

Miraculously, he survived his wounds and eventually ended up at the Combat Casualty Rehabilitation Center."

Sallow sneered. "Where you turned him into a freak."

"Where we made the surgical and bionic alterations that Kenneth Biggs designed himself," the doctor replied. "He wished to go down a new path in communications technology—"

At that moment, Bipolar turned around, and Sallow saw his face.

"Christ, what a mess."

The medical technician cleared her throat. "You see that his mouth and part of his throat have been replaced by a wave transmission disk of great power and range. The klystron and the magnetron tubes, along with the oscillators and resonators that control wave frequency, are all located behind the microwave emitter."

"Microwave?" Sallow cried. "Like an oven?"

"The same principle," the doctor replied. "Microwaves are short, high-frequency radio waves lying between the very-high-frequency and ultraviolet and conventional radio waves. But they have many applications beyond cooking—in radio and television, radar, satellite communications, and meteorology."

"So what's Bipolar going to do to Weapon X, deliver a weather report?"

"Let's return to your cooking analogy, Major," the woman suggested. "Microwave ovens operate by agitating the water molecules in food, causing them to vibrate, which produces heat. Microwaves can't penetrate metal, which is why you see sparks, then fire, if the two collide."

"You're losing me, Doc."

"Bipolar can function along the entire spectrum of energy waves. He can become a living maser, emitting waves that cause burns, cataracts, damage to the nervous system, and sterility. But he's particularly good at focusing energy in the microwave range to sear flesh and burn metal."

Sallow nodded. "I like the sound of that. Bipolar should do a fairly good job of knocking Weapon X down."

"If not killing it outright," the doctor replied. "If the regenerative powers of Weapon X are tied to its nervous system, which I believe they are, then Bipolar may inflict mortal wounds."

She paused to allow Major Sallow time to consider her words.

"At the very least, the creature will experience severe brain trauma, because its adamantium skull does not fully protect its brain from the damaging waves. Memory or even critical brain functions could be lost, even if Weapon X doesn't perish. "

Major Sallow focused his dead gray eyes on the diminutive doctor.

"The Director ordered me to take Weapon X dead or alive. Personally, I think dead is better."

34

LOGAN WAS RELUCTANT TO LEAVE HIS WARM BED and the woman curled up beside him. But not too long after the sun rose behind a veil of fog, he slipped out of her entwining arms.

Swaddled in wolf skin, Logan gathered up his meager tools—snares made from deer tendon, a leather rope to carry his catch, the spear he'd fashioned while Megan slept that first night when he brought her back to his cave.

Logan smiled at the memory.

In the beginning, he'd half suspected she was part of some elaborate scheme to capture him. Even now, suspicions lingered. But none of that mattered anymore. Whatever her motives, Megan had helped him reconnect with the human race and recoup some of his lost humanity.

For that, I'm grateful. Anything more would be a gift.

In truth, most of his doubts had melted away. Somehow, he trusted her. He only had to look into her eyes to stop doubting her—even when she said things that seemed to suggest she had some kind of secret agenda.

Like last night, when Megan urged him to consider surrendering to this woman, the Matron. Of course, Megan didn't call it surrender, but that's what it was.

Can't do it, Logan decided. *I can't trust anyone in Department K. Can't trust anyone in the government, period. Fortunately, there are other options.*

When the thaw comes, Megan and I can slip out of the forest, across the border to the United States. It's a big country, easy to get lost in. I have friends who can help me, and a few enemies I can shake down, too.

Who knows? Maybe we can find a place where the rest of the world will leave us alone.

Logan tried to imagine himself living an anonymous, workaday life in the suburbs, but the images just wouldn't come.

Of course not. It was crazy, preposterous.

Logan frowned.

So what am I supposed to do? he wondered. *I've always been able to take care of myself. I can fight, and there are always wars. I know how to make money, legally and illegally. And I don't need much in the way of material goods, anyway. Hell, I'm happy in a freakin' cave.*

Logan paused at the fork on the trail. He stood at the precipice and gazed into the abyss.

Things are different now. Confusing, too. In fact, it's a total

FUBAR from beginning to end. But Megan was right about one thing—I'm no longer alone. I have to do my thinking for two from now on, and I haven't quite wrapped my mind around that concept yet.

Still mulling the problem, Logan stepped away from the brink and descended the mountain.

The sun emerged from behind the clouds. Logan considered the weather and began to plan his day.

First, he would check out the snares he'd placed the last time he was in the forest. That meant crossing the road, and Logan knew he would have to proceed with caution. After the firefight the other day, he realized the road was still in use.

He considered returning to the scene, to see if anyone had come back to clear up the mess or lay a trap for him. He wouldn't mind tangling with a few armed men again—a nice morning romp. And he could use the exercise.

Logan mentally kicked himself.

Can't risk it, jackass. If something happened to me, Megan would be alone in the wilderness with no one to take care of her.

Logan groaned. *This thinking for two takes some getting used to.*

He scrambled across a patch of bare rocks, then descended into a narrow ravine that wound through the foothills to the road below. The breeze shifted, and the hairs stood up on his arms. Logan stopped in his tracks, suddenly alert.

He smelled soap. Stale beer. Mothballs. Tobacco smoke. *Men*.

Preoccupied with his thoughts, he'd blindly walked into an ambush. Now Logan whirled and ran back up the trail, trying to escape it.

"He knows we're here!" Jesse Lee yelled.

The bearded man popped up from behind a rock and fired. The rifle's noise boomed off the mountain. The slug tore a baseball-sized chunk out of Logan's back. Blood splattered the rocks, but the wound didn't even slow him down.

Logan spied movement and lurched sideways. Another bullet struck the ravine wall, kicking up snow.

Crouching low, he kept moving. All around him, Logan saw other figures moving from cover—middle-aged and old men, mostly, wearing a motley collection of army-surplus clothing and frayed hunting gear.

This isn't Department K. These are the people from Second Chance. What's their beef? What did I ever do to them?

Though the men were old, their guns worked just fine, and they were pretty good shots, too. Another bullet took Logan in the thigh. He cursed but limped forward until new muscle regenerated.

"He's coming your way, Jerry!" someone yelled.

Another shot bounced off the back of his skull. The impact scrambled Logan's brain for a split second, and he stumbled. He landed on his hands and knees and felt hot blood splash his back. The pain faded immediately, and the wound closed.

He was off and running a moment later, and the next shot ricocheted harmlessly off the stone cliff.

Logan reached the sheer slope and scrambled across the windswept rocks, his naked feet sure on the slippery surface. The men who pursued him were not so lucky. Their boots slipped on the icy stones; they fumbled their weapons when they were forced to use their hands to climb.

Bunch of freakin' amateurs.

Logan hated dealing with greenhorns. Anyone with street smarts could predict what a professional would do. It's the wannabes that were the biggest surprise—in a bad way.

This would be much easier if I could kill one or two of them.

But that was not an option, so Logan kept on moving, hoping to outrun them rather than fight. The last thing he wanted to do was hurt anyone from town, whatever their perceived problem was with him.

He reached the top of the windswept peak, clambered over the ledge that led to the trail—and a shadow loomed over him. Logan heard the click of a hammer, then the shotgun blast deafened him. Fiery pellets blasted through his chest, shoulders, and arms.

Logan slid backward. Then his claws leaped from their sheaths and dug into the rocks. The big man stepped backward, stumbled over his own feet, and tumbled to the ground. The empty shotgun clattered down the side of the hill and dropped out of sight.

A voice called from below. "Did you get him, Bill?"

Using his claws, Logan heaved himself over the ledge. The one called Bill seemed to wait for the fatal blow to come. Instead, Logan jumped over the fallen man and ran up the hill. The wounds from the shotgun blast were already closing as he disappeared among the boulders.

A few moments later, Logan reached the fork in the trail. From this point on, it was clear sailing all the way to the summit. He could run miles if he had to, while the geezers chasing him were already winded.

Logan slowed his pace but continued to climb.

He hoped the men who attacked him were not stupid enough to follow him up to his cave. But if they did, then he'd had no choice but to defend his home, even if it meant killing every single one of them.

Logan would never surrender, and he was tired of running. It was time to take a stand.

Thomas gambled that he'd be able to take the original trail up the mountain and beat the posse to Logan's cave. In his mind, it made more sense to warn Logan than to try to dissuade the thick heads led by Zen Master Marvin.

So the direct route made sense. He was a better mountain man than any one of the men in the posse, and he was at least a decade younger. Plus, Thomas had been climbing rocks since he was knee-high to a prairie dog. So while the posse took the long way around the mountain, he'd take a chance, and the shortcut.

So far, his gamble had paid off. He only hit two bad patches, one he already knew about. Now Thomas was close to the plateau, which meant he was close to Logan's cave, too. All he had to do was find it.

Thomas tensed when he heard a familiar sound—so close he barely had time to duck behind a tumble of rocks before the ebony Blackhawk roared over his head. The chopper quickly vanished behind a ridge, but from the sound of the blades, he knew the aircraft was hovering.

Thomas had a hunch that if he followed that Blackhawk, he'd find Logan's cave.

Logan reached the top of the ridge mere seconds after the Blackhawk roared away. He expected to see men in orange suits or another escapee from a freak show. But there was no one around.

Logan sniffed the air, but all he smelled was the exhaust spewed by the Blackhawk's turbine engines. Cautiously, he approached the cave. Everything appeared normal, but his spine tingled a warning. He spun on his heels, claws flashing silver.

The stranger who'd crept up on him was clad in sheets of black armor, a domed helmet over his head. His eyes were invisible behind a black visor, and he had what appeared to be a radar dish for a mouth.

"Not again," Logan growled. "Why don't you just go back to Department K and tell them all to leave me alone."

The cave was less than fifty feet away. Logan hoped the man didn't see the narrow entrance and didn't know Megan was inside. He also hoped she had the smarts to stay put until he dealt with Saucer Mouth.

"Are you just going to stand there?"

As if in response to his question, Logan heard an electronic hum that seemed to come from everywhere. The noise intensified, and Logan felt a strange pressure inside his ears.

His skin began to prickle, then curl. Finally, the pain registered, and Logan howled. By then, the flesh on his arms, chest, and torso was peeling back, the wolf hide on his back smoldered, the spear in his hand smoked. Logan tried to react, but his nervous system misfired. He reeled, his knees buckled, and he dropped to the snow.

Suddenly, a shrill cry cut through the electronic hum.

"No!" Megan screamed from the entrance of the cave.

Logan tried to cry out a warning, but the tongue bubbled inside his mouth, and only an incoherent bleat emerged.

The armored stranger heard her cry. He turned to face the woman—and the full power of the deadly waves washed over her. Megan threw up her arm, and the flesh seared instantly. She fell backward, back inside the cave.

In the split second the attacker was distracted, Logan's nerves and muscles regenerated enough for him to hurl the spear in his hand.

It struck their attacker in the heart, penetrating the layers of radiation-proof armor. The man's arms flew outward, and he fell backward. He landed in the snow, the spear sticking out of his chest like a flagpole.

Gasping, Logan stumbled to the cave. He paused for a moment, while more of his flesh reformed. Finally, he crawled through the cave mouth.

He found Megan lying facedown on the floor, still wrapped in the smoldering blanket. He touched her throat, felt for a pulse.

Nothing.

With trembling hands, Logan gently turned the body over. In the flickering firelight, he leaned close for a final kiss.

Logan howled when he saw the dead woman's face.

35

FIFTY MILES AWAY, MEGAN WOKE UP SCREAMING.

The Matron touched her arm. "Relax, you're safe now."

"My eyes!" Megan howled, shielding her face from the light.

"I have your glasses. Here . . ."

The Matron slipped them over her bionic eyes. Heart racing, Megan felt a rush of panic.

"Where am I? Where's Logan? He's in danger—"

"You were never with him," the Matron said softly. "You were right here, hooked up to the Reifying Encephalographic Monitor the whole time."

"Impossible," Megan said, her voice hoarse from disuse. She tried to rise but was stopped by electrodes hooked up to her head, her breasts, her arms.

The Matron pressed a button on a control panel. With a hissing sound, the electrodes fell away. Megan touched her face, her head, and discovered her scalp had been shaved; her hair was gone.

"It will grow back," the Matron assured her. "It was necessary, for the interface to work properly."

Megan sat up, and the sheet fell away from her body. She was naked on the cold metal slab.

"What interface?" Megan thought she knew the answer but asked anyway.

"She's dead now, so her name's not important. We called her Cypher."

The Matron handed Megan a lab smock, and she put it on.

"Cypher was the daughter of a military family. She was born . . . mentally challenged. A combination of extreme autism and a bizarre mutant psychic ability to mask her identity like a chameleon. It started when she was institutionalized. She made the nurses see her as a kitten, a turtle, a bird."

The Matron handed Megan a cup with lime-green liquid sloshing around in it. "Drink this. It will restore your electrolyte balance."

"I don't give a damn about my electrolytes. I want to know what happened."

"We brought Cypher to the CCRC. We worked long and hard. We tried everything to coax her buried personality to emerge. Eventually, we gave up. For a long time, we simply took care of her. Then the CCRC acquired an REM unit from SHIELD."

"You had one all along," croaked Megan.

"During our experiments, we discovered that the REM could be used to interface with Cypher's brain. That's what we did with you, Megan. When you were with Weapon X, it was really Cypher's body and her ability to mask her physical appearance, coupled with *your* mind."

Megan shook her head. "But Logan . . . he and I were together. . . ."

"You only thought you were. And your mind experienced all the physical pleasures because you felt what Cypher was feeling. But your body was never violated. I could not let that happen to you."

Tears sprang up in the tear ducts behind Megan's bionic eyes. "And Logan?"

"He saw what Cypher wanted him to see, which was you. With modifications, of course."

"My eyes, you mean?"

"And other things. We hoped that Weapon X would take you with him—either as a hostage or for his own physical gratification."

The Matron paused. "It was a risky scheme, of course. The creature could have killed you outright, which is why we set up that elaborate scenario on the road. We reasoned that if he saw you as vulnerable—as a victim of violence and not a perpetrator—he would not regard you as a threat. We never imagined in our wildest dreams that Weapon X would feel protectively toward you, that he would find you attractive and emotionally available."

"Then it never happened? The gunfight on the road, I mean."

"We had Cypher approach Corporal MacKenzie appearing as you. She convinced him that you were in danger and wished to flee this facility. The corporal did the rest."

"Then he's—"

"Dead. Along with a few members of my staff. The ruse was necessary to enable you to get close to Weapon X—"

Anger flashed across Megan's face. "Logan. His name is Logan."

"I understand the affection you feel for Weapon—I mean Logan. Trust me, these feelings will pass in time, like a bad dream."

Megan looked up. "Then you tinkered with my emotions, too?"

"Just a little. Your attraction to . . . Logan was real but magnified. His attraction to you was *very* real. I venture to say you'd have made an attractive couple . . . under very different circumstances, of course."

Megan wiped her cheek. "What happens now?"

The Matron shrugged. "By now, he may be dead. I lost all contact with him, in any case. When Cypher perished, the cameras and transmitters went with her."

Major Sallow stood on the steel platform, legs braced. Mr. Thorne leaned on the rail at his side, wearing a formfitting black uniform. In a display of helpless rage, Sallow shook his fist at the blank screens around the command center.

"What the hell is going on out there? Weapon X was face-to-face with Bipolar, then we lost all audio and visuals—"

The major faced the communications technician. "If this is a mutiny, I'll have you shot."

"It's no mutiny, sir." Lieutenant Pierce spoke from his command and control station. "I believe it was friendly fire. Bipolar fried the other operative, the woman in the cave. All our visual transmissions were coming through her. Now we've got nothing."

"What about satellites?"

The com tech shook her head. "We can't have one on station for twenty minutes."

Sallow bunched his fist. "So how do we know what happened?"

The chief medical officer looked up from her bio-monitor. "There's good news. I'm reading a heartbeat, respiration, blood pressure. Bipolar may be injured, but he's alive."

Sallow grinned. "If the freak is alive, then Weapon X is dead."

"Mr. Thorne, Lieutenant Pierce, follow me." The major descended the steel steps, boots clicking.

"Where to, Major?" Thorne asked.

"The airstrip. The Blackhawks will get us to the mountain in ten minutes. We're going up there to collect our prize."

• • •

Thomas scrambled to the top of the ledge. He paused, listening. More helicopters were roaring toward the mountain. He could hear them. They were getting close.

Thomas crossed a clearing and spied the dead man on the ground. He saw a spear jutting from the man's armored chest, and he gave the corpse a wide berth.

Finally, he spotted the narrow opening in the hillside, framed by two large boulders. Rifle at the ready, Thomas slowly advanced on the cave, pausing only after he heard a human noise from inside. It sounded like a sob of misery.

"Logan . . . is that you?"

There was no reply. "Logan, are you there?"

Silence.

"Okay, I'm coming in."

Cautiously, Thomas stuck his head through the cave mouth. It took a moment for his eyes to adjust to the darkness, but soon he knew he'd found the right place. He recognized the stone water trough, the deer-skin bed where he'd slept.

Then, in the flickering light of a dying fire, he saw Logan huddled on the dirt floor, cradling something in his arms.

Thomas crawled through the opening and carefully approached Logan until he stood over the man.

Logan looked up. Thomas thought he seemed dazed.

"She wasn't real," Logan muttered, his eyes haunted. "She didn't even exist. Just a lie . . . a freakin' trick."

Thomas got a good look at the figure wrapped in Logan's arms. It was a dead woman, small and thin and naked, her flesh darkened by burns. A deerskin blanket was tangled around her sprawled limbs.

The man on the ground shifted position, and Thomas saw the woman's features. Gagging, he took a step backward.

The woman's dead eyes stared at the ceiling, but that wasn't what shocked Thomas. It was her head, the way half of her skull had been cut away and replaced by a clear Plexiglas dome. Under the dome, penetrating the spongy pink brain, were a dozen electrodes of some kind. The brain itself floated in a milky white liquid, and there was a superminiaturized camera attached to the dead woman's temple.

"What the hell is it?" Thomas gasped.

Logan shook his head. "She wasn't real. She was a trick, an illusion. That's all. . . ."

Thomas crouched down. His fingers closed on the wild man's muscular shoulder. "Listen, Logan, we have to go. Men are coming. They'll be here any minute."

Logan blinked, then his eyes focused on Thomas as if he'd just awakened from a dream. "Soldier Boy, what are you doing here?"

"I came to warn you. Men are coming here. They're gunning for you."

"What? You mean that bunch of old geezers down in the valley. Already met up with them. Wasn't pretty."

Thomas wasn't sure what Logan meant, but he feared he was too late to save the posse. Knowing Logan's prowess, Thomas figured the men from Second Chance were all dead.

"Not those guys," Thomas said. "Soldiers are coming. Men in helicopters."

He heard a rumble emerge from deep in Logan's throat. "They're the ones who did this."

"They're going to do a lot worse if we don't get out of here right now," Thomas warned.

"I'm tired of running. I'm taking a stand. Right here."

Thomas squeezed the man's shoulder. "How about we move you to a new place? Like Second Chance? There might be a little problem with some of the folks at first, but I think I can smooth things out."

Logan shook off his hand. "Leave me alone."

"No. You saved me once, now I'm going to save you."

He tugged on Logan's arm. The man struggled against him at first, but finally Logan threw up his hands.

"All right, I'll go with you. Just stop yanking on my arm like a freakin' poodle or something."

"Come on. We have to move now."

Thomas climbed through the cave mouth, and Logan followed him.

"The old trail is still good, even after the firefight the other night," Thomas told Logan. "If I can walk it, you can. It's the fastest way off this rock—"

Thomas stopped talking when he heard a weird electronic humming.

"What's that—"

"Duck, kid!" Logan cried. He grabbed Thomas and threw him to the frozen ground. Then Logan threw himself in front of the youth, just as a rippling red-orange beam struck his chest. Thomas heard a sizzling sound and smelled burnt flesh.

Instantly, the layers of pink and brown muscles on Logan's chest cooked away, exposing a shiny metal rib cage. Behind the ribs, organs bubbled and cooked, spilling hot gore.

Logan turned his back on the ray, and the beam gnawed through slabs of muscle, sparking the metal-sheathed spine.

He looked down, and his eyes met Thomas's. As the youth watched, all awareness seemed to flee Logan's expression. Then the eyes themselves simmered and popped, spilling milky white liquid on the man's blistering cheeks.

Thomas screamed. "Logan!"

A shockwave of destructive energy reverberated through Logan's skull. He reeled as black jets of agony exploded inside him. Without eyes or ears, Logan was trapped in a swirling mind storm of a thousand memories, experiences, and emotions.

With total recall, Logan reexperienced moments from his life. He felt the touch of his mother's hand, tasted his first kiss, killed his first man. But each memory was its own eulogy—soon after it gripped him, it vanished forever as whole sections of his mind were burned away.

Time ceased to exist, each second an eternity. Logan desperately clawed at his disintegrating memories, but one after another they slipped from his grasp. Still Logan fought, until the last fire of his humanity sputtered and died like a match flame in a whirlwind, and he was cast into a formless, featureless void.

Logan pitched forward. Thomas scrambled aside so the burning corpse would not fall on him.

Thomas fumbled for his gun, still not sure who or what had killed Logan.

Finally, a shotgun boomed, the loud report ricocheting off the mountain.

Abruptly, the humming sound ceased. Thomas lifted his head and saw Ben standing in the middle of the clearing, a smoking shotgun in his beefy hands. The rest of the posse came up behind him—Jerry, Jesse Lee, Ben Lyons, Ray Creighton, Marvin the Zen Naturalist, and a few others from the town.

They were all staring, not at Logan but at the other dead man sprawled in the clearing.

"He had a b-big radar dish for a m-mouth," Ben stammered. "I watched him get up and pull a spear out of his chest. Then you and the wild man came out of the cave, and this guy fired some kind of ray. . . ."

His voice trailed off. Thomas followed Ben's troubled eyes and saw the thing he was staring at. If the spear didn't kill it, the shotgun blast sure did. The man's helmet was shattered, the top of his skull was gone, and his brains were splattered all over the ground.

"I just fired," Ben said, still staring. "I saw what he was doing to the wild man, and I pulled the trigger."

Thomas took the shotgun out of Ben's limp hand. "You did good, Ben."

The others gathered around the pair. No one said a word until Ben spoke again. "Did I do a good thing, Tommy? Did I? I don't know the man I shot from Adam. And the wild man . . . he killed Rachel, didn't he?"

Thomas glanced at Logan's smoking corpse, then shook his head. "You've got to believe me. I knew Logan, and I know he didn't kill Rachel—"

"No," a loud voice declared. "I did."

The men turned, surprised to see that a dozen armed soldiers had appeared in the clearing, guns trained on them. One of the soldiers was a major with a pockmarked face.

The man next to the officer wore a black form-fitting battle suit. "Yeah," he said with a toothy grin. "I cut the little brat's throat with these."

While the men from Second Chance watched, claws emerged from the man's wrist. They sprang up like grass, growing slowly, curling as they increased in length. Unlike Logan's claws, which popped out of a sheath in his forearms, these were made of a white bony material, not adamantium steel, the hardest metal in the world.

The man in black brandished his claws in front of the posse.

"Sharper than a diamond drill. I can cut your throats with a flick of my wrist. That's why they call me Thorne."

"You sonofa—" Jerry raised his rifle. A soldier fired, and he spun—the rifle flew from the bearded man's grip, and he hit the ground hard.

"Nobody move," the major commanded. "Drop your weapons, or we'll shoot you where you stand."

The men threw down their guns. Thomas reluctantly followed suit.

The officer approached them. "My name is Major Sallow, and I'm taking you all into custody."

Ben glanced at his brother on the ground. Jerry wasn't moving. "What do you want from us?"

Major Sallow paced the ground in front of them. Meanwhile, Thorne approached Logan's corpse.

"You men are from that town in the valley," Sallow said. "I think after we're done here, we're going to pay it a visit."

Marvin puffed out his chest. "Why don't you leave us alone?"

"You people have been way too busy for that," Sallow said. "Running all over the mountain. Sticking your noses where they don't belong. Now you're here, in the way again."

"What are you going to do with us?" Jesse Lee demanded.

"State secrets should remain secret," Sallow said. "We're going to clean up the mess and make sure nobody talks."

Thorne kicked the corpse at his feet. "Weapon X doesn't look so tough now, Major."

He crouched over the dead man and prodded Logan with his hand. Thorne snorted. "Just like that cute little girl. Weapon X is deader than—"

Logan's arm shot upward, his claws plunging into Thorne's throat. The man's taunting words ended in a wet gurgle. Eyes wide with shock, Thorne clutched at the blades penetrating his flesh.

With a maddened roar, Logan leaped to his feet. Legs kicking wildly, Thorne dangled on the steel claws like a fish on a hook. Logan tossed the still-struggling man across the clearing and over the edge of the cliff.

Major Sallow stepped back and raised his weapon. "Fire! Open fire!"

The clearing exploded with the sound of gunfire. Logan howled in surprise, then he surged forward, pushing against the tidal wave of hot lead.

"Scatter!" Thomas yelled.

The posse did. Some dived for their guns. Others took off, looking for a place to hide. Ben fell to his knees beside his brother, tried to rouse the man before he realized Jerry was gone.

The chatter of machine guns continued. While the soldiers concentrated on Logan, the posse systematically gunned them down.

Thomas spied Major Sallow running for cover and hurled his hunting knife. Thomas heard a wet smack. The spinning blade struck the major in the small of his back. Grunting, the officer took a few more steps, reaching backward to clutch at the blade.

Finally, Major Sallow's knees gave out, and he collapsed. Before Thomas could retrieve his knife, Bill Lyons stood over Sallow and finished him off with a pistol shot to the skull.

Meanwhile, Logan raced through the clearing, striking down soldiers one or two at a time. Claws flashed in the afternoon sun. Heads leaped from shoulders in red fountains of gore. Dismembered arms dropped to the blood-soaked ground.

A soldier slipped behind Logan, aiming a squad automatic weapon at the back of his head.

"Logan, look out!" Thomas cried.

Instead of reacting, Logan faced him. Thomas saw no humanity in his expression. Only the eyes of a wild, killer beast.

Something happened to Logan's mind, Thomas realized. When that thing attacked him, burned his flesh, it had burned something out of his brain, too. This just wasn't the same man who had saved his life.

The soldier pulled the trigger. The blast jerked Logan's head forward. Bullets ricocheted off his steel skull.

Logan lashed out with a backhand that slashed through the soldier's midsection. He screamed and dropped his rifle, clutched at the steaming intestines pouring out of his belly. Another slash, and the man's helmeted head rolled across the frozen ground.

The remaining soldiers took off in a run, but they didn't get far. Logan cut them down, one by one, until no one was left standing.

Hunched over his last victim, Logan grunted with animal satisfaction as he slashed at the corpse again and again, blood splashing the rocks.

The men from the posse gathered around Thomas. They watched Logan mutilate the corpse, oblivious to their presence.

Thomas studied Logan, who seemed either mad or crazy with grief. Either way, he was no longer the man Thomas had come to know.

"What do we do?" Ben whispered.

Thomas faced them. "Just back away, go down the hill, and don't make any noise."

"What if he sees us and attacks?" Marvin said softly.

Thomas picked up his Remington rifle. "Don't worry. I'll protect you."

"What about Jerry? We can't just leave him here," Ben cried, too loudly.

Logan heard the sound and whirled.

"Crap. He's coming," Bill Lyons moaned.

"Go," Thomas cried, pushing them onto the trail. The men hurried down the hill, and Thomas faced Logan again.

The wild man was moving on all fours, stalking him. Thomas clutched his rifle and placed his body between Logan and the rest of the posse.

Logan snarled, advancing slowly, like a predatory cat.

A voice called out behind him. "Come on, Thomas. If you stay, he'll kill you."

"Go home, Marvin," Thomas replied, eyes fixed on Logan. "You can't do any good here. You don't even have a gun."

"Yes, I do. I took it from one of the soldiers."

"Well, for God's sake, don't shoot. You can't hurt Logan, and you'll probably hit me."

Just when Thomas thought Logan was going to retreat, he sprang forward. Before Thomas could move, or even react, Logan had him in his grip.

One hand crushed Thomas's throat, cutting off his air. Claws dug into the tender flesh under his chin. A trickle of blood stained the razor-sharp points. Thomas bent his head back as far as it would go, but Logan's hand moved with him.

Thomas thought he saw a glint of understanding behind Logan's feral gaze. Unexpectedly, the man snarled, and his claws retracted, and the pressure on Thomas's throat disappeared. Thomas gasped, then faced his foe.

"I'm not going to fight you," Thomas hissed through gritted teeth. "You can kill me if you want to, but I'm not going to fight."

Logan turned and scrambled to the center of the clearing, where he paused. His movements seemed uncertain, pensive, as if waiting for something or someone. He turned his head and stared at the dark cave mouth.

Thomas called to him. "Logan? Are you there?"

This time, Thomas's words didn't seem to register. Without a second glance, Logan took off in a loping run, moving until he reached the opposite end of the clearing. He jumped onto another ledge, then vanished among the rocks.

"What rough beast is this," Thomas whispered.

"Huh?" Jesse Lee was beside him. The man scratched his scraggly head.

Thomas was surprised to find that the rest of the posse had returned, as well. The men surrounded him.

But Jesse Lee was still curious. "What did you say just now?"

"Forget it," Thomas replied. Then he faced them all. "I thought I told you guys to go home."

Jesse Lee threw an arm over Thomas's shoulder.

"Sorry to disobey a direct command, Tommy boy. But we're not going anywhere without you."

36

Ottawa, Ontario
Two days later

"DIRECTOR?"

The man looked up from the reports spread across his messy desk. His eyes were dull, his flesh sallow. His shock of white hair had yellowed like old parchment, all in the past few weeks.

"Why do you bother me?"

"Captain Von Trakker has made his final report," the Voice replied.

"And?"

"The Professor's facility is empty. There was no sign of Major Sallow or his men. Corporal MacKenzie and his team of engineers have also disappeared, and Captain Von Trakker could find no trace of Dr. Vigil, either."

"And the Matron?"

"She's gone, Director. She never returned to Shroud Lake. A Lieutenant Benteen is running things there. He's been very cooperative but claims to know nothing."

"And Weapon X?"

"He has also vanished. Captain Von Trakker has suggested we widen the satellite search."

"We don't have the resources for that. Can you imagine what such an endeavor would cost?"

"Approximately sixteen million Canadian dollars a month, Director."

"More than Department K's allotment for satellite surveillance, I'm afraid."

"Excuse me, Director. I believe we have guests."

The Director frowned. He wasn't expecting anyone, and he didn't like visitors just dropping in.

"Security reports that Corporal MacKenzie is here to see you, Director."

The Director closed the file. "Tell them to send the corporal up to my office immediately. I have several questions I'd like answered."

"Done, sir. But I'm confused. I believe Von Trakker said that Corporal—"

The Voice fell silent, and the lights inside the Director's plush office flickered. The man frowned, pushed his papers to the corner of the desk.

"Repeat your statement, please."

But the Director's command was greeted with silence. "I said repeat your statement."

The oak double doors opened, and the Matron entered, wearing the uniform of a Canadian Army corporal.

"What's the meaning of this outrage?" the Director fumed. "You're not MacKenzie."

"Of course I am." The Matron tapped the name tag on her uniform. "Corporal Angel MacKenzie reporting for duty."

The Director's eyes flashed, and he punched a button on his desk. "I've alerted security."

"I don't hear any alarms. And we won't, either. I'm afraid there's been a power failure. Nobody can hear you. Nobody will respond to your call. Dr. Vigil made sure of that."

"She's in on this, too?"

"Oh, yes. And she's also deleted that Personal Digital Manager of yours, the one with the unctuous voice."

The Director jerked in his chair. "Deleted! You're insane. You've effectively erased Department K's entire database! All the information collected through the years—on Weapons One through Ten and beyond. Data on Shroud Lake, the Weapon Null Program. It's—"

"Gone. Yes, I know. That was my intent." The Matron seemed pleased with herself, which only infuriated the Director.

"I'll have—"

A radio transmitter crackled.

"Excuse me, Director. I have to take this."

The Matron pulled the receiver from her belt and spoke. "Come in, Dr. Vigil."

"I've deactivated the security system and the alarms," Megan Vigil replied over the com. "The building is sealed. No one can get in or out unless I open the door."

The Matron smiled. "Good. Now I want you to leave."

"What?"

"Go, Megan. Live your life."

"But—"

The Matron cut the radio and dropped it onto the Persian rug.

The Director stared at the woman through wide, nervous eyes. "What do you want from me?"

"What do I want from you? What did you ever give me?"

The Director looked away.

"I did everything you've ever asked of me, Gideon. When you wanted me to leave, I left. When you told me never to see you again, I stayed away. Still you hate me. Why, Gideon? Why? I was a beautiful woman once. Desired by everyone . . . everyone but you."

"It was never you. It's what you let them do to you that made me hate you."

The Matron fought back tears. "I only wanted to serve the cause of freedom."

"By becoming a living weapon? A suicide bomber?"

"There was the Cold War. Freedom was threatened.

You know the strategy behind the program. With the beauty I possessed, I could seduce my way into the inner circle, then detonate at will, at a time and place where I could inflict the most damage."

The Director covered his ears. "I don't want to hear this."

"Do you know what they really did to me, Gideon? It's inside me, right now. One of the rarest chemical compounds in existence. Octanitrocubane—"

"Please, no more," the man begged.

"The largest supply of octanitrocubane in the world—not much more than a teardrop—is wrapped in an Apocalyne detonation sheath and attached to my heart."

She pressed her hands over her breasts.

"Why are you telling me this?" the Director demanded. "Is it because you blame me? You've always blamed me. But there was pain on both sides—"

"The detonation is keyed to a particular phrase. Ten words spoken in a combination that would never, ever come up in a normal conversation. Words I would never utter unless I was ready to set off the explosive."

The Director didn't want to listen, but he could no longer look away. With horrid facination, he watched his former lover's full, red lips form the deadly phrase.

"I love you, Gideon. And I will love you forever."

EPILOGUE

A SPRING STORM SUDDENLY DARKENED THE AFTER-
noon. The wind sprang up, and a warm rain began to
fall. Megan pulled the denim jacket tight around her
throat.

Tires hissed on the wet pavement, filling the air
with a fine mist. She fumbled in the backpack at her
feet and shoved a hat down over her shaggy mop
of short red hair. She pulled a newspaper from her
back pocket. Before she draped it over her head, she
glanced at the headline: "Separatist Bomb Destroys
Government Office; Three Dead in Blast."

I'm rid of them both. I'm free.

Of course, there was no way of knowing if she were
truly free. Though the Matron had deleted the Director's database, it was very possible that Department K
had servers off-site, where information about Weapon
X and the Weapon Null Program was still stored.

But in the chaos following the blast, Megan doubted anyone would take the time or trouble to search for her—especially since the world believed Megan Vigil was dead.

The wind increased, the rain intensified. Megan stuck out her thumb.

A massive truck rumbled by, then slowed to a halt on the side of the road.

The horn blared. Megan snatched up her backpack and dropped the newspaper. She ran to the front of the truck, sneakers squeaking on the wet pavement.

Through rain-speckled sunglasses, she read the logo emblazoned on the trailer and couldn't believe her good luck: "Yukon Alaska Shipping Company."

Megan slowed as she approached the cab. The passenger door opened.

If she'd expected the driver to be another rugged northern woodsman type, some blond man in a flannel shirt and a logger's mustache, Megan would have been disappointed. As she climbed into the cab, mariachi music blared from the radio, until the man behind the wheel politely turned the volume down.

Megan tossed the backpack onto the seat and climbed in after it. Then she looked at the driver. The man was about forty, short and squat, with slicked-back, ebony hair and dark eyes framed by laugh lines.

"Where to?" he asked.

"Are you heading north?"

The man grinned. "All the way."

"Do you know a town called Chichak?"

"Sure, I go through there every trip. It's a long ride, though." He paused. "I hope you like music. My name's Santiago, but folks call me Sam."

"I'm Megan." They shook hands.

Sam shifted gears and rolled onto the highway again. The sun broke through the clouds, and the rain stopped.

"Look around," Sam said. "You might see a rainbow."

Megan nodded. "Just might."

"So who do you know in Chichak? You got a boyfriend there?"

"It's just a stopping point, really. I'm moving on from there."

Sam shifted gears again, and the truck sped up. Megan sat back in her seat.

"I'm headed for another town," she said. "A place called Second Chance."

About the Author

Marc Cerasini lives in New York City and is the author of more than thirty books, including the *New York Times* nonfiction bestseller *O. J. Simpson: American Hero, American Tragedy,* plus *Heroes: U.S. Marine Corps Medal of Honor; The Future of War: The Face of 21st Century Warfare;* and *The Complete Idiot's Guide to U.S. Special Ops.*

He is also the author of the *USA Today* bestseller *AVP: Alien vs. Predator,* based on the motion picture, and four original *24: Declassified* novels, based on the Emmy Award–winning television series *24: Operation Hell Gate, Trojan Horse, Vanishing Point* and *Collateral Damage.*

With Alice Alfonsi, Marc is the coauthor of the nationally bestselling mystery novels *On What Grounds, Through the Grinder, Latte Trouble, Murder Most Froth, Decaffeinated Corpse, The Ghost and Mrs. McClure, The Ghost and the Dead Deb, The Ghost and the Dead Man's Library,* and *The Ghost and the Femme Fatale.* With Alice, he is also the coauthor of *24: The House Special Subcommittee Investigation of CTU,* a fictionalized guide to the show's first season.

He helped to create the *Tom Clancy's Power Plays*

series and wrote an essay analyzing Mr. Clancy's fiction for *The Tom Clancy Companion*. Marc's techno-thrillers include *Tom Clancy's NetForce: The Ultimate Escape* and five action/adventure novels based on Toho's Studios classic Godzilla, among them *Godzilla Returns, Godzilla 2000,* and *Godzilla at World's End*.

Marc is also the coauthor of a nonfiction look at the Godzilla film series, *The Official Godzilla Compendium,* with J. D. Lees. With Charles Hoffman, Marc is the coauthor of *Robert E. Howard, A Critical Study*.

Not sure what to read next?

Visit Pocket Books online at
www.simonsays.com

Reading suggestions for
you and your reading group
New release news
Author appearances
Online chats with your favorite writers
Special offers
Order books online
And much, much more!